the Goddess & MARTIN DAYSON

A Novel

STEPHEN HOLGATE

The Goddess and Martin Dayson, *A Novel*
by Stephen Holgate

ISBN-13:
979-8-9895687-0-3 (paperback)
979-8-9895687-9-6 (e-book)

Thank you for buying an authorized edition of this book.

PUBLISHING NOTE: This is a book of fiction. Names, characters, places and incidents either are the product of the author's imagination or are used fictitiously, and any resemblance to actual persons (living or dead), businesses, companies, events or locales is entirely coincidental. Every effort has been made to be accurate.

Cover layout, book layout & design by Suzanne Fyhrie Parrott
Cover art by Jeff Holgate

Registration number: TXu 2-402-309

Printed and bound
in the United States of America.

StephenHolgateWrite.com

Advance Praise for

"The Goddess and Martin Dayson"

"Where did we come from? Where are we going? . . . This sweet, intriguing novel offers wisdom in its story about political life, coming of age, family drama and archaeology – about those who came before, and a future of possibilities."

– **KRISTIN TUCKER**, former Executive Director
of the Washington State Arts Commission

"Martin Dayson is a multilayered story of discovery, change, and reconciliation . . . expertly conveys the sense of impending upheaval that the 1960s will represent in America. A skilled storyteller, Stephen Holgate vividly evokes Dayson and the people around him. It's sheer pleasure to read this novel as the author adroitly illuminates the mysteries that reside in his characters' hearts."

– **MARK JACOBS**, author of "**Silent Light**"

"One of the great delights of this always engaging novel is the skill with which each of the characters' secrets are revealed. And with each revelation we gain deeper insight into who they are."

– **MARK YORK**, Supervising Producer, Disney's "**Doug**"

Praise for Stephen Holgate

"Tangier" – Winner of the Silver Medal in Fiction by the Independent Publishers of America

Bookreporter Top Ten Mystery/Thrillers of the Year

"Stephen Holgate weaves an exquisite tapestry of wartime espionage, intrigue and mystery in his astounding debut novel." – L. Dean Murphy, *Bookreporter*

"Madagascar" – Finalist for Forward Reviews Book of the Year in Fiction.

Bookreporter Top Ten Mystery/Thrillers of the Year

"Le Carre fans won't want to miss this one." – *Publishers Weekly* starred review

Also by
Stephen Holgate

To Live and Die in the Floating World

Tangier

Madagascar

Sri Lanka

A Promise to Die For
(coming in Spring 2025)

Acknowledgments

Every book represents a team effort, and there are many people who have helped bring this one over the line. I especially want to thank Mark Jacobs, Kris Tucker, Mark York, Keith Scales, Kathy Randall, Suzanne Fyhrie Parrott and, as always, my dear wife, Felicia. I also want to thank my brother, Jeff, who has been of great help in putting this book together. And, as ever, I also want to thank Kimberley Cameron for believing in me. This work has been a long time in the making and I'm sure I must be forgetting others who have been of help. I can only ask forgiveness for any oversight.

For Dean Jeffress

Chapter One

The Idol in the Garden

"I found it out back while I was digging a garden." Martin Dayson registered the look Batch gave him and muttered, "They say old guys need a hobby." He nodded at the object in Batch's hands. "So, what do you think?"

Sitting in an armchair opposite his friend, Robert Bachelder, gazed at the stone figure barely larger than his outstretched hand. "What do I think? I think you need to stop calling yourself an old man."

"I'm sixty-two."

"I've got two years on you, Marty. Tell me how you're feeling when you catch up."

Dayson was staring out the window of the spare bedroom he had converted into a den, his mind elsewhere.

"When you get all this behind you"—Bachelder waved a hand to encompass the wreckage that had come to comprise his friend's life—"you'll feel ten years younger."

"Mmmmm." Dayson seemed about to say something, but only cocked his head at the stone figure. "Tell me what we've got here."

Bachelder turned the figurine over in his hands and squinted at the scratches left by its maker's tools, the marks worn almost smooth by time. With his fingertips he traced its contours, the prominent mounds of the breasts, the exaggerated breadth of the hips, the legs tapering to a rounded point. Were those lines on its head an attempt to fashion hair? Maybe a bit of color on the back. "How far down was it?"

"I dunno. A foot. Maybe a little more. The length of a shovel blade. I hit it pretty hard."

"I can see that." Bachelder rubbed at the fresh gouge on the figure's back. "So you thought you'd summon your old friend from the art museum to have a look."

"Even former rank hath its privileges. Is that what you're saying?" Dayson forced a laugh that came out more like a growl.

"No, Marty. I'm happy to come out, see your new place."

"Such as it is," Dayson said with a deprecating shrug.

Batch registered the defeat and loss of purpose he heard in his friend's tone. "Why don't we go outside and you can show me where you found it?"

With matching grunts, the two graying men levered themselves from their armchairs and went out through the utility room.

As they stepped outside, Bachelder gave a low whistle. "I didn't realize how much land you got with this place."

From the modest rise on which Dayson's small ranch-style house stood, they looked out through a line of fir trees toward open fields beyond, the view neatly bracketed by two clusters of ancient apple trees left to grow wild, slowly subsiding into the embrace of blackberry vines. To the west, beyond the fields, heavily wooded hills glowed a deep green.

"It's not all mine," Dayson said. "I've only got an acre and a half. Property line runs about fifty feet the other side of those firs to the west, there where the ground slopes down toward the fields. The view I get for free."

"A little bit of a comedown after the governor's residence, isn't it?" Batch got a grunt in reply. "Why did you move out here, to hell and gone? No one within half a mile of you."

"Want to be left alone."

"Other men have lost elections too, Marty."

Dayson grunted. "And other men have had their wives leave them. But they don't see it splashed across the front page."

They stood side by side—Dayson, short, compact, still powerful in the shoulders and chest, but his stomach growing prominent, Bachelder half a head taller, slim—each occupied with his own thoughts.

Bachelder didn't like the look in his old friend's eyes. Lost, angry, hurt. He'd let his hair grow long. And the beard—unkempt, almost entirely white.

A beard? Did he think this was the 1860s instead of the 1950s? Only Beat poets and bongo players grew beards. No, the beard, like Marty's moving out here, miles from anyone he knew, struck Bachelder as an attempt to hide from everyone, even from the mirror.

"Show me where you found it, Governor." He spoke lightly, trying to beguile his friend into a smile.

Unbeguiled, Dayson pointed toward a corner of his back yard. "Over here."

He led Bachelder to the large patch of upturned earth Dayson had set aside for a vegetable garden. The garden's long, straight lines were interrupted by a hole a couple of feet deep and maybe four in diameter.

"Found it right about here. I dug around to see if there might be something else. Nothing so far," Dayson said.

Lowering himself to one knee, Batch took up some dirt, kneaded it in his hand, let it fall back. There wasn't much point telling Dayson he should have left things alone until someone who knew what they were doing could come out take a look at it. "And you didn't find anything else? No pieces of stone? Bits of wood that didn't look quite natural?"

"Just dirt and a few potato bugs."

Bachelder crossed his arms over his upraised knee, looked around the yard and the nearby trees. "There, where the ground slopes away at the edge of your property, is there maybe a creek at the bottom?"

"A fast moving stream. Kinda small for a creek. Why?"

"Just thinking. Water can explain a lot. Could have been a little settlement here. Or some nomadic band pausing on its way to somewhere else. From here they could have seen quite a way, could spot anyone coming up on them. But who knows how things looked back then? We're talking a long time ago."

"You make it sound like thousands of years."

"It may have been." Bachelder rose to his feet, brushed the dirt off his hands. "The question is why they would leave your statue here? Maybe someone dropped it. Or, for some reason, they buried it here and moved on."

"Just visitors?" Dayson asked.

"We're all just visitors, Marty." Batch nodded toward the house, where they had left the figurine. "I've never seen anything like it in Oregon—or anywhere else in the Northwest. Fertility figures like that are more like something you'd find in the Middle East, Europe."

"Fertility figure?"

"The big breasts, the huge hips. Your parents didn't explain much to you, did they?'

Dayson made a face to keep from smiling. "I know about breasts, Bachelder. So you're saying—and hips—you're saying these things are always women? They didn't make figures of men?"

"They did. Warriors. Gods. Spirits. But mostly women. These little bands—that's what you'd have found around here—they lived close to the edge. If they suffered a drought, or a flood, or just ran into another group tougher than they were, they were gone. They couldn't assume their life as a tribe, a clan, would continue. They probably made these little idols, these icons, as a kind of juju, something to appease the Great Goddess, a plea for the continued life of their band. Anyway, that's what we think they were doing. Archaeologists find these things in other parts of the world."

"But not here."

"But not here." Bachelder shook his head. "No. Outside of some tools and arrowheads, early bands around here seem to have made everything out of wood, bone, hide, grasses. Things like that don't leave much trace. That's why we don't have many artifacts, why we have such a hard time figuring out when people first came here."

"Maybe they brought this thing with them from wherever they set out."

"From Mongolia? Siberia? Maybe they did. It wouldn't have been a day trip out here, coming across Alaska, Canada. We might be talking centuries."

"And they kept this with them all that time?" Dayson said, his voice hushed by the implication of his own words. He waved a hand to wipe the thought away. "Look, maybe it's just a prank. Someone buried it here to have a laugh at whoever dug it up and thought it was a big deal."

"Had you already broken the ground there, maybe left it for the night and came back the next day and found this thing?" Dayson shook his head. "Doesn't make much sense then. How could they know anyone would ever dig it up? No, I think it's the real thing."

Bachelder looked around his friend's property in a speculative way.

"What are you thinking?" Dayson asked.

"I'm not an archaeologist, just a curator of Indian artifacts, but I'm thinking someone should come out here and do a proper dig of this area."

Dayson pawed the earth with his foot. "Let's go back inside. I'll pour us a drink."

Martin Dayson handed Bachelder a scotch rocks and let him settle back into his chair while he stood at the window. "No, Batch, I don't want a bunch of people—archaeologists, or whatever—tromping around here digging things up."

"It wouldn't be a bunch. Probably just three or four." Bachelder squinted at Dayson. "But that's not it, is it?"

"If that thing's as unique as you say it is, the story'll get into the papers. 'Mysterious Artifact Found On Ex-Governor's Property.' Reporters calling up, asking all kinds of questions. And you know they wouldn't just stick to stuff about the figurine. They'd go after me about everything."

"You make it sound like the McCarthy hearings."

"McCarthy? Ike's problem. Not mine. Anyway, he's gone, thank God." He looked silently out the window at his yard before turning back to Bachelder. "No, I don't want anyone out here roaming around my place."

"You don't?" Bachelder nodded toward the big window. "Then what about her?"

"What?"

A girl—late teens—wearing an oddly old-fashioned dress, walked along the gap between the two stands of gnarled apple trees, occupied with something in her hands, perhaps twisting a blade of grass. She didn't glance at the house, walking by as if it didn't exist, and quickly disappeared from view.

"Goddammit! She crosses my place practically every day, first one way then the other. I can never get out there fast enough to tell her this is private property and to stay the hell off it."

"You're not turning into one of those old guys who yells, 'Get off my lawn,' to the neighborhood kids."

"She's trespassing," Dayson protested, looking at Bachelder for support and seeing he wasn't going to get any. "Should learn some respect . . ." he grumbled, his voice trailing away.

"Take it easy, Marty. You're out in the country. People take shortcuts. You're a farm boy. You know that."

"Trespassing . . ." Dayson muttered, adding something Batch couldn't catch.

That's new, Bachelder thought, the mumbling. He'd always spoken clearly, stated things decisively, able to hold an audience in his hand. Now he muttered like a man who had lost confidence in himself.

"How are your memoirs going?"

"Huh?" Dayson looked at his desk, scattered with papers. "They go," he lied. With sudden vehemence, he said, "Who the hell wants to know anything about a washed-up politician?"

"You have a story to tell. You've still got things to say to this state."

"Like a man shouting up from the bottom of a hole."

Each silence grew longer than the last. Batch knew not to intrude on his friend's thoughts.

When Dayson spoke again it seemed like the continuation of a dialogue he'd been conducting in his head. "I understand why she left me. Dorothy. Most people don't, but I do." He spoke softly, resigned. "Claimed desertion. So everyone figured I was playing around with another woman—even though no one actually said so. Put me in a hell of a spot. If I denied it without being accused, it would look like I was speaking from a guilty conscience. And when I didn't deny it . . . Well, then they were sure."

"Were you?"

Anger flared in Dayson's eyes before fading into weariness. "Nah. Or maybe just in love with myself." He blew out a long sigh. "Desertion. Maybe she was right. I was a farm boy. She was a farmer's daughter. We figured that's how we'd spend our lives. Until the war. When I came back I decided I wanted to run for office. She didn't sign up for this. Public life." He raised his eyes to the ceiling. "She hated it, Batch. Every moment of it."

"Yeah, I think I knew."

"That's why she never moved down to Salem from our place in Yamhill." He wagged his head. "I should have kept my House seat, stayed on the farm, raised corn and cows and Jocelyn. The party could've found someone else to run for governor. Plenty of other Republicans think they want it."

"You did a great job."

Drink in hand, Dayson caught his own reflection in the window and turned away from what he saw. "She had another man, Batch."

"Jesus, Marty."

"No one knew it. I didn't know until she told me. Someone we've known for years. Widower. Heck of a nice guy. I barely even want to kill him." He let out a mirthless chuckle. "Desertion. That's really what it was about. I worked hard, worked late, stayed down in Salem all week. She wanted someone who would be there in the evening, in the morning. Maybe it wasn't too much to ask."

"Jocelyn knows—about the other guy?"

Dayson nodded.

"What's she think?"

"Jocie's her mother's daughter. Tells me I should have paid her mom more attention." For a moment he thought to fight the accusation, but let it go. "Hell, she's right. Should have paid more attention to Jocie too."

"I had no idea about any of—"

"Thanks for coming out all this way," Dayson cut in, then softened. "It's good to see you, Batch."

Bachelder set his glass down and peered at the statue. "You want me to take your girl with me. Have someone look at it who knows more than I do?"

Dayson regarded the stone figure lying on the table next to Bachelder's empty glass, felt the strange pull it had held on him from the moment he'd dug it up. "No. I think she wants to stay here." A self-conscious smile flickered on and off for talking about the bit of rock as if it possessed life. He didn't want to tell Batch that he often held it in his hands, half expecting it to start speaking to him. People already thought he'd been acting strangely since Dorothy left him, since he'd lost his election. No one actually said anything, but he could see it in their eyes, just as he could see it in Bachelder's. "I'll keep her with me for now. Besides, like I say, I don't want anyone to know about her."

"Sure." When Dayson said nothing more, Bachelder rose from his seat.

"I suppose I should get going. Anne will start wondering where I am." He rose to his feet. "Let me know if you change your mind about the figure."

At the door he put his hand on Batch's shoulder, an uncharacteristically intimate gesture. "Thanks for coming out, Batch."

Bachelder regarded his old friend, saw the deep lines in his face, the dark circles under his eyes. "Sure thing, Marty. Good to see you."

After Dayson watched him drive away, he returned to his study and sat at his desk, thumbing through the few pages he'd written without registering any of it. After half an hour, he rose without writing a word, picked up the stone figure and wondered again who had made it, where it had come from and how it had come to rest in his garden.

Chapter Two

The Trespasser

Martin Dayson took off his gloves and felt around the blisters forming on his hands. Some farm boy, he thought. Years in the halls of the Capitol had made his hands go soft—his stomach too. A little shoveling left him winded. He rubbed his aching hip, which still held a fragment of a Japanese grenade, a souvenir of Okinawa, lodged too close to various nerves and arteries to allow safe extraction at the field hospital, and overlooked after he got to the Army hospital in Australia. He'd asked himself countless times if maybe he should have it cut out but, as always, a vague notion played at the edge of his conscience that this bit of metal was penance for something he never spoke about, and he had no right to remove it.

He chased the thought back into the dark corners of his mind from which it emerged, leaned against his shovel and looked at his morning's progress. He had enlarged the original hole but found nothing and had moved on to dig new ones, all without discernible pattern, their depth uneven, the work undertaken on hunch and impulse rather than plan as he sought something that might explain the presence of the figure sitting on his desk. His digging ended up looking like the handiwork of a madman lost in the grip of an obscure mania. He didn't like to think that maybe it was.

Whatever he did to fill the rest of the day, whether it was reading in his den, making some dinner, doing a little maintenance on his house, his thoughts were seldom far from the stone carving, turning it over in his mind like a man worrying his prayer beads.

Batch made the people who left it sound like primitive wanderers searching for more congenial climates, a place where they could end their journey and make a home. And somehow they had come here and left the little statue behind. Why? And why here? The figurine must have been important to them. They wouldn't have left it behind carelessly. Perhaps they had buried it during a time of peril, a desperate act of propitiation when they were hounded by enemies or starving during a hard winter, returning the icon to the earth from which it had come as a plea that the earth give something back. Or could things have become so bad that, in a fit of despair, they had given up on their gods and what the little figure had stood for and thrown it away? Maybe, as Batch said, another band, larger, more warlike, wiped them out, leaving their statuette on the ground, disdained as the unavailing icon of foreign spirits.

Occupied with these imaginings, a glimpse of bright color on the other side of the apple trees startled Dayson back into the present.

The young woman walked across his property with her head down as if she, like him, was lost in contemplation.

"Hey! You, girl!"

Dayson dropped his shovel and tried to hurry through the apple trees to intercept her, but by the time he got around the blackberry vines she had disappeared through the line of poplars that bordered his property to the north.

"Hey!" he shouted again.

No one heard him but the birds, who thought it wise to scatter toward quieter perches.

Puffing slightly, he thought of running after her, telling her she was to stay off his place, respect his boundaries. He snorted at his own foolishness. She was young and light-footed. If she heard him rumbling after her she would flit off, light as a butterfly.

Straining to catch a glimpse of the girl through the trees, Dayson rose on tiptoe. But she had already slipped from view.

"Hey," he sighed.

He tried to think of what lay in that direction—a couple of farms, a few houses and, a mile away, Topping, which was less a town than a pair of "Now Entering" signs posted a couple hundred yards apart on Highway 26 on the way to the coast.

As he set his heels back on the ground he looked down and found something he had not noticed in the few months since he had moved in, a footpath winding through the line of poplars to the north, crossing the length of his property and disappearing into the patch of woods to the south. Clearly, this girl wasn't the first person who felt entitled to cross his land. Batch was right. He lived in the country. People took shortcuts.

As he persuaded himself the girl hadn't committed any unique breach of his rights, he wondered again where she came from, where she was going. Or maybe she wasn't going anywhere, simply walking in the spring air, heedless of fusty notions about property lines, oblivious to old guys shouting into the trees.

Dayson put his gloves back on and slapped his hands together, telling himself he had work to do, though, as he headed back to his garden-cum-archaeological-site he knew his aimless digging hardly constituted work, though it might qualify as obsession.

Chapter Three

The Woman in the Blue Dress

In the weeks since his loss to Norman Gilkey, Dayson had come to dread things as simple as a trip to the grocery store. Whenever he drove the ten miles into Forest Grove someone would invariably recognize him, insist on shaking his hand and telling him what a damned shame it was he'd lost. If he took them all at their word he had yet to meet anyone who hadn't voted for him. Worse were the ones who looked away as he passed, until he felt like a cockroach who had crawled out from under the baseboard.

When he needed to buy only a few things, he avoided Forest Grove and drove down to the country store in Topping. Outside of a few locals in need of a loaf of bread or a traveler on his way to the beach, the store's aisles were blessedly empty of his fellow citizens. Better still, the graying couple who owned the place, the Greenburgs, never betrayed any sign of recognition when they toted up his purchases. Maybe it was the beard. Maybe they were Democrats. Maybe out here no one bothered to keep track of who was governor.

On a cool, gray spring morning, he'd been heading toward his car when he decided it was a good day for a walk. If time and custom had made the path that ran across his place into a sort of common law thoroughfare, he had as much right to walk it as anyone.

Once he had crossed the bounds of his property he felt a boyish thrill at doing something both perfectly acceptable and daringly illicit. Within a few yards, he began to marvel at the world he found when walking along the back of his neighbors' property. A glimpse of their unguarded selves revealed clothes on the line, children's toys in the grass, a broken-down car under a tree, all of it more interesting than the bland faces the houses presented from the road. Their broad tracts—virtually everyone lived on a couple acres or more—were divided from each other by scruffy hedges or wire fences, their decaying wooden posts twined with Queen Anne's lace and leaning at cockeyed angles amid the overgrown grass.

To the other side of the path, on his left, the open farmland showed a scrim of green so thin it appeared almost imaginary, seeming to float above the rich earth rather than growing from it.

After perhaps half a mile, the modest rise along which he walked dropped away and a thick growth of greenery intruded from the right-hand side of the path, its ragged height and impenetrable denseness almost obscuring the fact that it had once been a well-tended hedge, now neglected and left to grow wild. A few yards along its length, a narrow opening allowed a glimpse of the property behind the hedge.

Beyond the scraggly yard, thick with dandelions and dotted with unpruned rhododendrons, rose a two-story house, perhaps impressive at one time, but now, like its grounds, gone to seed, its weathered walls clad in a dark stain that had long ago lost its sheen. To each side, towering chestnuts had been left to grow unimpeded until their branches nearly met over the snaggle-toothed shingles. The low clouds drifting across the sky added their quantum of gloom to the dark house.

At first he thought the place deserted, then saw the glow of a lamp through a second story window. For an instant he imagined someone reading by its light.

Something about the place piqued his imagination. Who lived in this house, and what went on within its decaying walls?

He toyed with the notion that his sudden desire to leave his car behind and walk to the store had come on him precisely so he could discover this forbidding house. He scoffed at the notion, but couldn't quite let it go.

A stillness in the air spoke of approaching rain. Dayson hurried his pace and a few minutes later came through the stand of trees next to the old wooden store, which, with a scattering of houses and a gas station, comprised the whole of Topping. A sudden gust of wind and a rustling of leaves warned him the rain would be on him in a moment. He scampered across the open ground beyond the trees and skipped up onto the covered wooden porch that ran the length of the store.

On this quiet morning the place might have looked as deserted as the old house along the path but for the lighted sign out front advertising Hamm's beer. As Dayson stepped inside—the bell over the door tinkling its greeting, the air smelling pleasantly of dusty floors and aging vegetables—he found he wasn't the only customer. A graying, thick-waisted woman wearing an old raincoat over a faded blue housedress leaned across the counter, speaking in a low but insistent undertone to Mrs. Greenburg, who stood behind the register with one hand poised at the base of her throat, looking beseechingly toward her husband, who was stacking cigarettes in the rack behind the counter.

Something tense about the scene, Dayson thought absently.

He picked up coffee and potatoes and carrots and a package of stew meat that didn't look as if it had been in residence more than a couple days. When he headed toward the counter he found the woman in the blue dress still there. He noticed that her hair hadn't known a brush that morning, giving her the willfully unkempt appearance of a woman edging toward mental disorder. She stood as he'd first seen her, still shaking her head and muttering with increasing volume. Out of her tangle of words the word "cheat" broke through clearly.

Herb Greenburg, a tall thin man with wire-rimmed glasses, turned from the cigarette rack and set his hand on the counter. "That's how much it costs, Mrs. Tannehill," he said, his voice weary, as if he had discussed this with the woman many times. "The price is marked clearly on the cans. This isn't a car dealership where you can dicker over the price. It's not an auction. It's a grocery store, Sarah."

On the counter between Mrs. Tannehill and the Greenburgs lay an assortment of canned goods, a quart of milk, a weary-looking head of lettuce and a bottle of cheap Tokay. Beside these items, the woman—whom Dayson had at first thought older than himself, but on closer inspection appeared a badly-kept decade younger—had laid a pair of dollar bills and a small pile of change.

The woman glared at Dayson when he laid his own purchases next to hers, then returned to the beleaguered couple behind the counter.

Before she could resume her complaint, Dayson asked, "How much you charging her for all that?"

He expected a sharp look from Greenburg and got it. "Three dollars and twelve cents," the storekeeper said, more to Sarah Tannehill than to Dayson.

"And what's she got?"

"Two dollars and . . ." The grocer surveyed the small change. ". . . thirty-eight cents."

"Look, I'm in kind of a hurry. Let me throw in a buck for her things. Then you can check me out."

The woman in the blue dress lifted her chin. "I'm not in the habit of accepting charity from strangers," she said.

"I'm sure you're not, ma'am, but, like I say, I'm in a hurry. You can pay the Greenburgs the difference next time you're here, and they'll make it up to me."

After a guarded look at the Greenburgs the woman in the blue dress huffed indignantly but allowed Dayson to put his dollar on the counter.

Still mumbling invectives, she took her purchases, set her chin high and walked out.

Herb Greenburg watched her go and let loose a long sigh. "Thanks."

Dayson shrugged. "Glad to help."

The grocer nodded toward the door. "She's been coming here for years. Used to be all right. Never an easy person, but all right."

His wife added, "Her husband, Archie, now there was a dear man. But he's been gone—what is it?—nine years now?"

The awkwardness of their run-in with Mrs. Tannehill, especially in front of a relative stranger, had apparently shaken the couple from their normal reserve. Dayson wondered if, by helping them out in a difficult moment, they had for the first time seen him as a neighbor rather than simply someone who lived nearby.

Herb Greenburg added up Dayson's purchases on the big iron register. "Living alone in that big house—or nearly alone—the place falling down around her, has driven her kind of—"

"Herbert . . ." His wife warned, somehow drawing three syllables from the word.

He cocked his head to one side, acknowledging he was talking out of turn.

Dayson had seen no car out front, meaning this Tannehill woman must live within walking distance. Thinking that her disordered appearance might echo that of her home, he thought he knew where.

"Is that her place, the big old house on Hayward?"

"Yeah, that's hers." Mrs. Greenburg grimaced. "Used to be the place was kept up. But since Archie died . . ."

Her husband added, "I thought it might help her, having her nephew move in with her a few months ago."

"Niece," his wife corrected.

"Nephew."

"Niece."

"Anyway, it's not like he's ever come in here," Greenburg said with a mischievous glint in his eye. "But Sarah talks about him."

"Her," his wife insisted.

"Going to college in Forest Grove, Sarah says. But we've never seen her. Sometimes I wonder if this niece—" Greenburg looked at his wife with a little smile. "—isn't a figment of her imagination."

"And don't be making jokes, Herb. Maybe we haven't met her, but you know what people say about that girl's . . . reputation," she dredged up the word with a tone that indicated there was a lot she wasn't saying, though she had already managed to say it pretty clearly.

Greenburg lowered his head and said quietly, "People talk, Rose. But we don't know any of it for a fact, and shouldn't be saying anything."

"Well . . . you're right. Still . . . College girls," she concluded with a harrumph of disdain.

Greenburg replied, "Sarah Tannehill deserves our pity, not our criticism."

His wife allowed herself a faint smile. "A mighty hard thing to live with, the pity of a small town."

As Dayson picked up the sack and headed for the door, Rose called to him, "Thanks again for your help, Mr. Dayson."

Startled, Dayson stopped in the doorway. He was sure he had never mentioned his name to the Greenburgs, and had to confront the likelihood they'd always known who he was. While he thought he'd been playing things discreetly, they had, all along, been the ones giving a lesson in circumspection.

With a reminder to himself not to underestimate people, he managed a mute wave and backed through the door.

The rain had arrived, one of those soft showers that hardly rustles the leaves but soaks a person in minutes. He put his head down, hoping the rain didn't soak through his grocery bag, and started the mile-long trudge back to his place. Along the way he stopped for a moment to look at the house beside the path, wondering again what kind of life went on within its walls and reflecting on small town reputations—and the girl who so often crossed his property.

Chapter Four

Masks and Shamans

The same restlessness that had sent him down the path toward Topping and his glimpse of the decrepit house behind the hedge, nagged at Dayson all the next morning.

Finally, he grabbed a shovel and went outside. After a quarter hour of turning over the ground to prepare it for planting he gave into the urge to dig again, not even certain what he was looking for. It took nearly an hour for him to admit he was accomplishing nothing. He returned his shovel to the utility room and went inside.

Still agitated, he wandered into his study, picked up the stone figurine from his desk and held it tightly, as if trying to squeeze some revelation from its mute features. Then he wrapped it in a handkerchief, put it in his pocket and headed for his car.

It took Dayson an hour to drive into Portland from his place in the country. He hadn't been in the city since the last week of the campaign.

It had been a close election, not decided until after dawn the following day, when the last votes from Multnomah County were tallied. In the end, he had lost Portland by eight points and, with it, the state. His campaign manager and most of his election committee urged him to ask for a recount, but he'd told them no, he didn't believe it would change anything.

He didn't want to tell them the truth; he had no stomach for another fight. He'd lost his wife, perhaps his daughter, and, because of the still-pending divorce, the good opinion of many of those who had voted for him four years earlier. With the sometimes unbearable tensions of the Cold War and its threat to their way of life—to life itself—in the back of everyone's mind, a leader who couldn't keep his family together threatened the fabric of a country already under stress. No, he had lost, whatever the vote count.

When he got downtown he found a parking space near the art museum.

Robert Bachelder cleared away enough of the reed baskets, boxes of arrowheads and woven hats to allow the former governor to find a chair.

"Good to see you, Marty. Glad you tore yourself away from that place out in the sticks long enough for a visit."

Settling into the chair opposite Batch's desk, his hands folded over his stomach, Dayson surveyed the cluttered office with something that started as amusement but slowly turned to wonder.

Among the roomful of artifacts, Dayson found himself drawn to a wooden mask hanging from the wall of his friend's office. Perhaps three feet tall and nearly two wide, with a long half-open wooden beak held by leather hinges, it represented a bird of some sort, its stylized features conjuring a hidden essence.

The power of the mask filled the room. With its smooth surface and stark, flat colors—red, black, turquoise—it looked as if it might have been pulled from the center of a great tree just so, already formed, vibrating with an energy that beckoned to an atavistic region of the soul.

Struck by his friend's silence, Bachelder followed Dayson's gaze and regarded the mask, absorbing it anew or, rather, allowing it to once more absorb him.

"It's speaking to us, but in a language we don't understand anymore," Batch said quietly, as one might speak in church. "Shamans wore them in tribal ceremonies to invoke the spirits of the animals and birds that sur-rounded them in the forest."

The former governor squinted at Bachelder. "You're saying a medicine man took on the spirit of a bird with this thing?"

Still looking at the mask, Batch shook his head. "When the shaman put on the mask, it possessed him. He disappeared, and the spirit subsumed him—spirit of Eagle, of Bear, Beaver, Raven. That's why the beak could open, so he could show himself inside, his spirit taken over by that of the mask." He nodded at the great wooden bird. "When that happened, the tribe drew closer to the natural world until it was right there, inhabiting them, just like they inhabited it."

Dayson counterfeited a smile, donning his own mask to conceal how much the presence of the one on the wall moved him. As it must have done to the tribes Batch mentioned, it spoke to something within him that he could only barely discern, his understanding obscured by the clutter of modern life.

He nodded to indicate the artifacts cluttering the office. "Don't all these things crowding you like this, don't they give you nightmares?" He tried to say it with a laugh, unwilling to admit how they disturbed him.

Swiveling in his chair, Bachelder looked around the room and nodded. "I dream about them."

For a few moments they sat quietly, the mood not unlike the few seconds given in Sunday service for silent prayer.

Dayson reached into his pocket, unfolded the handkerchief from around the figurine he'd found in his garden and put it on Bachelder's desk.

"So, what can you tell me about my girl?" he asked.

His friend raised his eyebrows and sighed. "Not much more than I told you when I came out to your place. I made some phone calls. Seattle, Olympia, even down to San Francisco. No one knows of anything like it, at least not in this area. Some are skeptical about its authenticity. I don't blame them. We know the tribes could work stone. They made arrowheads and pestles and bowls, could even make smooth spheres almost like bowling balls. But we've never found anything like this."

"Bowling balls? What were they for?"

"For all we know they bowled with them. There's no one left to tell us. Even the members of the local tribes are just guessing."

"Or maybe they just don't want to tell you."

"I've wondered about that. Maybe they figure the meaning, the spirit from which it springs, has become so fragile that sharing it with strangers would kill it."

Dayson wanted to say, "What a bunch of hooey," but something held him back.

Sensing his friend's skepticism, Bachelder raised an eyebrow. "Scholars sit in their offices and puff their pipes and say these things were used for this or that, and this is how the old people thought of them. But we don't really know, and the deeper we get into it, the more we're just guessing. Maybe we're only projecting our own inner life onto a people we'll never know."

A small shiver of disquiet shuddered down Dayson's back. Still, he resisted. "You're getting all mystical on me, Batch. Makes me wonder if you've been hanging around these things too long."

Robert Bachelder leaned back in his chair and looked around once more at the artifacts that filled his office. "Maybe I have." His smile said he didn't believe it.

Dayson nodded at the figurine on the desk. "So you're saying there aren't any others like it."

Batch cocked his head to one side. "Over the years we've found a few carved stone figures, little thing. A fish. A cougar. Maybe they're funerary objects. Maybe not. It's a mystery. Or maybe the mystery is why they didn't make more of them. Maybe they didn't feel they needed to. They could, for their needs, more easily carve wood. Color it. Make it come alive. Or, better yet, summon the life already in it. Like our friend here." He indicated the mask on the wall. "Maybe they didn't think they had much need to make objects that would last long. The eternal lived all around them. They needed something for the here and now."

"So," Dayson nodded again at the figurine on the desk, "she might have been made for someone's funeral."

"The most honest answer is that I have no idea. But my gut tells me that you don't include a fertility image to accompany someone into the hereafter. In any case, around this region she's one of a kind. There's nothing like her."

"You're telling me she doesn't belong?"

"I just don't know, Marty." Bachelder clasped his hands behind his head and leaned back in his chair. "Now, aren't you glad you came to an expert?"

Dayson looked at the statuette, representing, he thought, not so much a woman as Woman, less life than Life.

His friend said, "Look, I know a young fellow working on his PhD from University of Washington. He's living here in Portland while he finishes his thesis. Name's Frank Persig. Anthropologist. He's worked on some archaeological digs in the Northwest. He knows more than I do about this stuff. Between bouts with his typewriter he needs something, a project he can feel is worthwhile."

"Why? Something wrong with him?"

"No. No. Just . . ." Bachelder shook his head rather than finish his thought. "Nothing like that. Look, why don't I have him come out, pay you a visit?"

Dayson growled, "And he'll just happen to be pulling a steam shovel behind his car with a couple of reporters at the levers."

"No, I promise you."

Dayson regarded the figurine for a long time, felt the need to change the subject. "You wouldn't believe it, Batch. I read that Norm Gilkey's talking about watering down those regulations we were drafting to clean up the Willamette. Him, a Democrat. He's kidding himself that it'll help him with downstate members of the legislature, get him some votes for tax reform." His tone betrayed a hunch that it might work, where his own efforts had come up short. "We sweated blood to get the cleanup bill passed, the regs drafted. Now he wants to toss half of it away."

"It doesn't leave your blood, does it? Politics. You're still drawn to it."

Dayson huffed a sardonic laugh. "Or it's still drawn to me." He lowered his head and turned the icon away, not liking the way it was looking at him. He slapped his knees, trying to act out a decisiveness he didn't feel. "No, I'm through with it." Knowing he had convinced neither his friend, nor himself, he glanced at Bachelder under his brow. "You know, a couple of years ago there was some talk about Ike dropping that SOB Nixon and taking me as his vice-president at the '56 convention."

"I think I heard something about that. You were tempted?"

With an unconvincing shrug of indifference, Dayson said, "No one ever talked to me directly. And Nixon hung on. You watch, he'll get the presidential nomination next year." He threw his head back and sighed. "Anyway, this vice-president stuff, you can't take it seriously. They'll whisper all sorts of names just to flatter someone into getting off the fence, or to make some state feel good about the presidential candidate. I mean, look at Stevenson's people a couple of years ago, floating the name of that pretty boy from Massachusetts. Whatsisname. He may not look like it yet, but he's running for president too."

"Kennedy?"

"Kennedy." Dayson blew out a dismissive breath.

"The guy's a war hero."

"War hero . . ." Dayson tried to pack the words with disdain, but ambivalence muted the bite. He caught Bachelder looking at him.

They both knew that folks had called Dayson the same thing and, though he had never tried to deny it, he'd never been comfortable with the label.

"No, I'm not talking about me, if that's what you're thinking. I never deserved . . ." But he didn't want to get into a discussion about what he deserved or didn't deserve. "This Kennedy guy, what did he ever do but get his boat sunk out from under him while he was sleeping? If Stevenson had been smart—" He stopped and threw up his hands. "Bah! I'm through with it!" He jerked his thumb toward the mask on the wall. "Can you get that guy to stop looking at me like that?" He tried to get his friend to share his laugh, but it smacked more of an unsettled mind than it did a joke.

"How you doing, Marty?"

"I'm fine," he said a little too quickly. "Fine. The divorce will be final one of these days. Maybe a couple more months. Lawyers . . ." he muttered. "Then Dorothy can let a decent interval pass and marry good old reliable Tommy Bayless. The sonofabitch."

"Has Jocie been out to see your new place?"

They both knew what the real question was.

"We've talked on the phone once or twice. Funny, it's her mother who asked for the divorce, but it's me Jocie's mad at."

Bachelder looked at his watch. "It's past noon. Let's go get some lunch."

"No, thanks, Batch. Not today."

"You didn't commit a crime, Marty. You just lost an election. You don't need to hide from the world."

"We'll do it another day, that's all." He wrapped his handkerchief around the figurine and put it back in his pocket, feeling better to have it on him. "Gotta go."

In the doorway, he stopped and turned back to his friend. "This guy Parsley, or Earwig…"

"Persig."

"Yeah. Go ahead and tell him to stop by."

Chapter Five

The Shack

Strong winds rocked Dayon's car as he drove back to his place. Ragged clouds cast dark shadows that gave way to moments of sunshine so bright it hurt the eyes, followed by sudden brief showers that pounded the roof of his car.

Already, Dayson regretted telling Bachelder to have Persig come by. The kid would tramp around the back yard shaking his head at the mess he, Dayson, had made, then patronize him by biting his tongue and saying it was all fine. He would bring one and then two and then who-knew-how-many others out to help him, and make clear to Dayson that he should stay out of the way, displacing him on his own property. The voters had booted him out of the governor's mansion. His wife had banished him from the farm in Yamhill. Damned if he would let some grad student push him around on his own place.

While showers passed one after another and the clouds rolled east, Dayson stood, mug in hand, looking out at the ground he'd torn up. The holes he'd dug after finding the icon were losing form in the rain, edges softening, mud slowly filling his half-assed excavations. The mess struck him as evidence of his foolishness as he searched for . . . what? Did he expect to find a trace of the vanished people who had left behind a figurine that countless years later would be discovered by a washed-up politician? And this washed-up politician would then tear the whole yard apart looking for something more—tools, beads, bones, anything—searching for what lay beneath it all. His mind slipped a cog, and he repeated out loud, "what lay beneath it all."

Drawn by the bright and rain-washed sky, Dayson wandered outside, walking past his would-be garden and between the clumps of apple trees to the edge of the path. He looked toward the line of poplars through which the girl so often emerged, then looked behind him toward the woods to the south where she disappeared, only to retrace her steps an hour or two later.

Before he could ask himself why, he was following the track of the young girl who treated his place as her own.

The woods grew silent as he entered, making him feel like an intruder, his presence upsetting the tranquility that existed in the absence of humans. Somehow, he imagined that it didn't go quiet like this when the girl walked through.

Within a few moments the woods were so dense Dayson lost sight of his house. He stopped in the shadow of a tall cedar still dripping with rain and breathed the cool, clean air. At his feet, he heard a rustling in the undergrowth—a mouse or squirrel edging away from his alien presence. He thought again of the mask in Bachelder's office, of the eerie power emanating from it. Could it have been carved from a cedar like the one in whose shelter he stood? Or did the spirit he felt when looking at the mask still live in these woods, the mask itself only its shadow? Maybe it lay inside this very tree, a mask sleeping in its great trunk.

For some minutes he stood as still as the mask itself until the birds again took up their chirping and cawing and the squirrels their chatter. He resumed walking, but trod more quietly now.

After a couple hundred yards, the path edged past a clearing on his left. In the center of the clearing stood the ruins of a house, long abandoned, nothing left but the chimney, a few bits of broken wall and some fallen beams blackened by age or a long-ago fire, hard to tell which now. The warming sun raised wisps of steam from the ruin. One day the place would entirely subside into the earth, betraying no trace of its presence, waiting for the day that a new landowner would, like Dayson, dig into the dirt and discover he was not the first one there.

Near the remains of the house stood a wooden shack bearing a few tatters of peeling paint, its small windows laced with cobwebs. From where he stood at the edge of the clearing, a barely discernible track led through the long grass to its door.

With a parting glance down the trail and a fleeting curiosity about what he might find if he continued walking, Dayson left the path and entered the clearing. The grass was long and his canvas shoes were soaked by the time he got to the door of the shack and pushed it open.

The shack smelled faintly of dust and tool oil and something unexpected, like the smell of fresh flowers.

Empty shelves, no more than dusty planks set on brackets, lined two of the walls. An old push-mower rusted in a corner. Yet the place was dry, even snug. A Primus stove, no bigger than a thermos, stood in the middle of the wooden floor—for heat, Dayson guessed, rather than cooking. Next to it a pair of blankets were laid out on a thin mattress.

Feeling that some last vestige of his own innocence had been plucked away, Dayson thought of the girl and muttered, "None of my business," then backed out, shutting the door behind him.

His hand still on the latch, he looked for another path, the one leading from the shack toward the other side of the clearing, from where her boyfriend came. But he found nothing. Maybe I'm wrong, he thought. Or maybe it doesn't matter. Yet, in his current mood, he felt a bite of disappointment that the girl was real and not some fairy that existed only on the bit of path that crossed his property.

"Reputation," Rose Greenburg had said. He'd learned a lot in his sixty-two years, much of it during the war, where there was no unknowing it later. Even then, people spoke of "bad girls" as if they were a menace to society. He'd come to think that the menace resided in those making the judgments—judgments founded in envy, or guilty yearning disguised as morality, and aimed at young women pushed by love or desperation or loneliness—or they simply liked boys. The condemnations heaped on them were almost always harsher than they deserved.

He stood at the door of the shack for some time before walking away, retracing his steps back into the woods, following the footpath toward his own place.

He was grateful no one had come along to shoo him off as a trespasser.

Deep in the night, the pain in his hip woke Dayson from a light sleep. He had thought that, freed of the burdens of office, he would sleep better in retirement, but it hadn't worked out that way. After years of marriage, he didn't like sleeping alone. Even during his time in Salem he had known that he could go home to Yamhill on the weekends, or Dorothy might occasionally come spend the night with him at the governor's residence. When filled with possibility, his bedroom had seemed less empty.

With a groan, he threw the covers off, got his feet under him and, more asleep than awake, stumbled toward the bathroom medicine cabinet, where he chewed a couple of aspirin, then cupped his hands under the faucet to wash them down.

Dr. Kimmel had told him he'd come to an age when he should have something on his stomach when he took the pills—when had he become old? which day had that been?—and, more awake than asleep now, wandered into the kitchen, stood at the sink and ate a couple of crackers, gazing out the window at his back yard, ghostly white in the moonlight.

Feeling his way along the wall—he hadn't lived in the place long enough to comfortably navigate it in the dark—Dayson walked past his bedroom and into the moonlit study. He found the carved figure lying on the desk, picked it up and carried it to the window.

Made of a light-colored stone, it glowed in the moonlight, leaving the illusion that it pulsed with a light from within, even breathed, animated by some force deep within itself.

He wasn't sure how much time passed before he let out a long breath and set it down.

"Dorothy," he whispered before turning back toward his empty bed.

Chapter Six

Tears in the Storm

The girl continued to cross his place most days. Sometimes he saw her going one way, sometimes the other, usually late in the morning—saw her because he watched for her now. After visiting the shack, he understood how she came by her reputation because surely he wasn't the first to see her passing, not the only one who knew how to add it up.

Herb Greenburg had said the pity of a small town was a hard thing to bear. How much heavier a burden might its censure prove?

Though he wondered what had changed—perhaps only the simple fact that she had become real to him, her motives the most human—he could no longer work up his previous annoyance at her trespass. His compulsion to shout her off his property had faded with the advancing spring.

Screened as she was by the trees and the blackberry vines, he never got more than a glimpse of her—tall, her hair light brown, what they used to call flaxen. She didn't wear the pleated skirts or toreador pants favored by other young women, but strangely anachronistic dresses that fell nearly to her ankles, as old-fashioned as Mother Hubbard. Always, she moved with the blithe grace of youth, seeming to glide more than walk.

Occasionally, as he puttered around the ground he still hoped to make into a garden, he would stop, seized by the sudden notion that she was standing behind the line of poplars or at the edge of the woods watching him. He would spin around, thinking to catch her spying on him, but would find nothing. Feeling ridiculous to imagine anyone would find him so interesting, he returned to his work and set his mind to other things.

* * *

For three days storms roared in off the Pacific, rolling over the Coast Range, carrying with them wind and rain and a sharp smell of the sea, sending Dayson inside to his study, where he turned on the lamp in middle of the day and read in his armchair, a warm brandy on the table beside him.

Through the window he watched the tops of the tall firs sway like the masts of a ship on a rolling sea. The poplars at the edge of his property rippled in waves, showing the tops of their leaves, then the bottoms, dark and light and then dark again. Twigs and bits of leaves swirled in the air. A rain squall approached from the west, scudding over the hills, crossing the fields, sweeping over his property, pounding on his roof before continuing east to bring rain to the city and snow to the mountains beyond.

Dayson picked up the stone figure lying on the table and gazed into its face, half-expecting it to start speaking to him. If it did, would he understand what it was trying to say?

Out of the corner of his eye he caught a fleeting movement crossing behind the apple trees and blackberry vines, hardly more than a bit of color flickering in the wind. He knew it was the girl, walking in the direction of Topping, heading back, he felt certain, toward the old house owned by Sarah Tannehill.

Dayson waited for the moment when she would cross the open ground between the stands of apple trees and he would catch a better glimpse of her. But the space between the trees remained empty. A couple of minutes passed and then a couple more.

Could he have imagined her, mistaken the movement of a wind-blown branch for the passing of a young woman? No, he was sure he had seen her. Seen someone in any case. And whoever it was had dropped from sight.

The rain, which had faded to a soft drizzle, picked up again and the dark firs groaned in the wind. Branches broke off in such winds, crashing to the ground, heavy enough to kill.

Dayson set down his coffee cup and, ignoring the voice telling him not to be a damned fool, went through the kitchen to the utility room, where he picked a rain slicker off its hook and went out through the back door.

Ducking his head against the force of the storm, he made his way across the yard toward the path.

He found her kneeling on the ground in the falling rain, her hair disheveled, her long skirt spread around her on the grass.

At his sudden appearance her hand went to her mouth.

The rain had darkened her hair. Black shadows ringed her reddened eyes. Her tears mingled with the rain streaming down her face. She looked eighteen, maybe nineteen.

For a heavy, wordless moment Dayson regarded her kneeling in the rain. He hadn't counted on her being pretty and it bothered him that her features, darkened by pain, moved him so.

"So, he left you."

She shook her head with startling ferocity, not, he sensed, in answer to his question, but as if by shaking her head hard enough she could make him vanish. The gesture failed and she hung her head. When she looked up again, their eyes met. The strength of her gaze made him take an involuntary step back. Yet he thought he saw in her eyes a flash of recognition and realized that, while he had so often seen her crossing his property, she, despite her seeming obliviousness, had seen him too.

He looked up into the roiling clouds, then back at the girl. "Listen, you can't stay out here in this."

"Because I'm trespassing?" she said, her voice sharp with mockery.

"Forget about trespassing for now," he said, raising his voice to be heard over the wind and the groaning of the trees. "Maybe you'd better come in and get dry." She didn't move. "If you want."

Her feral eyes flamed. "You have no idea what I want!"

"I'm not trying to—"

Before he could finish, she jumped to her feet and fled, running down the path in the direction of the old house behind the hedge.

"Hey!"

It was what he had always shouted at her, and it did as little good in bringing her back as it had in chasing her away.

Shaken by the girl's behavior, feeling vaguely accused—he had meant to help her, not run her off—Dayson returned his slicker to its hook in the utility room and went inside to change his soaked trousers.

Only as he crossed the living room did he see the car parked in the driveway. Its driver had probably got out and knocked on the door while he was in the back yard. But he had, no doubt, seen Dayson's car in the driveway and chosen to wait.

With a last glance out the kitchen window to where this odd girl had shouted at him and then disappeared, he continued toward his bedroom to get some dry clothes, mumbling, "Doesn't anyone call first?" and wondering how it was that, while he sought solitude, unbidden visitors came at him front and back.

He took his time changing his clothes before opening the door and waving toward the figure behind the wheel.

A thin, slope-shouldered young man got out of the car and came up the walkway as Dayson opened the door.

"How are you, Governor?"

"I'm fine, Art. I . . ." His mind still on the strange girl weeping in the rain, he found it hard to regain his bearings.

"If I've come at a bad time . . ."

Forcing a smile, Dayson said, "No, I'm only . . . Come on in out of the rain."

Art Thayer had been a college kid—young, smart, capable—when he signed on with Dayson's campaign nearly five years earlier. When he finished his degree, Dayson hired him as an assistant to his chief of staff. With half a dozen other staffers he had been a daily presence over those years, practically family. They hadn't seen each other since Norman Gilkey's inauguration back in January.

"Go find a chair in the study, Art. I'll be right there."

Dayson went into the kitchen and poured two cups of warmed-over coffee and again looked out the window at the rain, falling hard now, almost horizontal in the gusting wind. Was the girl still outside in this?

A mug in each hand, he joined Art in the study. For a few minutes they asked each other the usual, "How are you these days?" questions, both of them replying with a polite mix of trivialities and evasions.

When they had played out the string of their small talk Dayson asked, "So, what's on your mind, Art?"

Thayer cleared his throat, looked into his coffee cup. The young man's awkwardness spoke to Dayson of a need for help.

Though most of his senior staff had been well-established professionals before they went to work for him and had generally gone back to their former jobs after their time in Salem, his loss to Gilkey had been tough on the younger ones like Art. Some of them were still looking for work.

"Don't be shy. If you need me to write a letter of recommendation to someone or make a call for you, I'd be happy to do it."

"No, sir. That's not why I came."

"Then why—"

"It's about the Tyee Dam."

Dayson blinked in surprise. "What?"

"The Tyee Dam. The water reclamation project on the John Day River. They want to start construction next year and—"

"I know about the Tyee Dam. It's just . . ." With a bewildered laugh, he leaned back in his chair. "Why in the world are you here talking to me about the Tyee Dam? I thought maybe you needed some help finding a job, and I . . . The Tyee Dam?"

Art coughed into his hand as if the words didn't want to come out. "Thanks sir. It means a lot to me that you would be willing to help me out. But I think I've found a position. That is, I'm working for Governor Gilkey now."

Martin Dayson slumped in his chair. He saw the look on young Thayer's face and waved a hand in halfhearted absolution. "It's okay, Art. You needed a job. I'd have been happy to talk to Norm if you'd wanted me to." He made a small, deprecating gesture. "But I guess you didn't need that."

Dayson hadn't meant for it to sound accusatory, yet he felt a stab of pain at the fact that someone he regarded as part of his official family should so quickly sign on with the man who had taken his place.

Thayer seemed to sense this and again started to apologize.

Dayson raised a hand to stop him. "So, why has Gilkey sent you all the way out here to talk to me about the Tyee Dam?"

"He respects you a lot, sir."

"Sure he does. That's why he ran against me."

Thayer shifted in his chair and tried to smile. "Well, he wants your support for its construction."

"Hell, I always favored the Tyee Dam. He knows that. What does he want from me, a written affidavit?" But he knew the answer. Gilkey was a Democrat in a traditionally Republican state, with his own party in the minority in the state senate. Though water reclamation projects were primarily federal, the state legislature would need to find funds for the state's share of the work. Gilkey would need some Republican votes in the Senate to make that happen.

"So, he wants me for window-dressing."

Thayer looked stricken. "No, Governor. He respects your opinion and the standing you have in Oregon."

"If my standing was that great he wouldn't be governor. And maybe I'd be the one asking for his support." He huffed unhappily. "Like hell I would."

His former staffer tried to smile through their mutual discomfort. "Governor Gilkey thought maybe you'd like to come down to Salem and say a few words."

"Pose for a couple of pictures, smile and shake hands, just like I didn't care that he ran a dirty campaign."

Thayer set down his coffee cup. "I'm sorry, Governor. I didn't mean for my visit to—"

"And don't call me Governor. Or sir. That's all over."

"I'm sorry. I—"

"You can call me Dayson, or Mr. Dayson, or Martin if you have the nerve, or Pops, if that suits you." Dayson was surprised by his own bitterness and didn't want to inspect the likelihood he was taking out on Art the anger he nursed over all the trials of the past half-year.

He ran his hands over his face. "I'm sorry, Art. I don't know what gets into me." He made a little laugh as if none of this hurt. "You probably didn't want to come out here to begin with, but Gilkey left it to you to bell the cat."

"No. When Mr. Bremmer"—he named Gilkey's chief of staff—"asked if someone could talk to you, I volunteered. I figured you and I . . . Well . . ."

Dayson chuckled. Thayer was young and didn't know when he was being used. Of course he offered to be the one to see his old boss. They knew he would. Had been counting on it.

"Look, go back to Norm and tell him I was happy to see you. We had a good talk and you told me what you needed to tell me. And if he wants my help he can damn well call me himself." The young man's face went slack. "C'mon, Art, pick your chin off the floor. You're smart. You can find a way to say it without getting fired. It's fine. We're fine. You came out here with a message. You did your job great, and I'm sending you back with another message. That's all."

"Sure." Thayer nodded and tried to smile.

With the hardest part of the visit out of the way, Dayson let Thayer off the hook. With the storm still blowing outside, they talked about this and that, Thayer's old job and his new one, the gentler tone recalling the ease of their former relationship. Art had a funny story to tell about something that happened to the State Treasurer.

Dayson didn't realize he hadn't really been listening until the young man stopped speaking. He sensed a question hanging in the air.

"Sorry?" he asked

"Nothing. It's just that you were looking out the window, like there's someone out there."

"Huh? No. No one's there." He looked again out the window. "There's no one there."

After a few more minutes of cordiality Thayer rose to go. "Thanks for seeing me . . ." The young man stopped, embarrassed that he wasn't able to call him Governor nor able not to.

Dayson gave him a handshake and a simulation of his old smile. "Good to see you, Art. Congratulations on the new job. Gilkey's lucky to have you." He clapped the young man on the shoulder and guided him toward the front door. "But tell Norm to call me himself if he wants my help."

He stood in the shadows of his living room and watched his former aide get in his car and sit for some time before starting the engine. It wasn't going to be much fun reporting back to Bremmer that he hadn't been able to get a commitment out of his old boss. If Thayer had thoughts of offering himself up as the new administration's channel to the Republicans, based on his personal connections, this was a damned poor start and he knew it.

He was an ambitious young man, and that was fine, as far as it went. But was he anything else? Like most staffers, he must dream of running for office one day. If he imagined getting elected to the state House, a logical starting point, he'd better grow a thicker skin.

"Ah, hell," Dayson said aloud. He was getting old and grouchy. Art was a good kid. He shouldn't have sent him off looking like he'd been slapped in the face with a wet fish.

With a guilt-tinged sigh, Dayson went back to his study, where he sat at his desk shuffling through the scraps of notes he intended to somehow render into a volume of memoirs. For the hundredth time he asked himself why he had taken on the project. For the hundredth time he stumbled over the answer. He was doing it because everyone told him he should. He had a story to tell, people said. Such a fascinating life.

Maybe they hoped he would justify their own faith in him, give them something they could point to and insist they had dedicated themselves to a remarkable man. More likely, they couldn't think of anything better he could do with what years were left to him than go off into a corner and scribble. All he knew was that he couldn't match their enthusiasm to inspect his life and tell people what he found.

And there was the war, the war and what had happened to him—or, more rightly, what had not happened to him—and he didn't want to lie about that any more than he wanted to tell the truth.

After a while he put down his pen, picked up the little statue and sat for a long time gazing into its inscrutable features.

Chapter Seven

The Burning Bed

The weather broke the following day, leaving clear, cold nights and a light frost that melted in the morning sun.

Shovel in hand, bundled in a heavy sweater and thick gloves, Dayson stood at the edge of the torn-up earth of his intended garden, his breath steaming in the cold air, confronting the suspicion that all his haphazard digging—shallow here, deeper there, hopelessly unsystematic—was playing out like a pattern of the disorder that had become his life.

Even as he shoveled the damp earth, Art Thayer's visit continued to play at the edge of his mind. Why was Norm Gilkey suddenly angling for his support? And by proxy at that, sending someone who didn't seem to know much about whatever it was Gilkey had in mind. Art had said the new bill improved on the Tyee project, but couldn't tell him how. Dayson suspected the still-unknown changes would explain why Gilkey needed him, and why no one had told Art about them before sending him out to gain his support.

And the girl.

With a petulant kick at the ground, he told himself he should go back inside rather than waste his time working in the dirt with no plan and only the vaguest purpose.

Only as he turned to go back inside did Dayson become conscious that he had for some time smelled smoke on the air. Standing in the middle of his back yard, he searched the sky around him.

His breath caught at the sight of a column of black smoke rising beyond the patch of woods to the south of his house, its swirling cloud so emblematic of his own confused thoughts that he wondered if his mind had simply projected a mirage against the sky. But the quickly growing scent of burning wood told him it was real enough.

He shuffled toward the path that led into the woods, trying to think what could possibly burn after several days of rain. He broke into a clumsy trot as the answer came clear to him.

By the time he got to the edge of the clearing, the shack was wholly consumed in flames, the smoke growing thinner, turning from black to white as the fire burned more fiercely. Had the Primus stove somehow exploded, or its modest flame caught on something set too close? Or had a soul in despair purposely set the fire? These thoughts spoke to the possibility someone was still in the shack, and he feared who it might be.

Puffing from exertion and anxiety, Dayson walked rapidly across the clearing to within a few feet of the burning shack.

"Hey! Hey!" he called, the strength in his voice sapped by the knowledge that, if someone was still in the shack, he had come too late.

With a deep groan, one wall of the shack collapsed, bringing the roof down with it. Dayson's own groan followed it, then cut off in mid-breath.

The collapse of the shack revealed the girl standing at the opposite edge of the fire. Seen through the flames, her image shimmered like a dream. She stood with her feet apart, her eyes startlingly wide, as if she were an ancient vestal caught in the midst of a dark rite. At her feet lay a red five-gallon Jerrycan, tipped on its side.

Dayson scoffed at his own foolishness for thinking the girl might have immolated herself in the throes of despair. No, whatever her emotional state, this girl would be no one's victim.

By the time these thoughts raced through his head, she had seen him too. She opened her mouth and he thought he caught the sound of her voice above the crackling of the flames. He strained to catch what she was trying to tell him. Even as she called to him, she stood motionless, though her wavering image, seen through the lens of fire, made her appear to dance before him.

Then, as she had that day in the rain, and now before a fire, she fled, turning and running across the far side of the clearing into a line of trees and gone.

Suddenly alone, Martin Dayson tried to understand what had happened and what it meant. If not for the fire still burning in front of him, he might have wondered if he had imagined the whole thing.

He knew he should run back home and call the fire department. Any responsible citizen would. And he had always been the most responsible of citizens.

Still, he didn't move. If he called, he would have to tell the firemen what he had seen, or decide on some lie to protect the girl. Either way, they would have to investigate the fire. Deserted shacks don't spontaneously burst into flames.

If, as the Greenburgs hinted, the little community likely knew something of the girl's rendezvous at the shack, people would rightly suspect her of having set the fire.

He told himself he needed to make sure she was held accountable for her actions before she did any further harm. Yet he sensed that, for her own reasons, the girl who haunted the path behind his house had kindled a cleansing fire, expiated something he could not fathom. She had the courage to burn away her old life and start anew.

Fighting the guilt—and excitement—of transgressing important norms, Dayson decided he would allow her that. He would say nothing, make no call.

Dayson kept an eye on the fire for some time, watched the old shack's last wall collapse in a cloud of sparks. No neighbors came to investigate. With no trees near, surrounded only by the damp grass, the fire would not spread.

After the blaze had reduced itself to embers and a few sputtering flames, Dayson headed back to the path in the woods. Once he had regained the treeline, he stopped and looked back at the dying fire and knew, if he wanted to protect the girl, there was one more thing he needed to do.

He walked back toward the remains of the shack, staying away from its still-considerable heat, and crossed to where the girl had dropped the Jerrycan. Though empty, it still smelled of stove oil.

Setting the fire was arson. Never mind that no one but her cared about the shack. Tampering with evidence would make him an accessory. But leaving the can where an investigator might find it could send the girl to prison if anyone cared enough to press charges.

The loaded syllogism—if he was a good citizen, and good citizens report crimes, then . . . — played through his mind, challenging his sense of himself.

After a moment, not so much of hesitation as of steeling himself to do something both absolutely right and utterly wrong, he bent down, picked up the can and walked back to his house, knowing that, by doing so, he had forged an uncomfortable link with this enigmatic young woman.

Chapter Eight

The Keepers of the Old House

Martin Dayson stood at the counter while Rose Greenburg toted up his purchases. As she punched the "Total" button and the register dinged open, her husband came out from the back of the store. "I hope you haven't come looking for that dollar from Sarah Tannehill."

"I'm not worried about a buck."

"Anyway, she hasn't come by for a day or two," Herb Greenburg said. "Says she's not feeling well."

"It was her niece who come by to tell us, not Sarah," Mrs. Greenburg corrected him.

"I guess maybe it was her niece." The ghost of a smile played across the grocer's face. "I keep waiting for that nephew to show his face around here."

"You'll wait a long time, Greenburg," his wife told him, and added, "Sarah's got to be pretty bad again not to do her own shopping."

"Again?" Dayson asked.

"Kind of a regular thing." Herb raised his eyebrows to make clear there was a lot he wasn't saying.

"She need a doctor?" Dayson asked.

Mrs. Greenburg blew out a breath, and Dayson had the feeling he was missing something that should have been clear. "Can't afford a doctor. The girl only goes to college because of some scholarship or something. What she did to get it, Lord knows," she sniffed, giving her husband a loaded glance as broad as any wink.

"Now, Rose, we don't know anything about that," her husband said. "From what I hear, she's plenty bright enough to get a scholarship."

"Anyway," Rose Greenburg said, "it can't be good for a young girl to be living in that old place with Sarah."

Greenburg shrugged to close the topic. "Neither of them has two nickels to rub together. Sarah'll just have to ride it out. Don't know what the girl will do if something happens to her aunt."

The smell of hot tar filled the air as Dayson walked out of the store. A hundred yards up the highway a road crew worked in the spring sun, spreading the tar with long rakes while a guy at the controls of a steam roller waited for them to finish.

"Widening the goddamn road."

Dayson turned toward the sound of the voice and found a tall, sharp-featured man of about his own age standing on the porch of the Greenburgs' store. He wore muddy boots and bib overalls and an old shapeless hat, the whole of it spelling farmer as clearly as a sign around his neck.

"What's that?" Dayson asked.

"They're widening the goddamn road."

Dayson looked again at the road crew, then back at the farmer. "That's a good thing, isn't it?"

The man leaned over and spit in the dirt. "Sure, if you're from Portland." He invested the name with the locals' habitual note of contempt for the big city. "It's fine if all you want to do is tear through here a little faster on your way to the beach. It's only an hour away now. What do they want? Forty minutes? No time at all? And for what? To get some sand in their shoes. Folks'll roar through without even noticing we're here. And another thing—a big highway makes it easier for people from Forest Grove, Hillsboro, what-have-you, to come out here and put up a bunch of cheap houses, 'cause now they can race from here into work in no time. Price of land goes up. Taxes go up. Tell me what happens to the farmer then." Without waiting for a reply, he said, "It's already happening. People buying up land."

"Buying up land? Who?"

The farmer wagged his head. "Don't know. Don't matter. Not enough water. Only thing that holds 'em back from scooping up everything."

"But there's plenty of water around here."

The farmer shook his head, marveling at Dayson's ignorance. "All of it from wells. Can't build a bunch of houses with only well water. Thank God, I say."

For all the spending bills he'd signed for road improvements, highway repaving and new bridges, Dayson had never considered the possibility they were anything but a boon.

"I hadn't thought of it that way," he said, more to himself than to the man on the porch.

"'Bout time you did." The farmer took the edge off his comment with a grimace he may have thought looked like a smile. "You're probably from Portland yourself."

"No. Yamhill. Live up Hayward Road now."

"Yamhill." The farmer seemed to find this satisfactory. "Well, then," he said as if Dayson had acknowledged some irrefutable point. He climbed into his battered pickup, hauling himself into the cab with a hitch in his gait that spoke to an old injury. He gave Dayson a wave and pulled out onto the highway.

Dayson waved back and watched him disappear down the road.

Vaguely agitated, Dayson pulled into his driveway a few minutes later without any memory of the short drive home. After putting his groceries away he puttered aimlessly around the house, changed a light bulb, tightened a door knob, thumbed through his mail. Finally, he threw the bills and mailers onto his desk and, yielding to the impulse that had been eating at him since he had left the Greenburgs' store, headed back outside toward the path leading to Sarah Tannehill's crumbling dark house.

The distance was shorter than he'd remembered and he soon shouldered his way through the gap in the overgrown hedge, crossed the back yard and went around to the front of the house.

The faded and blistered door shook in its frame under his knocking. Though he got no response, he sensed someone inside, or perhaps imagined a troubling vibration radiating from the house itself, a structure as isolated and solitary as its inhabitants.

After waiting a few moments, Dayson knocked once more, then a third time before he grunted unhappily and turned to walk away.

He'd got no further than the bottom of the steps when he heard the door creak open behind him.

Illuminated in a sliver of sunlight stood the young woman he'd seen so many times and knew so little.

At the sight of the man whose land she so often crossed, she made a sharp intake of breath and raised her hand toward her face, like a delayed reaction to the heat of the burning shack where he had seen her last, or as if to wipe away the tears that had betrayed her when he found her weeping on the path behind his house.

Dayson searched her face for some trace of the wildness he had seen in her eyes through the wavering light of the fire, or the bitterness that had consumed her when she had shouted at him through the pouring rain that he had no idea what she wanted. He looked for the dark shadows he had seen around her eyes. But she had the physical resilience of youth and her smooth features betrayed no sign of her previous anguish. Instead, he found only wariness.

"What are you doing here?" she asked.

"I heard your aunt was sick."

In her hand she held a paperback book, her finger holding her place. He remembered the lamp he had noticed behind the lace curtains the first time he had seen the house. Was she the one he'd imagined reading by its light?

Her face dark with suspicion, she seemed about to say something—most likely, "Go away!"—when her eyes slid away from him and she glanced over her shoulder toward the second floor. Had a voice called from some corner of the old house?

When the girl turned back to him, she had made a decision.

"You may come in."

As he passed by her in the doorway, Dayson was startled to see she stood a good couple inches taller than himself. He had long been accustomed to being a touch shorter than most other men, but finding this girl looming over him sparked a tiny shiver of intimidation.

The spring morning had come on warm, but the house retained something of the winter's chill. Before him, a large living room, what would have been called a parlor in the era when the house was built, lay in shadow, its blinds drawn. To the right, a staircase led to the second floor.

The house was decently appointed with furniture of an earlier era. But the air was musty and a closer glance revealed a layer of dust on everything. Despite the two people who lived here, the place gave off an undertone of emptiness, like a museum exhibit of a domestic past.

"What do you want?" she asked.

She wore the long, plain dress he'd seen before, either badly out of date or emblematic of a new mode Dayson hadn't noticed yet. Her long straight flaxen hair hung loosely down her back—bold, even provocative, in an era of perms and curls and pony tails. And there was something else. Standing this close, he caught a hint of a flowery perfume that plucked a chord of memory. Yes, the scent he had noticed in the old shack in the clearing.

Each time he saw her she seemed a different person; the blithe lover flitting across his property, the fierce young woman crying in the rain, the wild spirit setting fire to her trysting place, and now the grave mistress of a dying house. All of them true, he sensed, and all of them disguises.

"What do I want?" Dayson replied. "I don't want anything."

But of course he did.

"I understand your aunt might need a doctor," he said, because he couldn't very well tell her, "I came to see if it was you who lived here with this batty dame."

"A doctor? Why would you think my—?" She stopped herself in mid-sentence and again looked over her shoulder toward the staircase, then turned back at Dayson. "I'm taking care of her."

"I understand she falls ill a lot."

The girl said nothing, but clasped her hands in front of her, her self-possession the fortress within which she stood.

With that, Dayson saw himself for the intruder he was, banging on the door, barging in, enquiring after the girl's aunt, trying to take charge as though he were, yes, the governor.

The girl raised her chin and parted her lips. Before she could speak, a voice came from upstairs.

"Mattie! Mattie! Who is that at the door? If he's another one of those men trying to buy my land you can tell him to go away and leave me alone." Despite her attempt to sound authoritative, her voice warbled on a high querulous note. "Mattie!" she cried again.

If Sarah Tannehill was unwell it had not diminished her voice.

The young woman—she had a name, Mattie—called up the stairs, "It's a neighbor."

"A what?" The idea surprised the older woman to silence, but only momentarily. "You are not to bring any men into my house without my leave," she called. "You know that. While you live in this house you will conduct yourself like a lady."

The girl pursed her lips, but betrayed no other sign of irritation at the older woman's words.

Her eyes still on Dayson, she called up the stairs, "I don't know him."

Perfectly true and perfectly false.

"What in the world . . .? Bring him up here."

Without a word, the young woman mounted the steps. Halfway up she stopped and looked back at Dayson, still standing near the door, and waited for him to follow her.

A row of closed doors added to the gloom of the upper hall, its darkness broken by a dim light spilling through the doorway nearest the stairs. The young woman, Mattie—Dayson felt oddly as if he had lost something in discovering her name—waited until he had caught up with her, then led him in.

A rumpled double bed with a nightstand took up one side of the room. On the other stood a wooden dresser. Over all of it hung a faint odor of decay. A lowered blind cast an orange glow over the room, a color intensified by the heat produced from the oil stove in the corner of the room. Next to it sat a red metal can, the twin of the one the girl had used to burn down the shack. Dayson looked from the can to the girl, who stood against the wall near the door. She made no reaction but for a slight arching of one eyebrow. He bit his lip to keep from smiling in admiration of her poise.

As Dayson's eyes adjusted to the dimness, he saw a figure sitting in a chair in front of the window, a blanket covering her legs and lap, her feet on a low wooden stool. Sarah Tannehill was not a large woman, but her upright posture and the bulkiness of the blanket gave her an outsized presence.

Silhouetted as she was against the window, Dayson couldn't see her features clearly, though he knew she would be able to see him. Did she recognize him from their meeting at the store?

"Yes?" She asked, though it was a demand, not a question.

"I understand you're not feeling well."

He expected her to deny any weakness or to dismiss his question as none of his affair. Instead, she turned her head away until she was looking at him out of the corner of one eye.

"I suppose those tiresome Greenburgs sent you," she said with a caginess that told Dayson she was fishing.

"No one sent me. They only mentioned you were ill because you're a neighbor and they're concerned."

She settled further back into the chair and said nothing.

Dayson glanced again at her niece, who stood with her back against the wall, silently watching. He turned back to the woman sitting in the chair. "I've got a friend, Dr. Kimmel, who could come by and see you."

"I am not the sort to accept charity."

Like hell you're not, Dayson wanted to say.

"If you'd like, Mrs. Tannehill, I could ask him to come by after his office hours today."

She weighed the value of his offer against the satisfaction of refusing him.

"If it would make you happy," she said.

"It would."

"All right. As it will make you feel better to send him, then send him." Again she turned her head away and flicked her hand to dismiss him.

Dayson struggled to swallow his irritation with the woman. Who the hell did she think she was? The answer came back to him with sudden clarity: No, who the hell do I think I am?

With a grunt that contained a legion of unspoken words, Dayson turned and walked out of the room. As he passed Mattie they exchanged a look. Did hers carry a hint of apology at her aunt's behavior?

He almost didn't hear Mattie following him downstairs. When they stood close enough to each other that he judged her aunt couldn't overhear them, he said, "Tell me, why did you think you had to burn down the—"

She cut him off with a quick, "Good day."

After putting up with her aunt's curt manner, Dayson was in no mood to take any more of it from her niece and thought to demand an answer from her. But her eyes betrayed unease behind the defiance. He decided to let it go.

When he said nothing more, she released a deep breath, and he realized that the scene in her aunt's room had taken more out of her than it had from him.

"I'll look after the doctor's charges," he told her. She seemed about to refuse. "Let me do this for you."

"I don't need—"

"Then for your aunt."

"For . . . my aunt." She regarded him for a long time, as silent as the house itself. At last, she relented. "That would be kind of you."

Dayson nodded up toward Sarah's room. "She says someone's trying to buy this place?" He hadn't meant to sound as if this were hard to believe.

The girl, Mattie, hesitated a moment before answering. "Yes. An agent continues to pester her, no matter how many times she says she's not selling. I suppose you get similar offers. They must come up to you while you're digging."

"No, I don't." An odd chord resonated in what the girl had said. "How do you know what I do?"

She clasped her hands in front of her. "What you do? Nothing. It's only that everyone here works their land a bit." She said this with such unruffled aplomb that Dayson almost believed her. He wondered again if she had been spying on him, but decided that anyone walking past his place as often as she had could see he'd been digging.

He looked around the weary rooms, saw the accumulating dust, felt the dead air. "Is there anything else I can do for you?"

"We're not charity cases."

"No." An awkward silence fell between them. "Are you all right?" he asked.

"All right? Why shouldn't I be?"

Why did she have to make everything so damn difficult? "I've been concerned about you, after . . ." He nodded in the direction of the burnt-out shack, and toward the place where he had found her crying in the rain. She could take her pick of which one might be the cause of his concern. "I thought maybe you—"

"I'm fine."

This wasn't how he wanted their conversation to end, and he decided to take a lighter tack. "I understand you're a college girl."

She cocked her head to one side as if trying to see around the question before answering. "Yes."

"English? Home Ec?"

Her eyes flared with indignation, and for a moment he caught an unexpected glimpse of the young woman who had set fire to the shack. "Just because I'm a woman doesn't mean I have to apply myself to someone's idea of tamed domesticity."

With a little pop of surprise, Dayson caught a glimmer, not of her limits, but of his own.

He covered with a smile. "You must be plenty smart. I understand you have a big scholarship."

To his surprise, she ducked her head and blushed a deep red. After taking his previous pointed remarks in stride, what seemed to him the most anodyne comment had thrown her off-center.

To the degree their exchange had been any sort of conversation at all, it had grown into an increasingly difficult one, sowing more confusion than clarity, leaving him perplexed and, against his will, further intrigued by this young woman.

"A scholarship isn't something to be ashamed of," he said, trying to fashion a disarming smile.

He felt the line of her vision slide away from him, refusing eye contact, until she was looking just over his head. With exquisite diction she said, "Why should you think I'm ashamed?"

And, like that, it came clear to him—why she saw her lover in such secrecy, why she would blush at obtaining a scholarship. "He was your professor, wasn't he? The one at the shack."

A momentary look of surprise lighted her eyes, but she betrayed nothing.

"Is that why your aunt doesn't want any men friends in her house?"

Her embarrassed blush turned to a flush of anger. "You have the most absurd notions. And I can't see how it would be any concern of yours. However, if you would send your Dr. Kimmel around, my aunt will be grateful."

"I doubt that. But I'll do it anyway."

Though he expected her to slam the door in his face at this remark, he saw instead a glimmer of suppressed laughter. From the tatters of their talk—what was said and what was left unsaid—emerged an unexpected hint of conspiracy between them about her aunt.

When she didn't dismiss him, it struck Dayson that, despite her icy distance and her show of temper, she didn't want him to leave. In this dark and crumbling house, with her aunt's domineering spirit squeezing into every corner, they must receive few visitors.

What was she doing here? Where were her parents? He knew that if he asked any of these questions she would reply with further evasions.

Suddenly he was weary of it, of her, of this fencing in the dark. He reminded himself he had come only to make an offer of assistance, helping a neighbor, nothing more. He could claim no reward, and their acceptance conferred no obligation.

"I'd better get going. I'm supposed to meet someone for lunch in Hillsboro," Dayson said, "I hope Dr. Kimmel can help your aunt."

As he put on his mask of formality, she took up hers as well.

"Thank you," she said, her manner again distant, protective of her aunt's privacy, and her own.

He nodded his goodbye, descended the stone steps, made his way again through the gap in the hedge and back up the path, somehow feeling more agitated than he had before he arrived.

Chapter Nine

Jocie

Dayson sat at a table in the little cafe, his hands folded around his coffee cup, and told himself he wasn't thinking of the young woman who lived in the old house on Hayward Road. Told himself several times.

He looked out the window to avoid making eye contact with the other customers. Even if no one said anything or tried to catch his eye, he could sense when people recognized him despite his unkempt beard and long hair and he heard their whispers.

As they finished their meals and walked out, a few of the patrons gave him a little wave or said a few words. Dayson smiled or nodded or lifted his chin in acknowledgment, always cordial, but heading off any further exchange. He told himself he'd have to let his beard grow longer.

He saw her through the window, head down, walking quickly, knowing she was late. When she came into the café he rose and held out his arms.

"Hi, Daddy."

Twenty-six years old and she still called him Daddy. And it still made him smile. A prick of conscience caused him to wonder if she called him that because she had only been a little girl, still calling him Daddy, when he had first gone off to war, then off to Salem, and his absence had prevented their relationship from maturing.

"Hi, Jocie. Good to see you."

He felt the reserve in her peck on the cheek, the half-hug. But he was happy to see her and told himself not to mind. If she was still sore at him, she had reason.

He hadn't seen her since Christmas, though he'd called a couple of times—short, awkward conversations with sudden goodbyes. So, he had been surprised when, a couple of days earlier, she had called him for the first time in months and said they should get together for lunch. "You need to get out of that house of yours. I'm afraid you're turning into some kind of anchorite."

You have to put down good money to send your daughter to a college where she comes out knowing words like that.

They had agreed to meet at a place off Main Street in Hillsboro, despite the fact that it was only a block away from the county courthouse, a place where government employees on their lunch hour were more likely to see past the hair and beard and recognize him. Maybe that was why she had picked the place. For all her bitterness at his absences, she liked to be recognized with him, was still proud of him.

They looked over the menu, talked about what they might order—the Reuben sandwich was supposed to be good—and how traffic had been and, no, she hadn't come out from Portland, where she worked at a law firm, but from the family's farm out at Yamhill, where she'd been visiting her mother.

The waitress came to take their order, giving Dayson a smile that said she knew who he was. He smiled back. When she left he and his daughter found they had nothing to say. Or many things to say but no way to say them.

Into the growing silence, he managed to ask, "How's Ed?"

"Fine. He works too hard." Her husband taught high school English, but didn't like it.

Looking away in a manner he wished to appear natural, he asked, "And how's your mother?"

A little pause, "She's fine."

"She doing okay?"

"Yes."

"Was Tommy there?"

"Daddy . . ."

"Just asking." He smiled, trying to make it seem like a joke. "Gotta say *something.*"

"What you gotta is you gotta stop hiding out at your place in— where?—Topping. I mean, really, Topping?"

"It's beautiful out there. You should come see my place."

For his sake, she smiled. "Mom's fine. Ed's fine. I'm fine. It's you who's the problem. You need to be doing something other than moping around that house."

"I'm not moping around the house."

"Yes, you are. Mom says so too. When I asked you to come to Hillsboro you sounded like I'd asked you to meet me in Outer Mongolia. You need to get out, get involved."

"Hell, Jocie, you hated it when I *was* involved."

She leaned back in her chair, putting distance between them. "Let's not go over all that again. I talked with Mom for a long time today, and maybe I understand better why you wanted to get into politics. How much it meant to you." She frowned. "What's the matter?"

"With me? Nothing."

Had Dorothy told her the real reason he'd run for office? It had always been just between the two of them, the thing he could tell no one but her.

Jocie put her hand over his. "I'm a little worried, that's all."

"Worried? I thought you were just mad at me."

"I'm not mad at you." She registered the look he gave her. "Okay. I have been, but I told myself that's all over."

"Sure. Now that I've lost my work and I'm humiliated, it's fine now. Maybe you're saying that's what you were hoping for." He knew the injustice in what he said and wondered why he was doing this.

"That's not fair."

"It seems to me you wanted—"

"Wanted? I wanted you. I wanted my daddy, without having to ask your secretary whether you had time for me, without having to share you with whoever came into your office and said they needed a minute."

"It wasn't like that. Maybe once I was governor, okay. But you were an adult by then. When I was in the House—"

"When you were in the House you'd leave before I got up and you'd work all day at the Capitol, then hang out at the Coaster with the other politicians and the lobbyists."

"C'mon, Joss, you were in college for a lot of that."

"But I still needed you! And before that it was the war, and I didn't see you for . . . How long was it?"

He felt the anger rising in him, knew its heat came from the fact that she was right but that she refused to understand him or the times in which he'd lived.

"I couldn't just stay home when other men were dying for our country. We all have things we have to do. I had to go."

"Just like you had to run for governor. Why did you think you needed to do that?"

He had never told her what had driven his ambition, and he vowed he never would.

"Daddy, anyone else could have been a soldier. Only you could be my father. And when you came back after the war you were always cross. You'd hardly say anything, and you'd go around acting like you were feeling guilty about something."

He looked away and shook his head. "I thought you said this was all behind us now."

She bit her lip and looked out the window, her face working with emotions that threatened to end in tears.

He reached across the table. She let him take her hands in his. "Jocie, I'm sorry. You're right, right about all of it."

She took a deep breath. "Mom wants to have the farm."

For a long time Dayson sat without moving.

"Daddy?"

"Look, the divorce is a long way from being settled."

"Because you don't do anything to settle it. And Mom will get her way on everything because you won't do anything to stop her. She wishes you'd stand up and show a little life. She doesn't want everything, but if you won't say what you want . . ."

"Tommy's got a farm. Why in the hell does she need two?"

"She doesn't. She wants the farm so she can give it to Ed and me."

"Oh." For a moment he couldn't say more, surprised by the arrangement his still-wife and forever-daughter had worked out between them. "Well, maybe I want the farm so I can be the one who gives it to you."

"Be serious, Daddy. You've never suggested anything like that."

"I never had the chance. Her lawyers have me so tied in knots . . ." He tilted his chair back and looked at the ceiling. "That's a bunch of baloney, isn't it? I've had plenty of chances."

"Daddy?"

"Yeah, Joss?"

"Ed and I would really like to have the farm."

"Sure."

"What's that mean? Sure we can have it? Sure, of course we'd want it?"

Still staring at the ceiling, he made a little shake of his head. "I dunno. Both, I guess. It's yours if you'd like it."

"Daddy?"

"Mmmm?"

"So why did you get into politics?"

"I thought you said your mom told you all about that."

"She thinks she did. But she was talking around something. I could tell. Something bigger than what she said."

"I guess we're always talking around the things we really want to say, aren't we? Hoping the other person will understand without us actually having to say the words." He didn't expect an answer. "I always loved your mother, y'know."

She bowed her head and said quietly, "I know."

"I'm sorry for all of it, Jocie. But I look back and I don't see where I could have done it any differently and still done the things I needed to do."

"That's sort of what Mom said."

"Smart lady, your mom." He poured a little milk in his coffee. "They tell you life is short, Joss. But it's not. It's really long. You can screw things up all kinds of ways, and maybe still have time to make it right in the end."

"I hope so, Daddy. I think you can. If you'll let yourself."

A cheery ding came from the kitchen, as the cook hit his handbell.

"Order up!"

Chapter Ten

The Seeker

Dayson had imagined, hoped, that the anthropologist Batch sent—this Frank Persig guy—would fit his notion of the typical academic, pale and thin, even shorter than himself, with a whiff of the library about him, someone he could browbeat and run off. All of which left him unprepared for the tall broad-shouldered fellow who appeared around the corner of his house one morning while he stood in the back yard with a hoe in his hand. Maybe twenty-five years old, wearing a Pendleton shirt and a wide-brimmed hat, Persig looked more like a lumberjack than a PhD candidate.

He introduced himself with a firm handshake, addressed Dayson as Governor and, after a brief exchange of courtesies, asked if he could see where he had discovered the figurine.

"I suppose so. And knock off the 'Governor' stuff. It's just Dayson," he grumbled.

The old pol expected—hoped for—a flash of anger from Persig, but got only a narrow-eyed frown. Something troubled behind his brown eyes, Dayson thought, a guardedness. And something more. A lack of sureness. In Dayson? In himself? He recalled Batch telling him that the young man needed something, though his friend had failed to specify what.

Standing at the edge of the half-finished garden plot, the two men regarded the haphazard collection of crumbling holes that dotted the ground like a case of acne. Persig pushed his hat back, thrust his hands in his back pockets and asked, "So, where did you dig up this carving?"

Dayson nodded toward the far corner of the plot. "Right around there somewhere, give or take a couple of feet."

Persig winced at Dayson's vagueness.

"I suppose you're going to tell me that all my digging has made a wreck of everything."

The young man looked at the torn up earth in a speculative way. "I don't know. Did you find anything more?"

"Not a thing."

"Then it doesn't really matter."

Dayson harrumphed to cover his relief, irritated by the realization that he wanted this kid's good opinion. "Now don't start telling me you want to tear up the whole area. You can have that half, but this half is my garden." The fact that, as yet, he had no garden made him all the more adamant.

Persig pursed his lips and nodded. "Okay."

His ready acquiescence grated on Dayson's nerves. "So, do you know what you're looking for?"

"Not really. We'll see what we can find and try to make some sense of it."

"And if you don't find anything."

"Then it doesn't make any sense."

Persig looked at the broken ground and the undisturbed area that edged it. "How about letting us dig into this grassy part next to your garden?"

Dayson felt the impulse to say no, but didn't want it getting back to Batch that he had agreed to let this guy come out then made it impossible for him to get his work done.

"Yeah, I guess that's all right," he allowed. "But what's this 'we' stuff?"

"I usually work with a couple of undergrads."

"Unh-unh." Dayson shook his head. "I told Bachelder I didn't want a bunch of people tramping around out here. Just one person. You or someone else, I don't care. But just one. That's the only way I'll say yes."

The tall young man's face darkened as he appeared to consider several possibilities, including getting back in his car and driving away. But after a moment he said, "Fair enough," and held out his hand. "Deal."

A little disappointed—he had been looking forward to an argument—Dayson reluctantly took his offered hand. "Deal."

They made a quick affirmative handshake, and Persig nodded toward the house. "Now, why don't you show me what you've found?"

* * *

Persig stood at the study window and let the morning light play on the stone figure in his hands. Like Robert Bachelder before him, he ran his hand over the statue's time-stippled surface. Yet the intensity in his gaze and the way he drew his fingers slowly over the features of the little fertility goddess—like a blind man reading the most arcane form of braille—suggested a different kind of search.

Behind him, Dayson stood with his hands in his pockets. "Well, what do you think?"

His eyes still on the bit of stone in his hand, Persig said, "I don't know what to make of it. How did something like this come to be here?" He ran his hand over the statuette again and tried to absorbed the message transmitted by its ancient features. "I'm surprised it was so close to the surface. About a foot down, you say." He hefted the figure, trying to judge its weight. "I suppose the earth can hold its treasures for many lifetimes, and then decide to give them up."

The young man had a touch of the poet about him, not an easy thing to bear in a world full of literalists. But there was something deeper eating at him.

Persig looked out at the back yard before turning to Dayson. "So, do you want me to go to work?"

The impulse to tell Persig to shove off and not come back felt clear and good. But Dayson's need to understand how this figurine had come into his life and what it meant to those who had carved it went deep.

Trying to sound off-hand, as if he were doing this for Persig's sake rather than his own, he said, "Yeah, let's have you get to work."

"I'll come out two or three days a week."

"Alone."

"If that's what you want. And we'll see what we find."

"All right," Dayson growled.

"Why don't I start today. My equipment is in the car."

"I'll meet you in the back yard."

* * *

While he walked out the back door and into the yard Dayson tried to imagine all the paraphernalia Persig would bring with him—picks, shovels, buckets and who knew what else—and realized how poorly formed were his notions of archaeologists, or anthropologists, or whatever it was this guy claimed to be.

As he waited for Persig, Dayson lifted his gaze toward the path that ran across his property, empty now. He hadn't seen his young trespasser for several days. If he expected to feel satisfaction from the thought, he found none. An image of the girl as an enigmatic avatar, like his statue, but of flesh, not stone, flitted half-formed through his mind.

Before he could pursue the thought further a clanking of metal drew his attention to Frank Persig coming around the corner of the house. Despite the clanging overture, he carried no pickax, no shovel, only some metal stakes, a hammer, a tape measure and what looked like a large ball of twine. A small box camera hung from a strap around his neck.

As Persig set to work, Dayson retrieved a spade from the utility room and for the next hour or so turned over ground for his garden—a plausible excuse to stick around and see what the young man might find.

To Dayson's surprise, Persig, whistling as he worked, spent a great deal of time taking photos of the back yard from various angles, and of the holes he had dug, even going down the short slope beyond the firs to the edge of the fields to take pictures of the far hills and the little stream at the base of the slope. When he returned he set his camera aside, stepped into the dirt plot and, using his tape measure to gauge the distance, began to drive his short stakes into the ground, connecting them with the twine to form a neat grid of two-foot squares.

Dayson didn't want to betray his curiosity nor complain about the kid's damned whistling, but couldn't keep from nodding at the half-finished grid and asking, "So, you going to dig, or play checkers?"

Dayson enjoyed getting the young man's goat. But if he resented Persig's presence, Persig appeared equally irritated at his.

As if talking to a child, Persig, said, "If I find anything I need to be able to document where it lay in relation to everything else. It helps me search in a more systematic way."

"You make digging a hole sound pretty complicated."

Wrapping twine around a stake, the younger man lifted his eyes toward Dayson's would-be garden. "You're preparing your ground. I'm preparing mine."

Dayson returned to his own digging until he again felt blisters forming on his too-soft hands and went inside for a while before coming out again, curious about what the young man had accomplished.

Persig had finished his grid and was brushing dirt off his hands. "That'll have to do for the day. I've got to get back into town, work on my dissertation."

As Dayson watched Persig walk around the corner of the house toward his car, he felt both anticipation and regret, dreading the idea of someone violating the bastion of solitude he had worked so hard to build around himself, yet tantalized by the possibility that this young man might find something that would shed light on the meaning of the stone figure.

Late that same afternoon Dr. Kimmel stopped by Dayson's house. A tall, slim man who evidently lived the advice of exercise and sensible diet he gave his patients, Josiah Kimmel was only a few months younger than Dayson, and in their brief acquaintance the two men had reached an intuitive understanding of each other.

After Dayson had waved the physician toward a chair in the living room and poured them each a scotch, he asked, "So, Doctor, how's our patient?"

Kimmel sipped his drink and looked dissatisfied. "Hard to say. She's a difficult woman."

"You know her?"

"It's a small community, Governor." Allowing Kimmel to call him Governor seemed to Dayson a fair exchange for calling him Doctor. "I knew her husband Archie much better. We were both members of Rotary. Good man, active, involved. I think it was always a difficult marriage. She was several years younger than Archie and better educated. I think she'd had a year of college. Wouldn't let him forget it. And she has a temper." Kimmel swirled the ice in his drink. "She didn't seem to care much for life on the farm. Now and then, after she'd had one of her fights with Archie, she'd take off, be gone a couple of weeks. I don't know what it was they argued about, but the lulls between fights never lasted very long. One time, years ago, she was gone for months and we wondered if they had split up. Even back then she never seemed entirely well. 'Indisposed,' Archie would say."

"Yet he died first."

Kimmel arched an eyebrow. "I think he may have preferred it that way. Died of a heart attack out in his fields. Sarah sold the farm—or most of it, anyway. Kept the house. Been living off the proceeds of the sale ever since. From the look of her place, I can't imagine there's much of the money left."

"How'd your visit with her go?"

Kimmel cocked his head to one side. As one of the few well-educated people in a small community, he carried a special status as a combination of healer, sage and father confessor, and his judgments went beyond the purely medical. "She's not entirely well. Her blood pressure's high. She's complaining of headaches, pains in her legs and feet, something about her stomach. But I had the feeling she was hiding more than she was telling me."

"Sounds like maybe she knows she's got something serious."

"Depends on what you want to call serious. It's her mental health I worry about. She admits she seldom goes out. She put her nose up when I asked her about it and told me, 'I have little need to go out.' Stays cooped up in her room most of the time, as far as I can tell. When I told her I wanted to draw some blood she refused. Wouldn't let me look at her feet. When I tried to insist, she flew into a temper and threw me out."

Dayson chuckled. "So I'm not the only one who's been shown the door by the old sweetheart. What do you suppose it's all about?"

"I'd wager she drinks. A lot. I didn't actually see her swigging gin, but I'd bet my license on it. The problems in her legs and feet sound like gout. That would likely be from the drinking. Like a lot of alcoholics, she keeps it hidden."

"But the girl must know."

"Her niece? Maybe not. She strikes me as mature for her years. But how much can you know at nineteen? I think she understands there's something wrong with her aunt that goes deeper than the immediate symptoms. Still, she's young and she's likely never been around something like this. Sarah might not have much problem hiding it from her."

"She's a bright girl. Scholarship at Pacific College."

"Yes, I guess maybe I'd heard that."

"How's she doing with all this?"

"The girl's strong. That's my impression. And yet . . ." Kimmel squinted, as if trying to see something more clearly. "She's somehow out of step with everything, everyone else. Something not entirely tame about her. Maybe that's what gives me the most hope for her." He looked up at Dayson from under his brow and said quietly, "You know people talk about her. Talk about her in that way where they say one thing, but with a nod or a wink, let you know they mean something else. I'm not sure exactly what it is they think they know. I don't suppose they do either. They know she's different. Could be it's nothing more than the usual envies and suspicions about a pretty young girl who has moved into the area and lives with one of its stranger characters." He gave his head a shake to let Dayson know that's all he had to say on the nature of local gossip and how Mattie had become its object. "Like I say, she's mature for her years, but this is hard on her. Maybe because she can't figure it out."

This would have been the moment for Dayson to share what he thought he had learned. But he decided to say nothing.

"And sometimes young people blame themselves for the problems of the adults around them," Kimmel said. He let out a long sigh. "It's a funny household. Just the two of them. In her way, she's very protective of her aunt. They seem very close and very distant at the same time. Not an ideal environment for the girl."

"But she seems to be holding up well?"

Josiah Kimmel leaned back into the sofa and gave Dayson a quizzical look. "Which of these two is supposed to be my patient?"

Dayson covered with a laugh. "I appreciate you going out there. Sorry for your trouble. What do I owe you?"

The doctor held up his hands. "Like I say, it's a small community. Sometimes we have to look after each other. This one's for Archie."

Chapter Eleven

A Garden Nymph

For several days the spring rains kept Dayson inside and Frank Persig from returning to the work he'd begun. The former governor wanted to get back to his garden, if only because it allowed him to ignore the call of the blank pages lying on his desk. Still, he enjoyed the restoration of his privacy.

On a quiet weekday morning he woke to sunny skies and a warm sun and knew that Persig would soon return, if not that day then the next.

He stood at his kitchen window asking himself if he regretted finding the little statue, or at least regretted telling anyone about it. Unable to come up with a clear answer on this and many other things, Dayson feared that ambivalence—the perpetual tick-tock of yes or no, do or don't, open or close—had become the mainspring propelling his life. The same irresolution stilled his pen when he thought of the war and the stain of his survival.

But he'd promised himself not to think of that.

To shove the war back into the shadows, he indulged a renewed distaste for the idea of anyone tramping around his place, digging up his yard. He found himself seized by the idea that if he renewed his own digging he might yet find the key to the presence of the figurine and could send Persig packing. Or he could make clear that no such key existed. Either way, he could make everyone go away.

Grabbing his shovel from the utility room, he hurried out to the yard. A moment later he stood by the patch of upturned earth, his foot poised on the shovel blade. And his resolution evaporated. If by a miracle he found something important, it would lead to further digging by Persig. And finding nothing would prove only that he had found nothing.

Dayson took his foot from the shovel, feeling cut adrift by his own indecision—and felt, too, an uncanny prickling of his scalp, an eerie sense of being watched. He looked behind him.

She made no effort to hide, but stood with her hands clasped in front of her, as if she had been waiting for some time, and that it was he, not she, who had suddenly appeared in his back yard.

For a moment they regarded each other in silence. Then she spoke.

"I want to apologize for the way I spoke to you when you came by the house. You were only trying to be helpful." She said it with odd formality, as if reciting lines from a play in which she was portraying a woman older than herself. Lifting her chin—the gesture reminiscent of her aunt's reaction when he offered to pay her grocery bill—she said, "And I wanted to tell you I was sorry for crossing your property without your permission." She seemed about to say something more, but apparently thought better of it and added nothing.

Dayson tried to size up the young woman before him. "Yes, I shouted after you a bunch of times, but I guess you never heard me."

"I always heard you," she said quietly.

"Then why—?" He stopped himself, the answer obvious. She had been following a call stronger than anything he could possibly derail by shouting at her. Now, deserted by her lover, their trysting place burned to the ground, she'd come to apologize.

"Your aunt's doing better?"

"Yes, thank you. And you're well?" she replied, prim as a schoolmarm.

How many different Mattie's did she have in her?

Before Dayson could think of how to reply, the girl peered over his shoulder at something behind him. Puzzled, he turned and realized her young ears had caught the sound of Frank Persig's whistling as he approached. A moment later the young man appeared around the corner of the house wearing his wide-brimmed hat, carrying a trowel and a notebook and a wide-mesh metal screen stretched over a wooden frame.

"Things are drying out," Persig called as he crossed the yard. "I thought I'd get back to work." He nodded at Dayson's shovel. "I guess you were thinking the same."

"I guess I was." He waved a hand to indicate the girl behind him. "And I suppose I should introduce . . ."

She was gone.

Persig dropped his equipment to the ground. "Sorry?"

His hand still outstretched, Dayson stared dumbly at the spot where Mattie had stood an instant earlier. A flash of color flickered briefly behind the blackberry vines and disappeared.

He looked again at the spot where she had been standing, almost ready to believe he had only imagined her. "Nothing."

The two men set to work under a warming sun. Dayson got his hoe from the utility room to make furrows for his garden, grateful that the rain had softened the earth. Meanwhile, Persig pulled several of his stakes from the ground, wound up the twine, took up Dayson's neglected shovel and began to dig a narrow trench that cut diagonally across his plot, throwing the shoveled dirt through the screen, which was propped on the ground at an angle.

"What are you doing?"

"Sifting the dirt through the screen. Sometimes important finds are very small."

After that exchange the morning passed in silence, broken only by the chunk and scrape of their tools against the earth. Yet it was a silence more comfortable than that of the first couple of days they had worked together. To his surprise, Dayson found his resentment at Persig's presence had lost its bite. He even allowed himself to borrow the kid's trowel to get under a stubborn bit of knotweed.

Propped in the dirt on one knee, Persig said, "Mr. Bachelder says you're working on your memoirs."

Batch had clearly failed to mention he didn't care to talk about it. "Does he?"

"Says you were in the Pacific during the war."

"Mr. Bachelder talks too much."

"He says you were decorated for—"

"Here's your trowel back."

He tossed the tool at Persig's feet and walked away.

Chapter Twelve

Grip and Grin

The call came late in the afternoon.

"Will you hold for the Governor?"

Dayson huffed at the need to hold for someone who had, after all, called him, but said, "Yeah, sure."

It wasn't the first time they'd spoken since the election. In February, Gilkey had called to invite him down for the commemoration of the state's centennial. They were planning a birthday observance in the Capitol rotunda and wanted him there, along with other dignitaries. The fact that the state's birthday fell on Valentine's Day seemed a deliberate dig at his now-solitary existence.

Yet, when he crossed the bridge over the Willamette and could see the dome of the Capitol he knew he couldn't do it, couldn't attend a celebration that only brought home to him that he too was a relic from the past, of no further consequence to the life of the state. Sitting solemnly under the rotunda with a bunch of other old guys would be like attending his own funeral. "No!" he'd said out loud, then turned the car around and drove back home, later calling Gilkey's office pleading sudden illness.

A series of clicks in the phone brought Dayson back to the present, and made him hope he had been disconnected.

"How are you, Governor?" Norman Gilkey asked, his voice singing with good cheer. Sincere or phony? Either way Dayson found it deeply aggravating.

"I'm okay, Norm. How are you?"

"Fine, fine." Nearly shouting over the weak connection, he said, "I'm told you've moved way out in the country."

"That's right."

"Why would you do that?"

"To get away from politicians."

"Still your old charming self." Dayson could hear the gritted teeth behind Gilkey's chuckle. "I understand Art Thayer paid you a visit the other day."

"Yeah, I guess he did."

"Good man, Art. You trained him well." When Dayson didn't respond, Gilkey continued. "He says the two of you talked about the Tyee Dam."

As if this was news to you, Dayson thought.

"I think he mentioned something about it."

"And he said you sounded very positive about it and you were just waiting for my call."

Ah, good for Art. Smart boy to put it to Gilkey that way.

"That's right, Norm."

"Well, look, Governor, I'm wondering if we might get you down here before the legislative session ends, and ask you to express your support for the project."

"A little grip and grin for the photographers? I suppose I could."

"That would be a big help. In fact, I was hoping you might say a few words in front of the Senate committee."

"Hell, Norm, my office introduced a bill on the reclamation project last session. What was it, Senate Bill 165? It was a little premature. The feds weren't ready, so it stayed in committee. But everyone knows where I stand."

"Yes, but you know how it is. It's a new session, so we need a new bill. I don't need to tell you."

But he just had.

"It's getting kind of late in the session to introduce a big bill, isn't it, Norm?"

"Once this gets thrown in the hopper it'll pass through committee and out onto the Senate floor pretty quickly, especially with good people like yourself behind it. Then through the House. There won't be much controversy. It's got a lot of support."

Why wasn't Gilkey starting the bill in the House, where the Democrats had a majority and it would enjoy a warmer welcome? Could he be so sure of getting Senate Republicans on board that it didn't matter to him where it started? And Dayson wanted to ask how a bill that hadn't even been introduced yet could have a lot of support.

"Who do you have carrying the bill in the Senate?"

"Sam Krieger's the chief sponsor," Gilkey replied. "Marlin Atteberry will carry it on the House side."

"Let me think about it. Why don't you shoot me a copy?"

Gilkey sounded startled. "Of the bill?"

What the hell?

"Yeah, of the bill, Norm."

"That's a lot of tedious reading. Why don't we just write up a summary and some talking points? You don't need to address the details of the bill. Your presence alone would speak volumes."

Especially when your staff has written my script, Dayson thought. He tried to find the fire behind Gilkey's cloud of smoke. "That's fine. Send me the talking points. And a copy of the bill."

A hesitation. "Happy to do it. Certainly. I'd be happy to do that for you. Very happy."

Dayson wanted to tell Gilkey that if he said happy one more time one of them might start to believe it, but it wouldn't be him.

Gilkey continued. "You'll like the new bill. In fact, we've made some improvements."

Here it comes.

"Yeah?"

"We're going to see if we can expand the project a little. More water for farmers, and maybe generate a bit of hydro power. Help them keep the lights on. Your own standing with the farmers of this state is terrific. You'll be helping them out a great deal."

There it is, Dayson thought, a play to farmers, most of them Republicans. So he's recruiting a Republican ex-governor to pretty literally help carry the water on this thing. Smart politics. No one ever said Norm was a dummy. Well, okay, he'd said it himself, and more than once, but that was in the heat of a campaign.

Before Dayson could reply, Gilkey went on. "The Eisenhower people have made some favorable noises, and we'd like to get this all lined up before the election next year so we don't have to start all over again with the next administration. I think there might even be one of the dams out your way."

Of course there would be.

"You don't say," Dayson deadpanned. "I look forward to seeing the bill."

"And those talking points too," Gilkey said a little too hurriedly. "Thanks, Governor. My office will let you know when the Senate sets a hearing. It'll be great to have you down here."

Sure it will.

"Fine, Norm. Who do I call if I've got some questions?"

"Questions?" Gilkey sounded nonplussed. Dayson smiled. "Well, I guess you could call Bob Bremmer. He's my chief of staff."

"I know Bob."

Dayson had already spoken to Gilkey longer than he'd wanted and his reserve of politeness was running dry. "Thanks for the call, Governor," he said. "I appreciate it."

"Quite all right, Martin. Goodbye."

"Good—" But the line was already dead.

He knew he could have told Gilkey no, probably should have. But, for all his grousing, he felt the urge to prove to the folks in Salem that he was still alive. Despite the hundred times he had told himself and others he wanted to be left alone, the prospect of getting a bit of limelight had its appeal, even if he insisted on backing into it.

Norm probably sensed his need for a taste of redemption. In addition to playing the farmers, his old rival had played him too.

Humming unhappily, he wandered into his study and glanced at his desk, but rather than sit at its scattering of papers he picked up the copy of "A Farewell to Arms" he'd been rereading and settled into his armchair, wishing he had thought to pour himself a drink.

Bothered by Gilkey's call, his eyes ran over a couple of pages before he realized he hadn't taken in any of it. Though he couldn't yet get a clear fix on things, he sensed something lay behind the new governor's play to his ego. Gilkey had sent Art out to talk to him about the Tyee Dam, a project he already favored, but the bill was turning out to be something more than that. How much did Art know about the project? And it was funny. For all Gilkey's enthusiasm about having him speak before the committee, he sounded reluctant to let him see an actual copy of the bill.

Trying to fit the pieces together, Dayson let his eyes drift toward the window facing on the back yard and started to let out a long, slow sigh. But what he saw made his breath catch in his throat.

Wanting to persuade himself he was upset, he rose from his armchair and headed outside.

Standing in the open doorway, Dayson asked, "Were you going to knock, or just stand there until I came out?"

Mattie looked behind her toward the path as if she were thinking of running off. But she stayed where she was.

"I came by to tell you that my aunt was feeling much better and to thank you again for sending your doctor to see my aunt."

Dayson didn't buy it. Kimmel had visited her aunt nearly a week earlier and she'd already told him her aunt was better. The fact that she had cooked up a phony pretext to come see him left Dayson with the startling thought that she might be as curious about him as he was about her. The older he got, the more the ways of young women baffled him.

"I'm glad about your aunt."

She nodded gravely. The wildness he had once seen in her eyes was occluded by a veil of formality that hid something vital about her, though Dayson was damned if he knew what it was.

"And how about you?" he asked.

Rather than reply, her eyes drifted toward the bit of ground where Dayson had found her crying in the rain. Catching herself, she turned back. "You've only lived here a few months."

He was again struck by an intimation that she had for some reason taken an interest in him. "That's right," he said. "I moved out here only a few months after you did."

A shift in her shoulders, a rapid eyeblink, gave him the satisfaction of knowing he had surprised her, though he cautioned himself that a show of interest on his part might leave her more alarmed than flattered.

The morning breeze sighed through the trees, tasting of the sea. All morning, clouds had scudded above the tall firs. Now the fields darkened with approaching rain.

Dayson looked into the sky and back at the girl. "It's going to pour in a minute. You'll get soaked."

She turned and looked toward the curtain of rain heading their way. A few wind-driven drops fell around them.

Only when she said, "Yes, I'd be grateful," did Dayson understand she had taken his warning as an invitation to come in.

Unnerved at the prospect of having this odd young woman in his home, but seeing no way out of it short of rudeness, he beckoned her in through the back door. Halfway toward the kitchen, she stopped, her eye caught by something in a corner of the utility room.

On top of a couple cases of books he hadn't unpacked yet, Dayson had set the red Jerry-can that she had dropped before fleeing the burning shack.

"I didn't want anyone to find it," Dayson said. "Or figure out where it came from."

The aplomb she had shown only moments earlier deserted her at the reminder of her act of arson.

Her thoughts unreadable, she shook her head but said nothing.

"Well, forget about it and come on in," he said and let her into the kitchen. "It's Mattie, isn't it? Your name."

"Mmm."

"You want a cup of coffee? Or does your aunt let you drink coffee yet?"

She frowned at his joke. "I prefer tea."

"Tea? I suppose I have some somewhere . . ."

He felt her eyes on him as he put the kettle on to boil and rummaged through the cupboards until he found a dusty box of Lipton. "I guess this is tea," he said "And I suppose you want a cookie with it. Isn't that how tea is done?"

"That won't be necessary."

"I know it's not *necessary*." Dayson searched through the cupboard again and came up with a package of Fig Newtons.

When her tea had brewed and he had reheated a cup of the morning's coffee for himself he felt at a loss about where to sit. The plastic-topped kitchen table struck him as unwelcoming, and he had piled the sofa with books he needed to sort through. So he led her back to his study and nodded her toward the armchair he gave to guests.

Mattie set her tea and cookie on the side table, wandered toward the window and looked out at the falling rain.

"It all looks different from here."

Dayson watched her with the fascination of a hiker who has come across a young doe. Trying to find a way to speak into the renewed silence, he could only come up with, "April showers bring May flowers."

"It's May now."

"Well, yeah, I know that."

She turned away from the window and trailed her hand across his desk, a gesture that evoked in Dayson an unsettling sense of intimacy, as if she had run her fingers up his back.

"What is this? 'An invitation to speak to the Republican Central Committee of...'"

The request was one of a couple dozen he had received since his loss. He had turned them all down.

"You're a Republican?" she asked.

How did she make it sound like something he should deny?

"Yeah, I'm a Republican. Something wrong with that?"

She didn't reply, but leaned over further to inspect the small glass-faced wooden box he'd set at a back corner of the desk.

"Is this some kind of medal?" When he didn't answer, she looked over her shoulder at him, demanding a response.

Dayson wondered why he didn't tell her to just leave his stuff alone and sit down and drink her tea.

"I got it for perfect attendance back in eighth grade."

Mattie didn't react to his quip but leaned closer to the little box. "That's your name, Martin Dayson?"

"Yeah."

"An army captain?"

"Used to be."

A few minutes earlier he had wondered if she might feel uncomfortable alone with a strange man. In fact he was the one who felt ill at ease, caught between a sense that this Mattie girl was overstepping her bounds and an unsettling desire to have her know a little more about him.

She drifted beyond the desk and looked at a framed photo on the wall. She glanced at him over her shoulder. He could sense her trying to see him with no beard and with hair that didn't spill over his collar. Her voice quiet with surprise, she said, "This is you with President Eisenhower."

"I won an essay contest."

She turned her back to Dayson and looked more closely at the photo. "You can stop treating me like a child anytime you like."

Dayson felt his face flush with a mix of embarrassment and annoyance. He opened his mouth to snap back at her, but found himself saying, "I'm sorry."

She finished her reconnaissance of the room and settled into the chair he'd offered her, sipped her tea and looked at him as coolly as if he were a painting on the wall. He frowned at his own unease, but could think of nothing to say. She glanced at the Hemingway on the table beside her, picked it up, read the back cover.

"So, you can read." He wondered why he wanted to provoke her.

A pause. A sigh. "Yes, quite well, thank you."

That she felt no need to defend herself made him feel small.

Trying to make up for his remark, he asked, "What do you like? To read, I mean."

She waited a moment, as if his words were in a foreign language she had to translate in her head before responding. "We have to read a lot for classes."

"Sure. But who do you like?"

"Katherine Anne Porter, Kerouac, James Joyce, the Existentialists . . ."

"The Exis— Great god! Whatever happened to Nancy Drew?"

". . . Simone de Beauvoir."

"Who she?"

"She and Jean-Paul Sartre are lovers."

"Sartre. Sartre. That French walleye?"

"They live together without being married."

"Well, isn't *that* original?"

His reaction was apparently not what she'd anticipated—had she thought he'd be scandalized?—and she added a little defensively, "She's a great woman."

Dayson grunted his skepticism. "Who has you reading that stuff?"

She turned her head and looked out the window. "I'd read some of it already." Her evasiveness spoke more strongly than her words.

He started to ask her why she didn't want to say anything about who encouraged her to read the rest, but stopped because he already knew. It was the man she met in the shack in the clearing. The man who had left her crying in the rain. One of her professors.

She sipped at her tea, said nothing.

More gently, he said, "I thought girls your age were all reading movie magazines and listening to Elvis."

She lowered an assessing gaze on him. "Elvis is yesterday."

He had thought to impress her with his knowledge of what was hip and current, and she had once again left him feeling like a relic from an older world.

"What do you mean?" He meant to throw down a challenge, but he could hear the querulous tone in his voice.

"There's something new coming. You can't see it. Not yet."

Her words hit him like a slap. But she had not said them to offend. For her it was a simple matter of fact.

"And what is that new thing?"

She took a bite of her cookie and looked out the window toward his garden, where tomato vines and carrot tops were poking through the earth. "I don't know. But I have this feeling, like the ice over a river is breaking up. Something's coming, and I'll be a part of it."

"Yeah?" He tried to hide the vague alarm her words provoked in him.

She cocked her head at him and said nothing. She had no fear of silence.

Dayson thought he had long ago passed the stage in life where he might sit with a pretty girl and be at a loss for words, and grew cross at the realization he hadn't. It seemed that everything about her left him cross.

Yet when she said, "It's stopped raining," and rose from her chair he felt a prick of regret.

"I must be going now," she said with the same odd formality with which they'd started.

Dayson accompanied her to the back door, or rather tried to keep up while she showed herself out. Yet, as she put her hand to the door knob, she stopped, turned, and gave Dayson a smile as bright as the sun.

"Goodbye, Mr. Dayson. Thank you for the tea," she said and dashed away.

He stood in the open doorway and watched her run along the footpath, through the trees and out of sight.

"Funny girl," Dayson muttered to himself.

Chapter Thirteen

A Frank Exchange of Evasions

Persig arrived early the following morning and went about preparing for work with his habitual deliberateness, laying out his tools, extending his grid to the farthest edges of his plot. From the kitchen, Dayson watched his slow, precise work and wondered how he had come by his perfectionism. What could it be about his life that he had to put everything exactly right?

At lunchtime Persig, as usual, sat in the grass to eat the sandwich he had packed, unmindful of the dark clouds coming in from the west, trailing a veil of rain.

Dayson thought about it once, twice, a third time before he cracked open the kitchen window and called out to him, "Rain coming. I guess you might as well come inside to eat."

The rain started a few minutes later, pounding on the roof hard enough to make conversation difficult before moving on.

Grudging the need to say anything, but put on edge by the silence, Dayson asked, "So, you getting anywhere?"

Persig allowed that he had mapped out a couple of places that definitely held nothing of interest. "So, yes, making real progress," he said with only a hint of irony.

Sitting with their elbows on the kitchen table, they exchanged a few anodyne words about the spring weather and the chance of more rain, each of them acting as if in competition to see who could be less forthcoming. Yet, almost by inadvertence, they threw a bit of light on their backgrounds and their work. With a few disjointed remarks, Persig sketched his academic career, a bachelor's degree from Reed, his work on his doctorate at the University of Washington, his hopes for a professorship.

In response to Dayson's half-hearted efforts to draw him out further, the younger man clammed up, saying nothing more than that he had grown up on the far side of the Cascades, near Bend, in central Oregon.

Once again Dayson sensed there was something Frank didn't want to talk about. Even as he wondered what it might be, he decided to leave it alone.

When it came his turn, Dayson too resisted bestowing any revelations to the young man. "I'm a farm boy from Yamhill. Fell in with bad companions. Ended up governor."

It was a condescending answer and Persig didn't try to hide his annoyance. "It's not like it happened by accident. You must have wanted it."

Dayson grunted. "Did I?"

"And you live up here, to hell and gone. I thought politicians liked nothing better than being around lots of people, glad-handing, working the crowds."

Dayson suppressed the urge to snap at him. "I suppose we all like some of that. People cheering, shouting your name. You make a grin and wave." To his own surprise, he realized he had somehow initiated a real conversation. "But I always felt better working on a problem, some issue that needed a solution. I liked putting together the votes to get something passed. Cracking a few heads when that's what it took."

Persig rolled his eyes. "Playing politics."

Dayson recognized the disdain for politics held by people who had no responsibility for turning their opinions into the tricky work of governing. "You bet I was playing politics. And it's the most serious game there is. What you do can affect every person in the state. You never forget that."

"I've heard people say you're arrogant."

"Damn right I'm arrogant. How else are you going to survive all the bullshit, hold onto those things you tell yourself are important and get something done?" He snorted. "Arrogant. I hope Norm Gilkey is too, or he's got no business being in the job."

As the conversation grew more serious both men found it increasingly difficult to look at the other. Gazing out the window, Persig said, "I saw you give a speech once. In Prineville. People were drawn to you." He sounded offended.

Dayson wondered how to respond. If he said to this kid, "Yeah, I'm charismatic," it would only add to Persig's notion that he thought too highly of himself. How could he admit to possessing a charlatan's gifts and at the same time insist that he had used them righteously? Call it what you like—presence, gravitas, charisma—it was an accident, like blue eyes or good hearing, something given, not earned. And he had it. People had cheered for him, jostled each other to shake his hand or, more unsettling, to simply touch him. Even while he lived off it he found it disturbing, making him wonder what people saw in him that remained hidden from himself—wondering too whether these same admirers would desert him if they knew why he was doing this, why he had felt driven to enter politics after the war.

Among those who crowded around him were some with an unsettling yearning in their eyes, the ones who, lacking the confidence or the courage or the imagination to follow their own dreams, lived through his until he became more important to them than they were to themselves. They swelled his crowds, volunteered for his campaigns. After he had won the governorship he hired a couple of them who possessed talent and competence, though he kept them at a distance, preferring people who saw his flaws.

Did he take advantage of these true believers? Sure he did. How else are you going to win elections, get bills passed, project your will into the bureaus and agencies? Besides, to have denied them would have been a form of cruelty. Or so he told himself. It had made him feel at times like an impostor, waiting for the deflating pop when they, and everyone else, saw through him.

When that moment had come, when his family life fell apart, when it became clear he couldn't hold onto his wife and daughter, many of those same people who admired him to the edge of idolatry felt betrayed, suddenly seeing him as a fraud who had played an unforgivable trick on them, while in fact it had always been a trick they had played on themselves.

Persig interrupted his thoughts. "I can't believe you're satisfied now, leaving all that behind, following a life like this."

Dayson squinted at this fellow digger of holes, this delver in the dirt, for signs of the misplaced adoration to which he owed so much. No, nothing. Good.

"It's stopped raining," he said. "Let's get back to work."

For the rest of the afternoon they worked in the specific silence of two men who didn't wish to talk further about themselves.

Chapter Fourteen

A Cup of Tea
with Simone de Boo-Boo

Again, Mattie had apparently stood in the garden until Dayson saw her and came to open the back door. He wondered how long she had waited for him to notice.

"Am I inviting you inside?"

As so often, she seemed not to have heard him. "My . . . My aunt says you used to be the governor."

"Yeah?"

"She says she didn't recognize you at first because of the beard." When Dayson didn't say anything to this, she asked, "Why didn't you tell me?"

"It didn't occur to me."

As unlikely as it sounded, it was the truth and she seemed to recognize it.

She nodded at something beside the door. "You shouldn't leave your tools outside."

He turned and found his hoe leaning against the house. "No, I suppose not. Shouldn't you be studying or going to class?"

"I've got time. And I have all evening to study."

Her remark made Dayson reflect again on the decaying and silent house, and the certainty that its days offered an abundance of empty hours.

"You want a cup of tea?"

She walked past him and into the house, trailing a smile.

This time he made tea for them both and carried it into the study. He no longer pretended her presence annoyed him, and she no longer offered any pretext for appearing at his door like a stray deer. And, as before, she didn't sit but, after glancing out the window, drifted toward his desk and again picked up the box that held his medal. "Did you get this for being governor?"

"No, that comes with a knife in the back."

"She says you were a war hero. My . . ."

"Your aunt?"

She looked out the window, said nothing.

Something morbid in the house Mattie shared with Sarah Tannehill, Dayson reflected. The girl must yearn to get out, breathe free air, feel the weight lift from her shoulders. But why, when she can get away, does she come here? Surely she has friends her own age she could hang out with. Yet he couldn't picture her sitting in a booth at the malt shop, gossiping with pony-tailed girlfriends about who was going out with whom and listening to the jukebox offerings of boy singers she already considered *passe*.

He thought of her having an affair with her professor. What better way to put herself outside the circle of the other girls' conventions? And all the while she waited for that something new she said was coming, a world more congenial to her spirit than the one in which she lived. Maybe when that world came, she would be the only one ready.

"War hero?" Dayson said, wondering why the hell everyone wanted to harp on that. "I never thought what I did . . ." As always, thinking about the war threatened to take him places he didn't want to go. He batted her question away with a wave of his hand.

"What's wrong?" Mattie asked.

"Wrong? Why should anything be wrong." A shiver pulsed through the plexus of his soul at the thought that this uncanny girl had the ability to sense his thoughts and that, however he might try, there would be no hiding from her.

"Something about the—"

"Just put the box down."

She set the medal back on his desk and started to turn away, but abruptly stopped. She reached down and touched the stone figurine that lay half-hidden beneath some papers. "What is this?"

"Leave it alone."

Why was he glad she ignored him?

As the others before her had done, she ran her hand over the smooth stone. Unlike Bachelder or Persig, though, she regarded its impassive features as if it were something—or someone—she recognized, something with which she shared a web of connection. The silence in the room took on a new texture as she traced the stone carving's broad hips, the over-generous breasts.

She turned her mouth into an ironic frown. "Men!"

"You don't think a woman did that?"

"No way."

"Well . . . Just put it down and drink your tea."

She continued to gaze at the figure in her hands, yet she gave Dayson the sense that, by some uncanny gift, she was regarding him rather than the stone, and that she fathomed something about his interest in the figure of which he himself was unaware.

"Put it back on the desk like a good girl," he said, trying to hide his discomfort.

"Like a good girl," she repeated, the words curdling in her mouth.

Mattie looked out the window at the torn-up earth, then at the object in her hand and, lastly, at Dayson before setting down the little statue and saying, "Lawrence said we look into the past and hope it will tell us the future. He says it never works."

"Lawrence?" Dayson asked. "Who's he?"

She stood very straight and gave him a look that told him he already knew.

"Ah. The one who pushed all these authors on you. Joyce, Sartre and—and what's her name?—Simone de Boo-boo."

As always, when he tried to mock her he ended up feeling like a brute and, at least about certain things, not as knowing or wise as the young woman standing before him.

How he wished he were back in politics where things were straightforward, where his skills matched his challenges.

"So, where is it you're going with your studies?" he asked. "What do you want to do?"

She settled into the chair opposite him, kicked off her shoes and curled her feet under her. He was sure she did it to aggravate him. "I don't want to be a Home Ec major, if that's what you're still thinking."

"I got over that."

"Maybe I'd want to be a professor." A glint of mischief lighted her eyes. "Or I could run for office."

"Run for—? Believe me, you don't want to get mixed up in that."

"Or a lawyer."

"A lawyer? Why would you want to be a lawyer?"

"That's just for boys, is it?"

"I'm not saying that."

"Yes you are."

He opened his mouth to scold her, but stopped and asked himself if maybe she was right. Though he left his words unsaid, a cloud of uncertainty appeared to eclipse her confidence.

"What's wrong?"

"Nothing," she said too quickly. "It's only . . ."

"What?"

"What if I'm the only one like me? If what I think is coming never arrives? Not for me, anyway. I see all the other girls—and the boys too—and they're not thinking about any of this. They're not thinking about anything at all."

For an instant, he thought she might cry.

"It must be a lonely business, being from the future." He spoke quietly, wanting her to know he wasn't making fun of her. "Everyone comes from their own time. I'm from mine—the Depression, the war. It makes me who I am."

"And you figure I'm from now, from the 50s?"

He cocked his head at an angle. "I'm not sure. Maybe like you say, you come from a time that hasn't happened yet."

"You make me sound like I've landed here from outer space." Her smile disappeared. "Sometimes I feel like it. And sometimes I think I'm ancient, a thousand years old. And I pity everyone who . . . who. . ."

"Who doesn't see coming what you see?"

"I don't *see* it. I don't know what it is. I just know it's coming."

"Does it scare you?"

He expected her to get her back up, claim that nothing scared her. Instead, she said, "Sometimes. Because it could be as bad as it is good." She chewed at her lip, an unsettled look in her eye. "Either way I'll be a part of it."

As gently as he could manage, he suggested, "Finish college. See what you want to do then. Maybe you could just be a young girl for a while longer."

As she had before, Dayson expected her to object, "I'm not a girl." Instead, she said, "No. I'm ready. And, anyway, the school doesn't offer what I want. No school does. I want to major in . . . in life. I want to understand it all, want to see it all, want to make it all new. Not just read little bits torn from it and pasted in a book. The classes I'm taking make me feel like a buzzard picking at road-kill." Her laugh faded to a quiet sigh. "Maybe I could be a writer. Like Simone de Boo-boo. Or I could write great poetry, like Ferlinghetti."

"Who?"

Her eyes popped in surprise. "The poet. He lives in San Francisco. Ferlinghetti."

"Sounds like a type of pasta."

"Lawrence Ferlinghetti. I can't believe you don't know him."

"I've been busy running the state, okay?"

"Too bad for you."

She looked at the scattered papers on his desk. "But you're trying to write something yourself."

Dayson grunted in reply.

"What is it you're working on?" she asked.

"Nothing." He waggled his head, relented. "Writing about my life." Before she could ask anything more, he steered the conversation to other topics. "Where are you from that you decided to go to school in Forest Grove, of all places?"

"I'm from Bakersfield, California."

"You've got a college there, haven't you? Why would you come all the way up here?"

"You ever been to Bakersfield?"

"Yeah. A couple of times."

She gave him a look that let him know he had answered his own question. "Wouldn't you leave there if you could?"

"Point taken. Okay, so your mom and dad sent you to Oregon. Sent you to live with your—"

"No!"

He was startled—and she apparently even more so—by the show of emotion behind her denial. She tried to walk it back. "They . . . They got divorced when I was small, and . . ." She made a little gesture as if throwing something away. "Anyway, I'm not close to my parents. Not anymore."

"No? What happened?"

Abruptly, she sat up and cocked her head toward the front of the house. "I think someone just pulled into your driveway."

This minor-league *deus ex machina* struck him as too neat to be credible. But the slamming of a car door in the driveway testified to her good faith and keener hearing.

Dayson looked at her, half-ready to believe she had conjured up this visitor to keep from having to say more.

He sensed Mattie following him as he walked into the living room. With a mind to appearances, he thought to tell her to go back into the study, but decided the teacup and saucer in her hands said enough about the innocence of her presence. As if his own gray hairs weren't testimony enough.

He saw the query in her eyes as she looked out the window.

"His name's Art Thayer. Used to work for me. He's just delivering something."

Wondering again how his attempts to establish privacy had somehow turned his house into a local mecca, he let Art in and made quick introductions.

"You could have just put it in the mail, Art," Dayson said as he took the envelope Thayer held out to him.

"The Governor said he wanted it delivered to you personally, and to let him know if you had any questions."

Dayson grunted unhappily. No doubt his former assistant had once again volunteered for the job. And he couldn't help but reflect that the last time he had heard Art Thayer address someone as "Governor," the young man had been referring to him.

Dayson waved Art into a chair and offered him a cup of tea, which he turned down.

"Those two pages in your hand, sir, are the talking points. I wrote them up myself."

Dayson glanced over them. "They look fine. Where's the bill?"

"Oh." As if caught by surprise, he reached into his inside coat pocket. "I've got it right here."

Clearly, Art had been told to hold it back unless specifically asked for it.

He handed the bill to his old boss and said, "I'm told to remind you this is just a draft."

"Let's look at this thing," Dayson murmured, putting on his reading glasses.

As he scanned the document, he caught Art glancing appreciatively at Mattie, and Mattie glaring at him until he looked away.

After a few minutes, Dayson said, "This first part looks quite a bit different from what we introduced last session."

"And it was a good bill, sir. The Governor is using it as the model for the new one."

Had Art been instructed to butter him up? He hoped not, as it would mean they were no longer being frank with each other, that their old relationship was gone. More cold-bloodedly, it also meant he couldn't call on that relationship to wedge out of Thayer anything he'd been told not to say.

"There seem to be several blank areas in this thing. There's a reference here, and again here, about amending the Oregon Revised Statutes, but nothing showing what the amendments are."

"Virtually every bill is an amendment to the ORS," Thayer said. They both knew he hadn't answered the question. "As I say, sir, it's just a draft."

Dayson wished he would stop with the "sir" stuff.

"May I see it too?"

Taken by surprise, both men looked at Mattie, who sat on the sofa, bland as butter, her hands clasped in her lap.

"It's a proposed law," Dayson said, with a tone he knew came off as patronizing.

"You mean it's not in English?"

She batted her eyes and made an ingenuous smile worthy of a Barbie doll.

Oh, she's good, Dayson thought. Barely suppressing a laugh, he looked at Art. "Can't do any harm to have an extra set of eyes on it." Ignoring Thayer's distress, he handed her the draft and turned to the other document in his hand. "And, here, in your talking points, you refer to dams, plural."

"The Governor says he mentioned to you there was going to be an expansion of the project beyond the Tyee."

"Yeah, I guess he did."

The lack of detail in both the bill and the talking points might be nothing more than an indication that, as Art said, it was still only in draft. Or it might be an attempt to make the proposal appear less complete than it really was. Dayson decided there was no point trying to press Art about it. He worked for someone else now.

"This looks fine—for starters. I'll hang onto this and wait for the final draft. Tell Norm thanks. But tell him I'm going to need more detail if I'm supposed to testify in front of a committee."

He wasn't sending Art back to Salem with his head tucked under his arm this time. But, once again he would have to go back to Gilkey—or more likely Bremmer, his chief of staff—and report mission not accomplished.

Dayson returned his glasses to his shirt pocket and rose briskly, once more, if only for a moment, the Governor.

"Good work, Art. Thanks for coming all the way out here." He clapped his former aide on the back and pushed him toward the door and out.

While Art backed out of the driveway, Mattie, teacup in hand, said, "I don't like him."

"Who, Art? He's a good kid."

"He's not being honest with you."

"He's just following his orders."

"Orders." She blew out a breath. "That's what I mean. You talk like he's a soldier."

"Like a soldier . . ." he muttered, ready to ask what she knew about soldiering. "You can't be showing all your cards at once. That's how it works. That's politics. Art used to follow my instructions. Now he works for someone else and follows his." She didn't seem satisfied with his answer, and he asked himself if he'd spent too many years in a career where a certain lack of candor was a hallmark of professional integrity. "The old saying about politics is that if you want a friend, buy a dog."

"It doesn't have to be that way."

"Since when did you start following politics? And don't try to tell me that you voted for me too."

"I don't follow politics." She was mad now. "But I believe in certain people. I believe in—"

"Don't tell me. Adlai Stevenson, the Illinois egghead."

"—John Kennedy."

"Kennedy? Kennedy! For a girl who doesn't follow politics—"

"He's not politics. He's a promise."

That stopped him. Despite the scars he'd earned in the battles and back rooms of politics, he believed he had retained his idealism. Maybe a couple of corners knocked off, but still . . . Yet, when confronted with the real thing, he realized his notion that she was naive only measured the thickness of his own shell of cynicism. And cynicism, he had long ago realized, was itself only the pernicious form of naivete.

Almost to himself, he asked, "He's that promise of something new?"

Her face reddened. "Maybe. A part of it, anyway."

"Well, your promise is going to be running for president. Nothing like that for getting your head out of the clouds. But don't get too excited. Nixon's going to win. You can bet your aunt's fall-y down-y house on it."

She stood there saying nothing, wearing her blue jeans like a boy, her long hair falling down her back. Where in the hell did she come from? Where was she going?

He knew she saw these questions in his eyes, but she didn't wish to answer, or didn't know how. Whichever it was, she said, "I've got to be going now. I have classes this afternoon."

She headed back into the study to get her shoes. Halfway across the room she stopped and said to him, "It mentions Bennett Creek."

"What?"

"That bill. It says something about Bennett Creek."

"Bennett Creek?"

"That's the name of the little stream that runs along the bottom of the hill," she said, nodding toward the trees and the fields out his back window.

How had she spotted what he had missed?

"I didn't even know it had a name," he said. "Anyway, that doesn't mean they'll build a dam along it. That would flood those fields. And this bill is designed to help farmers, not hurt them."

"Hunh!" He heard the note of skepticism in her voice. "There's something going on. I've told you. Men have been coming to the house, trying to get my aunt to sell what's left of her land."

"I'd understood she'd sold everything but the lot the house sits on."

"She's still got four acres along Hayward Road. Scrub woods that no one's ever wanted. Now someone does."

"There's not any real connection between that and this bill," he said and immediately wondered how he could know that.

She went into the study, where she sat on the edge of his desk and put her shoes on. While she tied her laces she looked at the short pile of written pages next to the stack of blank ones. "Page four. You're only on page four?"

"You can tell your professor my paper's going to be a little late."

"And I'll tell him to give you extra credit because it doesn't come naturally for you."

"Doesn't come naturally?" Dayson's mock exasperation was a clumsy screen for the real thing. "You think I can't write like Simone de Boo-boo or Ferlinspaghetti, or whatever his name is?"

"I have to go now," she said, prancing out of the room wearing the same maddening smirk she'd had when she came in.

He followed her across the house, trying to maintain his sense of outrage. "Extra credit, my eye!" Where did she get this ability to turn him into a spluttering old man?

By the time he got to the back door he expected to find her already skipping down the path and into the trees. Instead, she stood near Persig's plot of ground with his shovel in her hands.

"Where's your partner?" she asked.

"My what? He's not my partner. We're doing two different things."

"But in the same place. What are you looking for?"

"Buried treasure," Dayson snapped.

"Buried treasure!" Mattie gushed with sham excitement.

Apparently determined to drive him crazy, she danced over the broken ground, footed Dayson's shovel into the dirt and began to sing:

"Sixteen men on a dead man's chest,
Yo-ho-ho and a bottle of rum.
Drink and the devil have done for the rest . . ."

Desperate to be angry with her, Dayson thought to forge his most menacing scowl, but having lost any ability to resist her charm he could only throw his head back and laugh.

My god, he thought, when was the last time I laughed out loud?

"You're a card, Mattie Tannehill."

With an abruptness that shocked him, her head whipped around as if she'd been struck. She dropped the shovel, the smile vanished from her face.

"My name's not Tannehill!"

Baffled by her sudden change, Dayson tried to back up. "Okay. Okay. Your name's not Tannehill."

"That's her name, not mine."

"All right. But I don't understand why it's such—"

Before he could finish she had turned and disappeared down the path, running back to the house behind the hedge.

"Funny girl," he whispered to himself.

Chapter Fifteen

A Modest Proposal

Persig arrived after lunch the following day and for some time did little but stand at the edge of his dig with his head down and his arms crossed. After a few minutes, Dayson, watching from his study, saw him lower himself to his knees and run his hand along a part of his shallow trench, before rising to his feet again.

Despite the thaw between them, Dayson still nursed a last bolus of resentment at the young man's continuing imposition on his land, his time and his consciousness. Nevertheless, their relationship had, contrary to their common will, improved over the weeks. At times Dayson even caught himself looking forward to Persig's company. Yet he couldn't bring himself to go outside on this morning and ask him what was bothering him.

Sitting at his desk, Dayson's gaze wandered from the back yard to the carved figure before him and regarded its bland face—no more than a few lines, scratched into the stone, hinting at eyes, a mouth, a nose.

He reflected on how his discovery of the statuette had precipitated the crumbling of the defenses he had built up, bringing first Batch, and then Persig to his door. When he caught himself wondering if it hadn't also brought Mattie to him, he dismissed the thought as irrational. Or perhaps—and here he teetered on the edge of the fantastical—Mattie had, in her wandering across his property, somehow caused the figurine to come up from its hiding place in the earth and offer itself to him.

He set the stone idol back on his desk and looked out the window. He had barely registered the fact that he could no longer see Persig when he heard a tap at the open door of his study.

"Yeah?" He tried to maintain the gruffness he habitually adopted toward the younger man but, without quite meaning to, let his voice turn softer as he asked, "What do you want, Frank?"

It was the first time he had called him by his given name.

If Persig noticed he gave no sign, but only pointed to the object in Dayson's hand. "I want that."

Reflexively, Dayson clutched the stone to his chest.

"What for?"

Persig dropped into one of the armchairs and ran his fingers through his hair, his head sagging with a weariness less physical than emotional. "I've been getting nowhere. Maybe it's because there's nowhere to go. But in the last day or two I may have found something. A layer in the dirt. Black. At about the same depth as the figure you found. It might be a small patch of ash."

"Ash? That's important?"

"It could mark a place where someone—some group—regularly built campfires, built them often enough to leave behind a layer of ash."

"What's that got to do with her?" Dayson asked, squeezing the statuette a little more tightly.

"If it was a camp fire it might have been built by the same people who left the figure here."

"Or by someone else entirely."

"Or by someone else entirely." Persig nodded toward the stone carving. "You see the hints of color on its back? They might only be natural discoloration, some mineral in the soil that stuck to it. But I think it's more likely a sort of paint or dye, something organic that could be dated with a carbon-14 test. Then we could test the ash, if that's what it is, and see if it's from roughly the same time."

"What'll that prove?"

"Nothing. Not for sure. But it would indicate someone was here, someone who might have had that." He pointed to the figurine Dayson held against his chest. "It's not much, but it's all I've got."

"So, how are you going to do this dating?"

"The closest lab that can do what I need is up in Seattle at the university.

I need to go up there anyway, talk with my doctoral committee. It's getting time to present my dissertation."

Dayson regarded the figure in his hands, searching for the bit of color Persig described. "Can't you just scrape some off, test that?"

Persig shook his head. "There's so little there. I don't want to risk ruining it. Even if I take the whole thing up there, they may not find enough to test."

"And you'd be gone with it how long?"

"I'd have to wait in line. Probably a couple of weeks."

Dayson shook his head. "No." He hoped that taking an adamant position meant he was right. "I wouldn't let Batch take it, so I can't let you." The irrationality of his argument only made him more stubborn.

The young man looked at him hard, his mouth set tight. "All right. I understand." He rose from his chair and started to walk away, but with an impatient flip of his hand he turned on Dayson. "Actually, I don't understand at all. You've let me come out here to make my dig, to find some explanation for this," he said, cocking his chin at the figurine. "But neither of us will know anything unless I can take it with me to Seattle."

Dayson said nothing.

In exasperation, Persig asked, "What is it you want?"

It was the most elemental question, and Dayson realized with a shock that he had no answer. "Why can't you just test some of this black stuff you're talking about, this ash, and assume it comes from the same time as the statue?"

"No, I'm probably assuming too much already."

He could see Persig struggling to keep his anger in check.

Dayson realized how much he missed his old staff at the Capitol. They'd have taken care of this guy, eased him out the door, leaving him grateful to have shaken hands with the governor. But there was no one here but himself, and all he could do was clutch the stone carving as if it were the last thing left to him in this life.

"I'm sorry, Frank."

* * *

Too restless to go to bed that evening, he puttered around the house for a while, then went into the study to get a book, but instead picked up the stone figure of the woman from his desk. Yes, there was the discoloration Frank Persig had said might be paint or dye, and here the place he'd hit it with the shovel. The mute mouth mocked his yearning to know how she had come here and why. Surely there was a why.

He looked out the window and felt the night drawing him outside. Gripping the statue, he stepped out into the back yard and looked up at the stars. After a few moments he slowly raised his hand and looked at the rising moon over the top of the figurine, as a mariner might hold up a sextant to determine his position on a dark and unfamiliar sea.

Chapter Sixteen

Frank Persig's Story

Nearly a week passed without any sign of Persig, and Dayson wondered if, at the very moment he had finally accepted the young man's presence, he'd managed to drive him off. But late one morning, sitting at his desk, he heard a car pull into the drive, and a few minutes later the sound of Persig fetching his tools from the utility room.

Dayson took his time—paid some bills, did the dishes—before he grabbed his watering can and went out to the back yard.

He found Persig standing at the edge of his dig, arms crossed, his young face clouded with doubt. When he saw Dayson come out of the house he stepped down into the excavation and started to paw at the earth with his trowel.

Constrained by the weight of their last exchange, when Dayson had denied him the figurine, the two men made no greeting.

Dayson was filling his watering can at the tap by the side of the house when the sharp clink of metal hitting metal caught his ear. He looked over his shoulder toward the dig. Persig had dropped his trowel and stood up, staring at the ground before him.

As casually as he could manage, Dayson set his watering can on the grass and walked over to Persig's excavation. As he approached, the young man again knelt on the ground and with quick, deft movements began to extract from the dirt what appeared to be a bit of iron less than an inch thick and slightly curved.

Neither man spoke into the charged moment.

Persig got a camera and took a couple of pictures, then took up a brush to whisk the remaining dirt from the part he had exposed.

After a few minutes of rapid, careful work, Dayson saw the tension in Persig's back and shoulders go slack and his head slump. With a "Bah!" of disgust, he wrenched the object from the ground and tossed it onto the grass. A horseshoe.

"It was too close to the surface," Persig said between clenched teeth. "I should have known not to get . . ." Persig sat on the ground and released a sigh that ended in a dark laugh. "A goddamn horseshoe."

Grunting with the effort, Dayson sat on the grass a couple of feet from Persig and picked up the horseshoe, orange with rust. "Want me to toss it away for you?"

"No. Even if it doesn't mean much I need to tag it, catalogue it. Then you can nail it up somewhere. For good luck." He chuckled miserably and looked at the bit of iron. "From the amount of rust, it's probably fifty years old." He looked at Dayson's house. "When was your place built?"

"Forty-seven, I think."

"What was here before that?"

"No idea. You figure maybe some farmer with a few horses? One of them threw a shoe?"

Persig shrugged. "God knows. I don't. Could have just been left behind by a couple of guys playing horseshoes."

The two men sat quietly on the grass in the sun for a few minutes. Then Dayson asked, "So, why do you do this?"

Persig's head snapped up. "You saying this is a waste of time?"

"No. I'm just asking. You're a bright young guy. You could do lots of things. Go into business."

"Run for governor?"

Dayson refused to be provoked. "Sure, why not? Run for governor. Run for senate. Run for the border. Whatever you want. Why this?"

Persig kicked at his trowel and looked into the distance. "Beats me."

Dayson waited him out.

"We can't know where we are—who we are—unless we know where we came from, how we got here," Persig said with a passion that moved Dayson.

"Maybe I just want to get to the bottom of things" He gave Dayson a furtive look, as if he had revealed something he'd wished to keep back.

"What lay beneath it all," Dayson murmured, remembering the words he had said to himself weeks earlier as he looked out at the broken ground behind his house and contemplated the enigma of the figure he had found.

"Sorry?"

"Nothing." Dayson let out an ironic huff. "I suppose we don't want to look too closely at half the things we do."

"What are you saying?"

Dayson picked up a handful of dust, let it slip through his fingers. "What lay beneath it all," he said again quietly. He knew he would have to give up something of his own if he wanted anything from Persig. "Maybe I'm just talking about myself. The war. Why I went." The words came slowly, pried from a memory locked tight. For a while he said nothing more. But he knew he couldn't leave it there. "I was too old to fight. Wasn't going to get drafted. But I felt I needed to do my part. So I enlisted. They were taking a lot of people they shouldn't have back then, and they accepted me." He didn't add that Dorothy had pleaded with him not to go, telling him that Jocelyn needed her father and she needed her husband. But, as he had tried to tell Jocie in the cafe, he had, like so many other men, felt a duty larger than family. And so he had gone.

"I had some college. A year at Oregon State. They figured I was too well-educated to put to work washing dishes or driving a truck, and too old to be trusted with a firearm. So they gave me a commission and put me into G-2. Intelligence." He snorted. "Something I sadly lacked. I must have been the oldest lieutenant in the army."

However lightly sketched, it was more than he had said about the war to anyone in years. Unsure if any of this made sense to someone so young, he looked at Persig—and nearly laughed. While he had been spilling his guts, the young man was looking across the fields toward the hills, not listening.

"Well, enough about me," Dayson said.

Persig blinked. "Sorry. What?"

"Nothing." He nodded toward the fields on the other side of the trees. "What do you think? If someone dammed up the little stream at the bottom of the rise there, would it flood those fields?"

"I suppose so."

"Yeah, that's what I was thinking. Wouldn't make much sense, would it?" He slapped his hands together to change the subject. "So, you were born in Bend?"

The effect of the simple question startled Dayson. Persig's head dropped and his brow creased in pain.

Puzzled, Dayson said, "Sorry, Frank. I . . . Is that such a tough question?"

"I . . . I don't really . . ." Persig seemed as puzzled as Dayson by his inability to answer. He took a short, sharp breath, raised his head and said, "I'm not sure where I was born. I was adopted." His words carried a tone of defiance that withered as soon as he spoke them, bearing witness to an internal battle of his own that he was not winning.

Adopted, Dayson thought. He wanted to tell the young kid it was no big deal. Clearly, though, for Frank Persig, it was.

How could it be otherwise? They lived in a society in which nuclear Armageddon lurked just over the horizon. Conformity had become the only real source of reassurance, the only glue holding the country together. Letting his own family break apart, violating the norms of a society under siege, had cost him the governorship. Persig, by being adopted, with its suggestion of having been conceived on the wrong side of the sheet, presented a living challenge to those same strictures.

"I'm sorry, Frank. You don't have to talk about it if you don't want."

Having started, though, the young man, like Dayson a moment earlier, needed to continue. "I remember my mother, I think. Some things about her. She was very pretty. I try to make up stories about why she gave me away." He waved his hand in dismissal, though Dayson wondered what he wanted to dismiss. His birth? Its circumstances? Himself? "I lived with two or three foster families. They treated me like I was a criminal, like I'd come to them straight from prison. I got fed. I had clothes on my back. But I was kept at a distance, like there was this circle of barbed wire around me. No one wanted to risk getting snagged on it. Finally, I ended up with Mom and Dad. That's what I've always called them. And they've been wonderful to me. They adopted me, called me their son. And they told me I was better off not thinking about the past. Maybe they were right, but it makes me . . ." He looked across the fields toward the forested hills, and shrugged.

Neither man knew how to fill the silence. The cliches that occurred to Dayson—"Someone must have really cared about you to adopt you." and "I'm sure your mother loved you."—rang too hollow to utter.

He had so often given this kid nothing but the back of his hand he wondered why Frank had shared this. It came to Dayson that maybe he had no one else to tell. Yet, he knew there was something more behind the story, something larger that colored everything he did, said, thought.

In the end, he could only say, "Thanks, Frank, for telling me."

Dayson got to his feet and retrieved his watering can, pausing for a moment as if thinking he should apologize, though he wasn't sure for what, then went back to tending his garden, giving the younger man his privacy.

Persig tried fitfully to take up his work again, but after a while gathered up his things and started toward the utility room.

"Frank."

The young man stopped.

"Look, about the statue. Maybe you're right. You need to take it up to Seattle for those tests. I was being a pain in the ass when I said no."

To his annoyance, the young man didn't appear grateful. "If you think you have to do this because you're suddenly feeling sorry for me . . ."

"That's not it. I made up my mind a few days ago. Stay here. I'll go get it for you."

He went inside and looked at the statuette on his desk. Despite the promise he had made moments earlier, he hesitated, suddenly unwilling to do what he knew he had to do. With a sharp exhalation of breath, he broke through some barrier within himself, grabbed the stone figure and walked back outside.

"You say you'll be gone a couple of weeks with it?"

"Something like that."

"Okay. Just let me know what you—" He stopped in mid-sentence.

This time he saw her coming, gliding through the poplars and along the path toward his house.

When Mattie saw the two men she stopped, Persig's presence apparently taking her by surprise. After a moment, she again advanced toward them, holding a bit of tinfoil in her hand. When she saw that Dayson had noticed it, she stuffed it in the pocket of her blue jeans.

"Hello, Mattie."

Approaching cautiously, she returned Dayson's greeting without taking her eyes off Persig.

What a welter of contradictions she was, Dayson thought, bold and timid, confident and insecure, wild as a tempest, self-possessed as a prophet. Or was her reaction far simpler than he wished to acknowledge? Persig was a tall, broad-shouldered good-looking fellow who, despite his torments—or perhaps because of them—possessed a strong presence.

For his part, Persig's flushed face indicated something more elemental about the sight of this tall young woman.

With a wry twist of his mouth, Dayson made introductions, nodding at the two young people in turn. "Mattie, Frank Persig. Frank, this is Mattie—" He stopped, struck by the fact that he didn't know her last name, only knew it wasn't Tannehill.

He raised his eyes enquiringly.

She frowned, as if he were forcing her to give up a secret. "Reed."

"Reed," he repeated, trying to fit the word to the young woman before him. Reed in the wind. Reed growing wild. "Mattie Reed," he said to Persig. "Neighbor girl."

They both knew it was more than that, though neither could have said what.

Maybe it didn't matter how he characterized her. Persig didn't seem to have heard him, but simply gazed at her as if she were some new and fascinating icon uncovered only this moment.

"You're the one who digs everything up," she said to bring him back to earth.

Persig realized he was staring. He laughed and turned away to hide his embarrassment, which only managed to underline it.

"I guess I am."

"You're the one who found the statue."

He coughed into his hand. "No, that was Mr. Dayson."

"Ah."

Her expression spoke to a readjustment of her thinking.

"And you've been digging up more things since then."

Now it was Persig who looked at Dayson. Both he and Mattie were behaving as if the older man were the only medium through which they could speak to each other.

"No. I haven't found anything more," Persig confessed.

She cocked her head to one side like a curious bird. "But you keep digging."

"Yeah."

"What is it you're looking for?"

"I . . . I'm not sure."

Dayson marveled at how the girl's presence had so undone the young man. To get him off the hook, and change the subject, he asked, "What brings you out here, Mattie?"

"Nothing. I just came by to say hello."

He nodded to the pocket where she had put the tinfoil. "You have something you were going to show me."

She put her hand over her pocket as if afraid whatever she'd hidden there might pop out and start singing.

"No. Well, yes. Another time." She smiled to cover her discomfort. "I've got class in a little bit. I'd better get going."

Dayson knew she hadn't walked all the way up the path to tell him she had to be leaving, but decided to let it go.

She said goodbye and politely told Persig it had been nice to make his acquaintance.

Before the young man could reply she ran off.

Persig looked at Dayson, saw the question his face.

"Neighbor girl," Dayson said again. "Stops by now and then." He found he didn't want to talk about her to the young man. "Look, go ahead and take the thing up to Seattle. Do what you need to do."

Persig took the statue before Dayson could change his mind.

That night, without its presence in the house, Dayson found it difficult to sleep.

Chapter Seventeen

The Last Wise Man

The following morning Dayson sat at his desk, bleary-eyed, looking over the latest exchange between his lawyers and Dorothy's, one side asking for the moon, the other offering green cheese. An enclosed note from one of his attorneys pleaded to Dayson for clearer guidance. The dissolution of a twenty-seven year marriage necessitated complex financial negotiations, the attorney wrote plaintively, requiring an exchange of demands and concessions regarding real and personal property as well as the apportionment of blame for the divorce. Regarding the last point, the lawyer had, a week earlier, tried to persuade Dayson to make an issue of his wife's unfaithfulness, saying it would help him in any settlement and save him thousands of dollars. "And lose my daughter forever," Dayson had replied, and refused.

What, then, asked the law firm of Huber, Hoselton and Fennell, did he want?

Dayson tossed the letter onto his desk. "Hell, I don't know," he said out loud.

The whole thing was like a boxing match in which the boxers—the lawyers—never got hurt and only the spectators ended up with their noses broken. He shoved the papers aside, picked up the phone and dialed the familiar number.

"Hi, Ernie. Martin Dayson."

"Good morning, Governor. It's good to hear your voice. To what do I owe the honor?"

Dayson had plucked Ernie Fonseca from Oregon State University three years earlier to head up the Department of State Lands. If anyone outside Gilkey's office had details on the bill, he figured it would be Ernie.

Dayson cradled the receiver against his ear and leaned back in his chair. "I'm curious about this new proposal on the reclamation project that includes the Tyee Dam. I don't have a bill number. I don't think it's been introduced yet. But I'm told the project's being expanded beyond what we had last session."

"Believe it or not, we haven't seen the bill, Governor."

"You're kidding me."

"Normally they'd have asked my office to draft it, but I think someone in the governor's office is working on it instead. I don't know if they'll even run it by us before they send it to Legislative Counsel for the final draft. Very odd."

"I was hoping you could help me out. I'm supposed to testify when the bill comes up in committee. But they want to avoid telling me what's in it."

"Join the club. The Tyee's part of it. But I'm pretty sure the bill doesn't stop there. They've been asking us for maps of rural areas in the Willamette Valley."

"That's a helluva long way from the John Day River. Look, there seems to be something in the bill about a Bennett Creek. Have they asked for any maps that might include Bennett Creek?"

"I wish I could tell you. There are ten thousand creeks in this state, and I'm afraid I don't know all of them. Why?"

"Something a friend said."

"Your friend seems to know more about it than I do."

"What do you think, Ernie? You figure Gilkey's making a play for farmers with this bill?"

Fonseca chuckled. "I try to stay out of the politics of these things. I figure the Governor's office makes policy and I carry it out. That way I sleep better and keep my job longer."

"You're the last wise man in Salem, Ernie."

"No, I just moved up a notch when you left."

"Look, let me know if you find out anything more on this bill."

"Happy to do it. But, honestly? I think there's something going on there that they don't want to talk about. They seem to think they can line up all the support they need without telling anyone what the bill actually does. But you didn't hear that from me."

"Thanks, Ernie."

"I'm thinking you probably don't want me telling anyone about this call."

"You'll sleep better and keep your job longer. So long."

Chapter Eighteen

The End of Something

Two o'clock came and went. Martin Dayson straightened a chair in the living room, checked twice then a third time whether he had enough water in the coffee pot, put a few dishes away, checked again about the water. Finally, he stood in the middle of the living room, hands on his hips, unable to think of what else to do.

When Dorothy insisted over the phone that they needed to talk, he'd thought she would ask him to come out to the farm. She might have understood how hard that might be on him as, when he pre-empted her by asking her to come out to his place, she surprised him by saying yes.

And now she was late.

At two-twenty the familiar Buick pulled into the driveway. Despite his insistence, to her and to himself, that their meeting was purely business, his heart caught for a moment as she came up to the door. He hadn't seen her in three months.

Both teams of lawyers had advised them, implored them, not to meet, each side afraid their client would give the farm away—in her case figuratively, in his literally—and reach an agreement without their appropriately remunerated assistance.

He noticed his hand shaking as he opened the door for her.

"Hi, Dot."

"Hi, Marty."

She accepted a kiss on the cheek but didn't return it, let him take her coat, but held onto her purse as if she might need to hit him with it later.

Did she want a cup of coffee? She considered it for a moment, as if looking for a trap behind the offer, before saying, "Sure."

While he went into the kitchen, she took a seat on the sofa. Even with his back to her, he could feel her looking the place over.

"So, how do you like it out here?" she asked.

Every movement, every word, felt excruciatingly unnatural.

"Well, it's quiet," he said over his shoulder.

She allowed herself a laugh, and the chill eased a little.

"What do you do all day?"

Coming in from the kitchen, he looked around the room as if he might find the answer written on the wall. "I dunno, answer some mail, read, look after my garden."

"You're growing a garden?" She punctuated the question with a sardonic smile. "Doing anything with those memoirs?"

"Why the hell is everyone plaguing me about my memoirs?" He handed Dorothy her cup, set his on the coffee table and took the armchair. "If they think my life's so damn interesting, they can write it themselves."

She looked around the room and shook her head. "I don't like to see you out here by yourself."

"If you're so concerned about me being by myself, you shouldn't have taken up with Tommy." He wanted to make it sound like a joke.

"Stop it, Marty."

"I'm just saying . . ."

"You said it."

He made a rumbling in his throat, but he knew he'd already stepped over a line he'd sworn not to even approach.

"So, what's on your mind?" he asked.

"You're on my mind. And on my lawyer's mind. And on your own lawyer's mind. And you're driving us all crazy. We need to settle this thing, and no one knows what you want."

"Want? I don't give a damn."

"Yes you do. Or this would be settled by now."

It irritated him, her genius for seeing through him—and reminded him why he loved her. She was right. Not only did he not know what he wanted, he refused to think about it except to wish it would all go away.

"What would make you happy?" he asked.

She crossed her legs and fished a cigarette from a pack in her purse.

"I was going to ask for the farm, but only so I can give it to Jocie and Ed."

"Yeah, Jocie said something to me about it the other day. That's fine. What else?"

"We can split the bank accounts and the bonds. I don't want your pension. It's yours, you earned it."

He wanted to say something sarcastic, but knew she was being generous.

"Alimony?"

"No," she shook her head and exhaled a plume of smoke. "I don't need any alimony."

"Child support?"

"Be serious, Marty."

He chuckled. "Fine. That's all fine." He let twenty-seven years go with a sigh. "Your lawyer's going to be okay with this?"

"No."

"Mine either." They regarded each other silently for a moment, then they both laughed.

"Well, that was quick," Dayson said, smiling. "You haven't even finished your coffee."

Her smile in return, a tentative and fleeting thing, spoke to her own surprise at how abruptly the wall between them had not so much fallen as simply disappeared.

And it left them both at a loss about what to say next.

Funny, he thought, how the most familiar presence in his life could leave him feeling so undone. It was exactly this jarring collision of her old-shoe familiarity with the paradox of her otherness that threw him so badly.

"You want a little tour of the place?"

She eyed him narrowly, guarded again, and Dayson wondered if they had already started building a new wall to replace the one they'd just torn down.

"Yes. Why not?"

Dayson stood and indicated the room around them. "This is the living room. That area there is a sort of dining area. And there's the kitchen." He held up his hands in a there-you-have-it gesture. "Any questions?"

She gave him a sardonic smile. "Well, that was quick."

"It's not exactly the governor's mansion, is it?"

"What's through there?"

"There? Just my . . . C'mon, I'll show you."

Leaving their coffee to grow cold, he led her back to his study.

"It's kind of a mess," he said with a shrug she could read as either apology or indifference.

She looked at the familiar books in new shelves, trailed her hand along the familiar desk piled with unfamiliar papers.

She picked up the medal in its glass-fronted case and glanced at Dayson.

"How's Tommy?" he asked before she could ask why he had the medal out.

Another sidelong glance. "Tommy's fine."

"He's gotten over Helen's death?"

"You don't get over something like that."

Dayson nodded. Unable to leave it alone, he said, "Hell, Dorothy, Tommy Bayless is boring. A nice guy, but maybe the most boring man I've ever known. I think he bored Helen to death. Should have been indicted for it. Same thing could happen to you."

"I'll take my chances."

"Dorothy . . ."

"I could use boring."

"I'm retired now. Finished with all that. I'm sure I could be just as boring as Tommy if I put my mind to it."

She awarded him a smile for trying. "It's too late, Marty."

"You told me you loved me because I was exciting, wanted to get out and get things done. And then you divorced me for the same reason."

She chewed on her lip, something he had marked years earlier as a sure sign she was angry.

"You know it's not that simple."

"Didn't I love you?"

"Why are you asking me?" she said. "It's like you saw yourself as a knight of the Round Table. Always off on a holy quest, especially after the war. I was left at home, admiring you. That wears thin after a while. I needed you there, with me." She folded her arms over her chest and said with false brightness, "So, you had lunch with Jocie the other day."

"Yeah, she gave me a call. I didn't realize she was still speaking to me." He cocked his head to one side. "I sound like I'm feeling sorry for myself, don't I?"

"Are you?"

Unable to speak and look at her at the same time, he turned toward the window, his back to Dorothy, for the moment still husband and wife. "I'm one sorry-assed sonofabitch, if that's what you mean. Sorry about not being a good enough father."

"Tell Jocie. She needs you to do that."

"I tried, but . . ."

"Try again."

He nodded, unable to trust himself to speak around the lump in his throat.

He heard her step up behind him, felt her arms around his chest. He put a hand on her arm and held it there.

With a pat on his hand, she pulled away. "Why don't you show me your garden?"

A cloudless sky. The sun warm on their backs.

"And the peas are just about ready," Dayson continued. "You can see the beans are looking good. Those are the tomatoes coming along." He saw her smile. "But I guess you know what a tomato plant looks like."

"Pretty much."

"Am I showing off?"

"It's all right." She nodded toward the other half of the plot. "What's going on here? Why have you got it all dug out like this?"

"Nothing really." He made an unconvincing shrug. "I may plant this part yet. Squash. Maybe some late vegetables."

"You're not going to tell me what these holes are about?"

"No." He tried to laugh, as if it were a joke between them.

"Why not?"

"I don't know." He watched her trying to piece it together. He didn't know how to tell her, "I found a goddess and no one knows how it came to be there." Or how to say that there was this young girl who kept crossing his property, showing up at his door, and she was as great a mystery to him, and perhaps to herself, as the stone icon?

He looked out across the garden, between the apple trees toward the path, empty now. "I still love you, Dot."

Her sigh cut through his heart, telling him it was no good.

"I know. I still love you too, Marty. Some. Not enough to . . ."

Dayson raised his hand to stop her. "Spare me the percentages. You needed me around more. I know that. Knew it even then. But I still had so much I needed to do. I had obligations."

"You had obligations to us too." She put her hand to her mouth and closed her eyes, as if the remark had pained her as much as it had him. "It's been fifteen years, Marty. You've done enough for him."

"I'm not talking about Ben Rosloff!"

"Yes, you are."

Dayson felt himself panting, his chest odd, hollow.

"He's dead, Marty."

"You think I don't know that?"

"But you've never accepted it. Marty, you can't keep living someone else's life. You had me and Jocie and the farm. And you put us all aside to follow your idea of what some other guy might maybe possibly could have done."

The gorge rose in Dayson's throat and he felt light-headed. He wanted to tell Dorothy how mistaken she was, how she had it all wrong. But he had spent too many nights staring at the ceiling telling himself that, yes, he could live his own life and Ben Rosloff's too. And all that time he was the one who'd had it all wrong.

Usually, the light-headedness, when it came, passed quickly. Not today. He sat down on the grass, his feet in Persig's dig. The thought occurred to him that they could bury him right here.

"You all right, Marty?"

"Sure. Just kind of tired."

"Your blood pressure's still too high?"

He worked to slow his breathing. More natural now. There, it had passed. "Ah, Dot, why did you want to bring me so low?"

"I didn't want to, Marty. I really didn't. I thought you would still win."

"Your political instincts were never the best."

"I voted for you."

He chuckled miserably.

"Maybe it's a good thing you lost, Marty. You can start leading your own life now. Find out where that takes you."

"If it makes you feel better to think that's true . . ."

"It should make you feel better."

"Well, it doesn't."

After twenty-seven years, he knew when he was making her angry and he asked himself why he was doing it. Right when they were finally having the talk they needed to have, he was managing to wreck it.

Like sailors steering away from the rocks, they moved the conversation onto safer topics, the weather and the growing season, how the old Buick was holding up. After a while she said she had to be going. She would talk to her lawyers about what they'd worked out and Dayson would talk to his, and to hell with what any of them thought. She gave him a peck on the cheek, said goodbye, and walked away.

Dayson couldn't bring himself to watch her go.

Chapter Nineteen

Further Evasions

Bob Bremmer, Gilkey's chief of staff, tried to laugh, just to show how much he enjoyed speaking over the phone with the former governor. Couldn't think of any better way to pass his morning. And nothing could please him more than answering—or not answering—his questions.

Even ex-governors are formidable political beings, in part because current governors understand that they will themselves be ex-governors one day, so can be particularly solicitous of their predecessors. Bremmer clearly didn't want to get caught between them.

Yes, there would be six dams built, he said, each one constructed to aid local farmers. That was what the bill was all about, helping Oregon's farmers. No, he didn't know off the top of his head where each one would go. Dayson should call the committee staff. Well, that's true, the committee staff didn't have the bill yet. But as soon as they did . . . No, there's no secrecy about the bill. Yes, the Department of State Lands would normally have drafted the bill, but they had a lot on their plate and the Governor decided to draw it up through his own office. No, he couldn't say if anyone from outside had a hand in drafting it. The Senate hearing? Scheduled for sometime in June. Yes, of course they were looking forward to his presence. And of course the Governor would love to speak to him. However, he isn't available right now.

"You don't want to be talking about this with me, do you?"

"What? Of course I do. It's just that you have so many questions, Governor."

"Is that a problem?"

"Problem? No. No—though your appearance before the committee is seen as something more ceremonial than substantive."

"Yeah? Who decided that?"

"I've got another call coming in, Governor. So . . ."

"For a routine bill, you guys seem awfully antsy."

"I'd love to talk about this further, but I really must—" Bremmer hung up without finishing his sentence.

Chapter Twenty

A Handful of Ashes

Two weeks had passed since he had seen Persig, the time he had said he would need to go up to Seattle to run a test on the statue and deal with his dissertation committee. Yet looking out the kitchen window as he washed some dishes, it took Dayson by surprise to see the young man standing in the back yard again, hands in his pockets, toeing the edge of his modest dig.

Dayson asked himself what it was with people that they couldn't come up and knock on his door. From day one, Persig had always walked around to the back yard without showing himself at the door. And that first time Art Thayer came, the youngster might have sat in his car until he starved if he, Dayson, hadn't gone to the door and waved him in. And Mattie, appearing in the back yard as if from nowhere, ineluctable as Poe's raven—or a plastic lawn elf. Was everyone so in awe of a defeated politician that they couldn't take him head-on? Or had he become such an ogre in his exile that people hoped to tiptoe past his cave without waking him?

Or maybe he had it all wrong. Rather than refusing to come to his door, they were conspiring to draw him out.

Whatever the answer, the contrarian in Dayson told him he should stay put and ignore Persig. But his wish to see what the lab boys in Seattle might have gleaned from the figurine pulled him out the back door.

As Dayson walked across the yard the expression on Persig's face told him that, whatever he had done in Seattle, it hadn't gone well. So he said nothing and the two men stood together looking down at the torn-up earth like mourners at a gravesite.

"Good to see you, Frank."

"I only came out for a few minutes," he said, his voice flat. "Just to tell you what they said about . . ." He nodded at the small cloth sack that lay at his feet, betraying the familiar shape within.

"Okay, so tell me, what did you find out about my girl?"

Persig looked down at the sack for some time, as if working up the will to speak. "Not much we didn't know before. Which is practically nothing. There wasn't enough of the coloring, whatever it is, to get any results from the carbon-14 test. They analyzed the stone itself, and they tell me it's not found in the Northwest. They're looking into that, trying to figure out its provenance. They'll likely tell me it could have come from anywhere in Siberia or East Asia. Timbuktu. The moon."

"How about the black stuff?"

"Ash. Had that right. Something like three thousand years old."

"So it was a campfire?"

"Don't know. If I keep digging maybe I'll find more of it spread around here and decide it's just the remains of an old forest fire. Either way, I can't prove any connection between the ash and the statue without knowing the statue's age." He gave Dayson a sidelong glance. "Or exactly how far down you found it."

Dayson shrugged. Some things can't be helped.

Persig leaned down, picked up a handful of dirt, appeared to search for something in it, then threw it back and rose to his feet. "No one gives a damn about this thing. I've talked to the guys in Seattle, sent letters to Berkeley, UCLA, telling them about it, asking if they could think of anything that would make sense of it. Nothing. Not a word from anyone. If it was another mask or some fish hooks or one more petroglyph they'd be running here with their magnifying glasses, shoving each other out of the way to write articles explaining why it's slightly different from the fish hooks just like it, show how brilliant they are at making distinctions that don't make a damn bit of difference. But this thing is so inexplicable that it doesn't even register with them. They have no place in their mind to put it. So they do nothing. Won't even talk to me."

"Maybe we'll never know what it's about, Frank."

"No!" Forcing a calmness more harrowing than his outburst, he said between clenched teeth, "All I need to do is work harder, dig deeper. I'll prove where it came from, why it's here. I'll prove it. I'll make them treat me like I'm as good as—"

He staggered away from his dig, his hand clutching his brow.

"Sounds like something a lot bigger than academic politics is bothering you. Maybe you should—"

"She was raped!" He bent over, gagging as if about to vomit. But he couldn't get it out.

"Frank . . ."

He shot upright, his face white, gasping for air. "She was raped!"

"What? Who was—"

"My mother!"

"Migod. If you don't want to talk—"

But he had gone past any point of stopping and the words came pouring out as if they were what he finally needed to bring up. "Raped by a railroad worker. She was a Warm Springs Indian. Helped her family by selling salmon to the passenger trains that stopped along the Columbia Gorge. And this guy told her to come up to the caboose to sell him a salmon. And he . . . She gave me away when I was four, five." He turned on Dayson. "Why did she wait so long? Why did she wait years, and then give me away?"

For a long, stunned moment, the only word Dayson could get out was, "Jesus." He knew this boy at this moment needed so much more than that. "I can't tell you why, Frank. I would never have guessed. No one would. I mean, you don't—"

"Don't look like an Indian? Well, you're right. I look like him. I look like this . . . criminal. Maybe I should be asking why she kept me around for as long as she did when I looked like the man who had done this to her. That's why the foster families looked at me the way they did. They saw the criminal in me."

"Frank, they probably didn't even know."

"They could see it. If I could see it, they could too. I keep looking in the mirror and asking myself, 'Where's the other part of me—the part of me that's her, my mother?' Maybe that's why she gave me away. She couldn't find it either. Sometimes I think I can feel it, inside me, the part that belongs to her. The part that belongs. . . somewhere. I keep looking for it. Digging to find it." He heard his own words and stopped.

The older man wondered what he was supposed to tell him. That if he couldn't find anything more here in his garden, couldn't discover where the statue came from and what it meant, then he'd never figure out anything about himself? The notion was absurd. Yet wasn't he, with his own obsessions about the icon, doing the same thing?

Both men looked at the torn earth that refused to yield its secrets, looked at the orderly depths of the tightly planned, thoroughly controlled dig, and realized Persig had discovered even less than Dayson's helter-skelter shoveling had done. The chances he ever would were too small to think about.

That realization, though, wouldn't be enough to make either of them stop looking. It would take something greater than failure to make them halt their search. And there would be no point in continuing this conversation until they knew what that something might be.

"So, how did the meeting with your dissertation committee go?"

Persig shrugged. "It went."

Dayson reached down, picked up the sack and retrieved from it the hunk of stone. A surge of comfort coursed through him at holding it once again in his hand, having it home.

He wondered again why this thing meant so much to him. Had he lost something that it could bring back? Maybe everyone had so lost that ancient intuition of some greater force around them—an intuition once as real and as common as the sense of smell or sight—that they no longer understood the power embedded in objects like the stone goddess and the ability of these avatars to restore us to ourselves.

A vision of the great wooden mask trapped in Batch's office passed through the unknown region between the mind and consciousness. He wondered if, for both Persig and himself, all their searching simply led them further and further away from what they were looking for. Perhaps they'd never find what they sought until they stopped looking.

Dayson skipped past these imponderables long enough to ask, "So what are you going to do now?"

And he found that while he had hoped so often that Persig would say he was giving up, he now hoped he wouldn't.

The young man shook his head as if to expel the incubus of defeat. "Maybe I won't find any more ash around the site. That could indicate what I have is from a campfire." He looked across the fields to the silent hills. "I'm going to keep digging. I only came out to tell you the tests didn't go well."

After Persig had left, Dayson walked over to the boy's dig and sat on the grass, his feet on the bare dirt, trying to decipher the mystery of why someone would yearn to do so much with his life, hoping that by doing great things he could fill the great hole inside him—and wondering if he were thinking of Persig or himself.

The day had grown warm. Birds called in the distance—from the fields, from the woods, from the sky. But a great drowsiness had come over him and he was too sleepy to answer.

Like a lazy cat in the sun, Dayson stretched and lay back on the grass and closed his eyes. The sun felt good on his face. Its light, turned red by the filter of his eyelids, pulsed with his heartbeat. His breathing slowed, his thoughts lost focus. He sensed the great bird soaring above him, its beak held wide, the face of the shaman peeking out at him, trying to tell him something. But he couldn't quite catch what it was.

When he felt the bird's shadow pass over him, he opened his eyes.

Chapter Twenty-One

Scotch and Sinatra

Standing between Dayson and the sun, Mattie leaned over him, smiling.

"I woke you up."

"What? No. I . . . No." He didn't want to admit to her that he had fallen asleep in the sun like an old man.

He sat up with a grunt, woozy from his doze. As she backed away a step he saw she was holding something behind her back.

Dayson rubbed his hands over his face and nodded at her. "What have you got there?"

She pulled it out to show him. "A record album. Joan Baez."

"Joe Baeza?"

"Joan— You've really never heard of Joan Baez?"

Dayson murmured something noncommittal.

"Have you got a stereo?" she asked. She spoke with an odd, mischievous smile that seemed to be about something more than a stereo.

"Stereo? I've got a record player somewhere, if that's what you want."

"That will do."

While Mattie prepared tea, Dayson rummaged through a closet until he found his inexpensive portable turntable and brought it into the living room.

While he plugged the machine in and switched it on, Mattie, smiling slyly, carried in the tea and cookies and set them on the coffee table. Her peculiar exhilaration bothered and intrigued Dayson.

She took the record from its sleeve. "I thought you needed to know what was going on in the world beyond Topping."

This was something between a recurring topic and a running joke, the young college girl chiding the former governor about how little he knew of the world. Though he scoffed at her insistence that he'd become a troglodyte, he felt keenly his lack of familiarity with the things important to her—the writers she mentioned, the foreign films she had seen on campus, the musicians she spoke of. At the same time, she knew little, and apparently cared even less, about the life he had left behind—or, more accurately, from which he had been expelled. Her disdain for the achievements in which he had taken such pride renewed his secret fear that they were as ephemeral as the prevailing winds and that they, and he too, would soon be forgotten.

"You figure I'm an old fuddy-duddy?" he asked.

"Fuddy-duddy?" she repeated, wrinkling her nose at the unfamiliar term. "If that means you're letting yourself turn into a cranky old man who never goes out, then yes."

Dayson managed not to wince at the accuracy of the barb she'd thrown. He nodded toward the record Mattie was placing on the turntable. "You figure this is going to do the trick? Have me rocking and rolling in the streets?"

"It's a start. She's become very important this year." Again, she flashed a peculiar smile, both searching and beguiling, as she leaned over the turntable and set the needle on the record.

Rather than settling onto the sofa opposite Dayson's chair, she sat on the floor next to his feet, something that normally would not have bothered him but at that moment felt uncomfortably close.

After a momentary hiss as the needle searched for the groove, the room filled with the sound of a simple guitar and a voice like an angel, something both surprisingly old-fashioned in its melody and disturbingly new in its boldness. They listened in silence to a ballad about a dead labor organizer. Dayson wanted to ask Mattie if this Baez girl thought the Depression was still on, but when he looked down he found her, eyes closed, entirely absorbed in the music. No sidelong glances in his direction, no appeal for his approval. She had left him on his own to sense the spell of the music or not. Then came a song about the folly of war. As if the young singer knew anything about it, Dayson thought. Just as he was ready to cross her off as a self-righteous dilettante the next song entirely disarmed him.

Sensing his change, Mattie looked up at him. "What?"

"My mother used to sing this around the house when I was a boy."

He meant to say it dismissively, to let Mattie know that, whatever she might think, this was nothing new. But he sensed the cruelty of his impulse. Her youth made the song as new as herself. And he caught the tone of his own voice, colored by unexpected wonder.

"Yes," Mattie whispered. "She's calling to us."

Unsettled, he asked, "Calling us? To do what?"

She gave him a piercing look but said nothing.

Where, he wondered, did she get this ability to make him feel as if she were the teacher and he the callow student?

Still, he resisted. "Okay, but what's so special about this?" he asked, trying not to reveal how much the song had affected him, and at the same time hoping she had an answer for him.

In fact, she did. But it wasn't one he'd anticipated.

"There's a way to help you go deeper into it, make it go deeper into you."

She was looking directly into his eyes, searching his face.

He forced a frown to hide the disquiet her cryptic words raised in him. "Yeah? What's that?"

Biting her lip, she reached into the pocket of her blue jeans. Her eyes still holding his, her own expression a singular mix of daring and uncertainty, she pulled out the bit of tinfoil she had hidden in her pocket the other day and carefully unwrapped it.

Dayson squinted at the contents of the tinfoil. "A cigarette. You smoke?"

She made no answer but continued to look at him with that ineffable smile.

"You even roll your own," he said with a laugh. "What are you some kind of cowboy?" Even as he spoke, the truth dawned on him and his laugh went hollow.

"It's not a cigarette." Her face lit up with an elfin grin. "At least not a regular one."

He tried to hide his shock behind a mask of gruffness. "What's a girl like you doing taking this stuff?" He realized he was posing the question more to himself than to her, and marveled at the genius this girl possessed for making him feel out of his depth.

She managed not to roll her eyes. "Taking? It's not a pill. Just something to relax you, make your soul feel larger."

"My soul fits fine, thank you. And I don't need some slip of a girl to . . ." To do what, he wondered. "What are you, some kind of beatnik?"

With a laugh, she reached up and plucked at his beard. "I was going to ask you the same thing."

Dayson knew he should act offended, but couldn't help but laugh. "Does your aunt know about this?"

The joy left her face. "Be quiet about her. You know nothing about her."

When was the last time anyone had spoken to him like this? Again, he wanted to take offense, but knew he was the one who had somehow overstepped a bound.

He looked at the cigarette she had taken from its bit of tinfoil. A couple of friends had tried the stuff in college and told him it did them no harm, leaving him with a vague curiosity. But he had never thought he would be in a position to say yes or no to it.

He saw the dare in her eyes. Despite his astonishment that she would possess something he associated with dope fiends and goateed musicians, he knew that if he didn't accept her challenge something important between them would be lost.

"Okay," he grumped, trying to cover his uncertainty. He raised a warning hand. "But you have to promise never to tell anyone about this."

She laughed. "Even if I'm called in front of a senate committee?"

"Especially if."

"It's a promise," she whispered.

She put the cigarette in her mouth, retrieved a match from her pocket and struck it with an impressive flick of her fingernail.

The anticipation sent a shiver of expectation through Dayson, so much like when he'd been a kid taking his first drink, or running a trembling hand over the thigh of his first girlfriend. He struggled with the temptation of thinking youth was somehow mutable, a state he could regain.

She took a deep breath of the marijuana and passed it to him.

Like Macbeth gazing at the dagger hovering before his eyes, he eyed it warily.

She expelled the stream of smoke with a laugh. "You're afraid!" she declared with a mocking smile.

"Afraid!? I landed at Saipan, Okinawa."

"But you're afraid of this." She handed the joint to him. "Quick, before it goes out."

Frowning, he inhaled the harsh-tasting smoke and, as she had, held it in his lungs for a few seconds, then passed it back to her before going into a coughing fit that left his eyes watering.

"Not exactly a Marlboro filter," he choked.

Mattie indicated they should smoke it in turns. Dayson chuckled that such an outlaw act should possess an established etiquette. For the next few minutes they silently passed the smoke back and forth, each exchange laying down a growing layer of intimacy.

As she turned the record over she asked, "What do you think? Do you feel anything?"

"A runny nose."

"That's it?"

"So this is marijuana and folk singers?" Dayson harrumphed. "I'll stick to scotch and Sinatra."

Her expression wavered between disappointment and skepticism. "Nothing at all?"

"Nothing at all." Dayson sat back and folded his hands over his belly. "But I might have been wrong about the music. It's . . . fascinating." He sighed contentedly. "Could you pass me one of those cookies? Actually, maybe a couple of 'em. What's so funny?"

"Nothing at all," she said, gazing at him with an unsettling intensity. "I know what people think about . . . about her."

"Are you talking about . . . ?" The rest of the question slipped away like smoke up a chimney.

"Sarah. They think she's crazy. It makes it easy for people. They want to look down at her because she's difficult and upsets folks. And I know what they think about me. They judge me because of who I am—or what they think I've done. They want to put a label on me so they can dismiss me."

His thoughts had grown both strangely vague and compellingly insistent. He groped for words. "How did you become so old? And I'm feeling so young. Like I don't know anything. When did you pass me up? I mean, I know what you're talking about. Who you're talking about? That professor who . . ." He couldn't find the words to finish his thought.

"Lawrence made me feel free. He knows how much I want to see the world, all of it, and he tried to help me do it. He said he loved me. But I think he only saw something in me that he wished he had in himself. He liked to say he was free, but he wasn't and he knew it. And he thought he could get free through me."

Dayson let her words roll around in his mind until he understood them, and was struck again at how this girl understood so much, could see so clearly.

"So, he left you and you were angry and you burned the shack down."

Her eyes turned deadly earnest. "No." She shook her head. "No. I set it on fire because something of me was trapped in there and I had to let it out. And that was the only way."

Suddenly shy, she extinguished the joint between two fingers and said, "Maybe this is enough for a first time," she said.

"But . . ." He couldn't think of what came next.

She took what remained of the cigarette, folded the tinfoil around it and slid it back into her pocket.

"You think too much." Mattie said it simply, a statement of fact.

Of course he thought too much, he wanted to tell her. Impulses and sentiment were not the tools needed to lead a state, bring order to the bureaucracies, move important legislation. But these occupations were lost to him now, and he felt a shadow of regret that he had allowed impulse and sentiment so little room in his life. Might he have kept Dorothy's love, Jocie's affection if he had allowed those qualities freer rein?"

“And you stay in your house too much.”

“Why shouldn’t I? Everyone seems to come to me.”

“For their own reasons.”

“I wish I knew what they were.”

Their conversation was playing out like contrapuntal melodies, curling around each other, never quite merging.

“There’s a dance at the grange hall tonight,” she said.

“A dance?”

“You should go.”

His pleasant torpor rocked on a wave of surprise.

“Me? I don’t think …” His next words, whatever they might have been, darted down a rabbit hole, leaving him with nothing to say.

“You think too much.”

“You said that. Didn’t you?”

“I should say it again.”

“I’m too old to be going to any dance with you.”

“You’re not going *with* me. It’s just dance. Besides, the difference in our ages doesn’t matter.”

Could he find a way to tell her she didn’t mean it in the same way he did?

“You figure I should go to a ‘hop’ and make a fool of myself?

“Yes.”

“I won’t know anyone.”

“You’ll know me.”

“Yeah, well …”

“When was the last time you allowed yourself to have any fun?”

“Fun? I still have fun. I just don’t enjoy it anymore. Gives me heartburn.”

“You’re afraid to enjoy yourself.”

“You seem to think I’m afraid of ‘most everything.”

“You’ll come?”

Her smirk goaded him into saying, “I will.”

The certainty in his tone took him by surprise. He’d meant it as a question.

“It starts at eight. I’ll see you there.”

Before he could rally his intention to reverse course she was gone.

Chapter Twenty-Two

At the Hop

Dayson tried to remember who it was who said, "Do sober what you said you'd promised to do drunk. That'll teach you to keep your mouth shut."

Though he still wanted to persuade himself the marijuana hadn't affected him, he felt its spell dissipate only slowly, leaving him washed up on the shore of his own folly, knowing he had made a promise he shouldn't have made. He wondered if this was why she had brought that stuff with her, to put him in a position of saying yes to something when he needed to say no. Surely he couldn't be held to a promise made in a state of diminished responsibility.

By eight that evening he had put on a tie and a sport coat and headed for the door.

The grange hall, a long, low white building that looked like a country church without a steeple, lay on Highway 26, a mile outside of Topping. It consisted of a large kitchen and a larger meeting hall with a stage that, on this night, featured a five-piece band of middle-aged musicians pretending to be younger. At the other end of the hall, grange members served up punch and homemade cookies.

Nervously fingering the knot of his tie, Martin Dayson gave his fifty-cent admission fee to a woman at a table near the front door and slouched into the large hall, its ceiling lights decorated with Chinese lanterns that dimmed the room to a muted pink. He paid a dime for a glass of punch and stood in the shadows and listened while the band played a polka, then a foxtrot, followed by a denatured rock and roll number that the group somehow made to sound like another polka.

Roughly four-score locals filled the large room, ranging in age from little kids to gray-hairs like himself.

Among the multitude, though, he couldn't find the one face he had expected to see. Of course he hadn't come to the dance in order to see Mattie, but only to get out of the house, meet his neighbors. So he told himself. In her absence, he buttoned and unbuttoned his sport coat, tugged at his shirt collar, put a hand in his pocket, took it out again, all the time feeling like what he was, a stranger pretending to belong. How could he have been governor of the state, he wondered, when he felt so out of place among its people?

He told himself again that he would never have agreed to come if he hadn't been smoking that stuff. And, most likely, she would never have made the suggestion if she hadn't been smoking it too. Now, of the two of them, she was the one who'd had enough sense to stay home. Lesson learned.

Dayson laughed to himself, trying to remember when he'd last been stood up, and had started toward the exit when he caught a movement or, rather, a stillness out of the corner of his eye.

Mattie stood five feet away. Funny, he thought, how often he saw her like that, at the edge of his vision, like a wraith at the margins of his mind. She stood with her hands clasped before her, a gesture he had once thought a mark of her unshakable aplomb, but had begun to understand as a mask for her moments of uncertainty.

"I was about to give up on you," he said.

"I didn't mean to be so late."

She appeared distracted, as if she had left some part of herself behind and was waiting for it to catch up. Dayson was about to ask what was bothering her when he saw it for himself. In the dim light of the grange hall, a couple of the locals were eyeing Mattie, making furtive comments behind their hands, then looking quickly away when she turned toward them.

She lifted her chin in defiance.

"Don't get your back up. Maybe they're looking at me," Dayson said with a forced laugh. "And I'll bet every one of 'em will claim they voted for me."

They both knew the truth. None of these people could know anything but the sketchiest facts about her, which only made it easier to gossip, freeing them from the need to see her as anything but a girl of easy virtue, reducing her to grist for the local scandal mill. That she lived with the most notable eccentric around, an old woman hiding in an old dark house, made it perfect.

"Ignore them," Dayson said quietly. "I, for one, am glad you're here."

Mattie looked around the roomful of people laughing, talking, dancing. After making their whispered comments the gossips had turned to other topics, switching easily from judging Mattie to ignoring her.

She said again that she had urged him to come in order to get him out of the house. It occurred to him that the dance offered her the same opportunity. It suggested an idea that began to form in his mind of why she came by his place so often. And behind that idea he caught a shadowy glimpse of the life she led in that gloomy and decaying house with her aunt. Her aunt. More than once she had stumbled over the word, as though it were a relationship she needed to deny. And there was something not quite right in Mattie's insistence that she had come up from Bakersfield simply to go to school. Years in politics had taught Dayson how seldom people actually lied to you, and how they even more rarely told the whole truth. Something unspoken lay buried in the middle of her story.

The little group on stage struck up a dance tune from the big band era. Dayson leaned in toward Mattie. "I don't suppose you've ever seen a foxtrot?"

"Are you kidding? They made the boys dance with us every Friday for gym class. Foxtrot, waltz, you name it." She smiled, daring him. "C'mon, Mr. Governor."

Seized by the kind of pleasurable awkwardness he hadn't felt since adolescence, Dayson followed her onto the dance floor, his heart racing like a teenager's as they merged into the other dancers. He put a chaste hand against Mattie's back, took her right hand in his left and looked her in the eye, confirming once more that, yes, she was a good couple of inches taller than him.

Those Friday high school gym classes had done their job admirably, he thought, as Mattie danced skillfully around the floor of the grange hall. More wondrously, he found himself smiling so broadly that the corners of his mouth ached as they stretched beyond the demands of his habitual frown.

When the music stopped they stayed on the dance floor. The band turned to a tame version of a pop hit, and Mattie quickly showed him a dance step not so different from the foxtrot. They laughed together at his clumsiness in trying to pick it up.

As the number ended, Dayson mopped his forehead with the back of his hand. "I think I'd better get this coat off," he said, not wanting to admit that after only a couple of dance he needed to take a break.

Glowing with good-feeling, he retreated with her toward the edge of the room, draped his coat over the back of one of the folding chairs lined against the wall and pulled out his handkerchief to dab at his face. "Let's see if I can get us a glass of punch. I'll treat you the dime. And maybe we can wait for a song I know."

When she said nothing, he repeated, "I said, let's see if I can . . ."

But she wasn't listening.

He followed her gaze to the double doors at the entrance and saw that, while a few dancers were stepping out to catch some fresh air, a new couple had only now arrived.

Mattie, so at ease a moment earlier, stood absolutely still. Dayson started to ask her what was wrong, but stopped before he could form the words. He knew.

The man, perhaps thirty-five, looked almost the parody of a college professor, tweed coat with—oh, yes—leather patches at the elbows, and the self-assurance of a man accustomed to being listened to more often than he needed to listen. He probably smoked a pipe. Coincidentally, if such a thing could be coincidence, he too had a beard, though dark, curly and neatly trimmed, in contrast to Dayson's, scruffy and gray.

The woman on the man's arm—pretty, younger than him, wearing a string of pearls and cats-eye glasses—appeared uncomfortable. Clearly, coming to the dance had been his idea. As she turned to look toward the dance floor, Mattie made a barely audible gasp. The woman was obviously pregnant.

Mattie grasped Dayson's arm and started to lean on him, but recovered herself and took a step away from him. Her eyes, though, remained on the newly-arrived couple.

As they paid their admission and came into the hall, the man saw Mattie. Had he been looking for her? He stopped, seemingly unable to decide if he should come closer or go the other way. Finally, he said something in his wife's ear and led her over to the bearded old man who was standing with a girl young enough to be his granddaughter.

"Hello, Mattie," he said as he approached, his voice that of a man trying hard to sound natural. Without quite taking his eyes off Mattie, he inclined his head toward his wife and explained, "Mattie has been one of my students the last couple of quarters."

His wife's smile flickered like a candle. "Hello, Mattie. I think Donny has mentioned you."

Donny? Dayson barely managed not to laugh.

The young professor frowned at his wife's use of this diminutive and offered his hand to Dayson as if Dayson should be honored to shake it. "Dr. Donald Lawrence, professor of English," he said, adding in a lower register, "and my wife, Sandy."

The realization that all this time Mattie had been calling her professor by his last name, not his first, cast a different light on their relationship, implied a certain distance, whatever their intimacy.

"Nice to meet you. I'm Marty. Retired."

After handshakes all around, Lawrence patted his wife's bulging new life in a proprietorial way, "Sandy's probably only good for a couple of dances, but we wanted to come this evening, support the community," he said, unable to keep a patronizing tone from his voice, as if the community were a convalescing patient he might cheer up with his presence.

Dayson put on a smile and gestured toward the dance floor. "Enjoy yourselves."

During this brief exchange, Mattie had said nothing. Nor had she, for even a moment, taken her eyes off her professor.

A twinge of something dark that he didn't wish to inspect, coursed through Martin Dayson's gut.

"Let me get you that glass of punch," he mumbled, though he doubted Mattie heard him.

He drifted toward the refreshment table, where, as the room grew warmer, it seemed half the town had congregated. By the time he bought the two glasses and shuffled back, Lawrence and his wife were coming off the dance floor.

With a little laugh, Sandy Lawrence fanned her face. "Oh, I've got to sit down!" she said as she took one of the chairs against the wall.

Lawrence smiled at Mattie. "Maybe a former student would agree to dance with her old professor."

Mattie dipped her head in a barely perceptible nod.

Dayson understood. Despite burning down their trysting place, she had not completely exorcised whatever part of her had been trapped in that shack.

Taking her by the hand, Lawrence led Mattie into the crowd of dancers. While the band took up a slow romantic number popular on the radio that spring, they put their arms around each other like a pair of teenagers.

Holding the two cups of punch in his hands, Dayson watched them dance, trying to pretend he found the whole scene amusing. After he'd seen all he wanted to see he turned away and said to Sandy Lawrence, "You look like you could use a cold drink."

She accepted the glass, her smile rising and then fading as she too watched her husband dance with Mattie.

Dayson felt certain he would catch in Lawrence's eye the gleaming leer of the predator, something he could despise and warn Mattie against. Instead, he found only honest affection in the way he gazed at her, an affection shared by the girl in his arms. His wife had to see it too.

For a moment longer, the professor's pregnant wife and the retired politician watched the dancing couple in silence, then Dayson handed his own cup to Sandy, saying, "Would you mind holding this for a minute?" and walked out onto the dance floor, wondering if his judgement was still clouded by the stuff Mattie had got him to smoke that day, because even as he approached them this seemed like folly.

He knew enough to paste a broad and indulgent smile on his face as he tapped Lawrence on the shoulder.

"How about letting me cut in?"

The subdued yet exalted look Mattie and her professor had been sharing gave way to mutual astonishment.

"Cut in?" Lawrence clearly thought this was some kind of joke.

"Yeah, a customary bit of etiquette at dances."

Struggling for a reply, Lawrence looked to Mattie for an explanation.

Her voice flat, she said, "He's a neighbor."

Thinking he understood now, the professor turned his brightest smile on Dayson and cocked his chin toward Mattie. "Sure, old-timer, but let's wait until the end of this dance and then she can decide for herself."

Dayson matched the other man's smile, watt for watt.

"Let her decide now."

The exchange had become a contest to see who could best hide his animus behind a smokescreen of civility.

Both men turned toward Mattie. With a dead-eyed look at Dayson she said, "Let us finish this dance."

Lawrence smiled and winked at Dayson.

Struggling to find a reply other than popping this supercilious sonofabitch in the nose, Dayson covered his retreat with one more dishonest smile. Muttering something that was unintelligible even to himself, he made his way back to where Sandy Lawrence sat in a folding chair against the wall.

The look in the young woman's eyes, her fixed smile bent like a blue note, made him think she wanted to say something. But she allowed herself only an enigmatic shake of the head.

Dayson was ready to bet his mortgage that she too had been one of Donny's students.

A few moments later the band took a break and Lawrence led Mattie back to where Dayson waited with his wife. Sandy Lawrence reached out a hand to her husband, who took it in both of his and gazed at her fondly.

Dayson was forced to admit to himself that the guy loved his wife. The bastard.

With a wan smile, she said to him, "I'm afraid I'm getting a little tired, darling."

"Really, honey?" For an instant he looked as if he might try to talk her into staying, but in the end said only, "I'm glad we did this. It was good for both of us."

Dayson thought of looking at Mattie to see how she was taking this little scene of marital affection, but decided he didn't want to know.

Lawrence said goodnight to Mattie, their lack of physical contact—no handshake, no peck on the cheek—somehow speaking to their intimacy. With a smile as magnanimous as it was insufferable, Lawrence held out his hand to Dayson. "Nice to meet you, Marty."

"Sure thing. Donny."

Dayson enjoyed watching Lawrence's face redden.

The young couple departed, Lawrence lending his wife a supportive and affectionate arm around her waist.

The moment they were out of earshot Mattie turned on Dayson. "What did you think you were doing, saying you wanted to cut in?" she asked, her voice tight with anger. "And you didn't have to call him Donny."

"You're right. I did it for sheer pleasure. Besides, he was taking advantage of you, playing on your emotions. He dumps you a few weeks ago, then wants to make all lovey-dovey like nothing happened."

Her lips twitched as if she had a lot to say, but left it at, "I can decide for myself when someone's trying to take advantage of me."

"I'm just saying he shouldn't treat a girl like that."

"I told you before. I'm not a girl!"

"What?" His bafflement testified to his own cluelessness. Trying to cover, he said, "You knew he was going to be here this evening."

"No!" she snapped, undercutting the effect by adding, "Not really."

"But you wanted to be here. Just in case."

"I only wanted you to get out of your house a little. I didn't think you'd make a big scene."

"I didn't make a scene."

She lowered her head, unable to look at him.

He asked quietly, "Did you know his wife was pregnant?"

She started to say something, stopped, but it burst out of her. "I get so frustrated with you! And all the things you think you understand. But you don't understand anything. Not anything important." Her eyes made clear she meant her remark to sting, but the plaintiveness in her voice somehow made it come out as a plea—a plea for what, Dayson couldn't tell. "Lawrence helped me to go farther down a path I didn't realize I'd already chosen. He's the one who showed me where I was going. The books he gave me, the writers he introduced me to . . ." She stopped, and he thought she might cry. "It was so I didn't have to go alone."

"And of course he offered himself in the same spirit."

"Stop it! Just stop it! You're not my father! You're not my boyfriend! You're not anything to me!"

Furious with Dayson and with herself, she spun away. As she did, she caught a look at the clock on the wall.

"My god! I've got to go. She'll know I've been gone."

Agitated beyond endurance, she made for the door, then turned back to Dayson and shouted, "Damn you!"

"Mattie—"

"Just leave me alone!"

Trailing a comet's tail of frustration and anger, she ran out the door.

Chapter Twenty-Three

Awakened by the Idol

By the time Dayson got home that evening his hip hurt like hell. And the conviction that he had behaved badly at the dance left him with a nasty emotional hangover.

He turned on the television but, as usual, poor reception made everything appear to be occurring in a heavy snowstorm. He turned it off and drifted into the study but could not bring himself to either sit at his desk or pick up a book. Instead, he stood at the study window and looked out toward his back yard, its broken ground lost to sight in the darkness of the moonless night. He didn't need moonlight, though, to see Frank's excavations, sterile as the moon itself. The earth had rendered up only one worthwhile find—and even that discovered by Dayson, not the young scholar—the stone icon, as uncertain in its meaning as it was inexplicable in its presence, an object most likely lost by a band of wanderers, who may themselves have been lost.

"Lost," he said aloud, wondering how, at his age, his life had come so badly adrift. For years he had followed the path that appeared so clearly before him, a path that presented itself as duty and had led him to a measure of renown and a position of influence his younger self could not have imagined. In speeches and conversation he had often said, and wished to believe, that his journey began in the soil of the family farm. But the nightmares from which he woke in a cold sweat took him back to the heat, death and terror of Okinawa. And to Ben Rosloff. The nightmares filled him with guilt and fear, the twin demons that had come to rule his life and been the true impetus toward the life he had chosen. Now the path had abruptly given out, leaving him with no idea where he was or what direction he should take.

Disturbed, distracted, he absently picked up the figurine from his desk and wandered into the living room, unable to escape the thought that, like whoever had left the icon behind, he too was a wanderer. He set the crude sculpture on the coffee table and sat on the couch gazing at its impassive features as if it might yet speak to him, or at least give him a wink, a chuck under the chin, spit in his face, something, anything.

But he was asking too much. At the very moment he wanted so much from it, the statue had turned back into a simple piece of stone, with nothing to say to him or anyone else. After a while he gave it up and went to bed.

The little statue tapped at his door, beckoning him, demanding that he get up and follow.

"No. I can't," he mumbled, then, more forcefully, "Go away!"

Awakened by the sound of his own voice, he looked around, confused, still living half in his dream. The tapping, though, did not cease. He looked at his clock. Nearly eleven.

There it was again, a knocking somewhere in the house.

Expelling an unhappy grunt, Dayson threw off his covers and took his robe from its hook on the door. He lurched into the living room while trying to sort through a muddled notion that it was too late at night for a door-to-door salesman, and burglars don't knock.

"Just a minute!" he shouted to the renewed knocking which, he realized, was not coming from the front door but the back.

Chasing the last cobwebs of sleep from his mind, he turned on a table lamp as he crossed the living room, went out through the kitchen into the utility room and opened the back door.

Astonished, he took a step back. "What in the hell are you—?"

But she had already darted past him and through the kitchen, heading toward the one light in the house.

Dayson followed her into the living room, where Mattie stood without a coat or sweater, hugging herself tightly, her eyes wide, her gaze inward.

"Mattie, what's wrong?"

"I'm sorry," she said, her voice choked with confusion and unhappiness.

142

"I didn't know where else to go." She shook her head, or shivered, Dayson wasn't sure which.

"Sit down. I'll fix you a cup of tea," he said. "Tell me what's going on."

She seemed not to have heard him.

By the time he returned from the kitchen she was sitting on the couch, her arms still wrapped tightly around herself. He handed her the tea, took the chair opposite her and waited for her to decide when she was ready to speak.

The girl—she had never looked so young, he thought—took a shuddering breath. "I'm not supposed to leave in the evening. So I had to sneak out of the house to go to the dance. And that's why I had to run away when I saw what time it was. I had to get back before she locked up. She says she's worried about my safety. But that's not it. It's at night it comes on her, this terror of being left alone. She's afraid I'll leave her someday." Mattie paused, her head down. "And someday I will."

Dayson wanted to shout, "Yes, leave. Now! If you want to be free, run before she wraps you in guilt so tightly you'll never get away." He had become convinced that, as she said, she belonged to the future, a future neither of them could see yet, but one that would require her to cut her ties to Sarah and Donny Lawrence—and himself—and run from Topping as fast as she could. But he said none of this.

"The evenings pass so slowly. My life passes so slowly." A sad, distracted smile played across her face. "I left the light on in my room this evening to make her think I was staying up reading. I figured I could sneak back in. But I came back too late. I tried to find a door or window that maybe she'd left unlocked, but I couldn't. So I stood outside the house for a long time, trying to think of what to do. And I got cold."

"Couldn't you just knock on the door? Tell her the time slipped away?"

Mattie shook her head. "You don't understand. She'd go crazy, knowing I'd snuck out." She took a deep breath and let it go. "I couldn't think of anything else to do, anywhere else to go."

"It's okay, Mattie. I'm glad you came."

He watched her shaman's spirit abandon her, leaving a sad and frightened girl.

"I'm really, really sorry."

Were the words directed at him, or was she commenting on her own life?

"It's all right," he said.

She took a sip of her tea, and he felt her eyes truly registering him for the first time since she had come in. She was here now, with him, no longer out in the cold.

"She's just . . ." Mattie searched for the words that would explain her aunt, and found there were none. "This is how she is."

Dayson thought of telling her that her aunt was half-crazy and drank too much, but knew it wouldn't really be an answer, only another way of asking the question of why she stayed.

"You need a place to spend the night."

After a bit she nodded. "I can go back in the morning. After she's opened up, she always goes back to her room. If I come in quietly she may not notice I was gone." She looked at him from the depths of her sadness. "We live in that house, the two of us. But we both live alone."

Dayson found a spare blanket and a sheet she could fold over herself, and took one of the pillows from his own bed.

When he brought them out to her she insisted on making the bed herself.

"It gets cold in this part of the house," he told her, "Let me turn up the heat."

"No. You don't have to heat up the whole house for me."

"At least let me put a fire in the fireplace."

By the time she had sipped the last of her tea he'd built a decent fire and she had regained something of her composure.

"Is he coming back in the morning?" she asked.

"Sorry?"

"The guy you work with."

"Frank?" He didn't want to ask why she was thinking of him. "Yeah, I expect he is."

"But he doesn't come every day."

"No. Just sometimes."

"He's the one who's helping you dig for buried treasure," she said, trying to smile.

"Yes, I guess so."

"That medal of yours."

"Yeah?"

"Sarah . . . My aunt says it was for bravery during the war."

Dayson thought it over for a long time. Usually, he dismissed any remark about the war with a flick of the hand or a caustic remark. Tonight, though, he owed her something more. "Bravery? No. We all just wanted to stay alive, Mattie. That's all. That's what war is, a bunch of guys trying to stay alive. That piece of ribbon might be a sign of hysteria as much as anything else."

Mattie lowered her eyes. "I'm sorry for what I said at the dance. You . . . You mean a lot to me."

"It's forgotten. I was being a pain in the ass."

He watched the thought turning in her mind, saw it chased by another, one she hesitated to bring up.

"What is it?" he asked.

"Can I ask you something?"

"Sure."

"You wear a wedding ring, but I never see your wife."

Startled, he looked at the band on his finger, so taken for granted, like the marriage itself, that it hadn't occurred to him to take it off.

Her young eyes gazed at him, unblinking. He knew he had to tell her the truth.

"She left me."

"Even though you were the governor?"

"Maybe because I was the governor. And not much of a husband. Not much of a father either."

"That's hard for me to believe."

"Bless your heart."

"I'm sorry that she . . . that . . ."

"Yeah, me too."

He watched her thinking about something else.

"That law," she said.

"What? You mean the bill you read?"

"Yes, the bill."

"What about it?"

"Does it have something to do with why people want to buy my aunt's property?"

"I'm not sure. Like you say, someone's buying land around here. I'm not sure who, but I think they want to build a lot of houses. Maybe it has something to do with the bill." He shrugged. "Maybe it doesn't."

"It's farmland. It needs to stay farmland."

Even as he had supported farmers—had been a farmer—Dayson had for years vaguely regarded the valley's open fields as empty space, waiting for someone to make better use of it. Yet her words puzzled him even as he sensed they were true. "Why do you say that?"

"It's so green. I come from Bakersfield. Nothing's green there. It's all dead and we're living in the middle of it. Green means life. People shouldn't be able to take it away. It's like killing."

"I never thought of it that way." Curious, he thought, how his words echoed those he had spoken to the farmer in front of Greenburgs' store about widening the highway. For the first time it occurred to him that the decisiveness and assurance in which he took pride, the responsibilities he had shouldered, had kept him at such a high pitch of activity that he could avoid seeing things for what they really were. "Maybe you're right. Maybe there's a lot I need to look at differently."

"Can you do something about it?" she asked.

"About what? This bill?"

"Yes."

"They want me to come down and speak in favor of it. I'm not sure I want to."

"But can't you do something?"

He shook his head. "I don't carry much weight down there anymore."

"More than anyone else around here has."

"I figure it's someone else's turn."

"There's no one else here who can do it."

"Maybe you're too impressed with what I used to be. You think it gives me some kind of status down there. It doesn't. I'm just a former somebody." He saw the disappointment in her face. "Well, let me think about it."

Standing near the couch, he looked down at her in the light of the flickering fire and thought of beauty, not so much whether or not she was beautiful, but simply of beauty and how easy it was to miss it when it was all around, the beauty of the hills and the land, the sky. And, yes, of Mattie Reed.

"I'll let you get to sleep now," he said and turned to leave.

"This is it, isn't it?"

"What?"

She was looking at the figurine he had left on the coffee table earlier that evening.

"You said you were looking for buried treasure. I saw you with it in your hand the other day. The day I met Frank. This is it, the thing you found?"

Dayson regarded the statuette and recalled how she had been fascinated with it the day she had picked it up from his desk. "I guess maybe it is."

"So, what is it?"

"Not sure. A fertility figure of some sort. A goddess," he said, a little embarrassed at employing such a word. "That's what they tell me." He gestured toward the stone figure. "It's because of this that I asked Frank to come out and make his excavations."

"But he hasn't found anything else."

"No. Well, a horseshoe."

The color had returned to her face. She lay down on the couch and pulled the sheet and the blanket over her. "A horseshoe," she repeated.

She stared into the fire, its shadows playing across her face in the dimly lighted room. Her eyes drifted from the fire to Dayson. "Don't be too hard on Lawrence." The flicker of a smile crossed her face. "On Donny."

He waited for more. But there was no more. He thought of several things he could say, starting with, "Why the hell not?" He settled for the only decent thing he could. "Okay." Quietly, he added, "What do you think, Mattie, is it maybe time for you to go back to Bakersfield, back to your mom and dad?" He caught the tone of his own voice and feared he had said this only because she had mentioned Lawrence—and Frank.

"No!" Then, less certainly, "No." He thought that was the end of it, but after a moment she said, "My father doesn't want me around. And my . . . mom. She resents everything I do, everything I am. It's always been like that."

He thought of how she had said that she and her aunt both lived alone in that great dark house. It must have been the same in Bakersfield. Was it any wonder she wanted the future to arrive quickly? The past had nothing to offer.

"So you ran off to live with your aunt?"

She nodded, then shook her head again, leaving her response ambiguous. "We came up here once or twice, my father and me, when I was a kid. My parents were already divorced. They were short visits. And I remember them being tense. Even as a kid I could tell. It made me wonder why we came at all."

"Why did she offer to put you through college?"

"Maybe because she never got to finish." That sad little smile again. "I guess I'm supposed to do the things she didn't get to do, be the person she didn't get to be. But I don't want to be her. That's the part she doesn't understand."

Dayson asked himself if Mattie understood how her aunt wasn't simply trying to give Mattie the life she didn't get to lead, but was living through her in some sense, trying to absorb the girl into her own impoverished soul. "So you started college and you met Lawrence and he arranged the scholarship for you."

"I deserved it."

"I'm sure you did."

They both took a deep breath.

"Thanks for never telling my aunt—or anyone—about the shack."

He gave a deprecating lift of the shoulder. "I hear your aunt and uncle weren't always happy together. A difficult marriage. Like for most of us, maybe."

"Yes."

"She even left him for several months. Have I got that right?"

Her reaction startled him. "What business is that of anyone's?" she said, her voice both sullen and defiant.

What a puzzling girl. Dayson wondered if who she was and who she was trying to be might all make sense if he could only see it from the right angle.

"It's only my business because I care about you."

For a long time she said nothing. Dayson wondered if she was thinking of what he'd said, or trying to ignore it. Eventually, like water finding its own level, her eyes returned to the little statue.

"How did she get here?"

"I dug it up and brought it in."

"No. I mean what's she doing here?"

She sounded as if she might be asking about herself.

"No one can figure that out."

She blinked, sleep pulling at her.

"But what do you think?" she asked.

"The best anyone can do is guess. Sometimes I think she was waiting here all this time for me to come along and dig her up. Waiting to say something to me. But I still don't know what it is."

"Maybe you have to listen the right way."

Dayson didn't want her to see how much her words affected him. It made him realize he didn't know how to listen to a nineteen-year-old girl, much less a goddess.

"It's so quiet," she said softly, her whispered words somehow adding to the silence.

"Maybe you'd like me to put Joe Baeza back on the record player?"

Her smile glowed like the fire at the other end of the room. "No, I'm fine."

As the silence between them lengthened, he looked down and saw she had fallen asleep. For a moment he thought to lean over and kiss her on the forehead as he had done so many years ago with Jocie. But he feared he would wake her.

He turned out the lamp, drew the screen in front of the fireplace and went back to bed.

* * *

A few hours later he woke, his hip throbbing. He got up and took two aspirin, then padded toward the kitchen for a couple of crackers.

As he passed through the living room, he saw by the glow of the dying fire that Mattie had kicked her blanket onto the floor and she lay tightly curled up with nothing more than the sheet over her.

As he bent down to pick up the blanket, he saw in her clasped hands the little figurine, pressed to her chest. She was breathing softly, evenly, as if taking comfort from the sculpted stone. Perhaps, he thought, it took comfort from her as well.

He lifted the blanket high and let it settle over her.

Even before he returned from the kitchen, she had uncurled under the warmth of the blanket and was sleeping peacefully.

When he looked for her in the morning, she was gone.

Chapter Twenty-Four

Okinawa and After

Young people and their problems.

Both Mattie and Persig had, for reasons Dayson couldn't fathom, trusted him with their secrets. He should remind them of how the voters felt after trusting him.

His gifts and determination had taken him to the most powerful office in the state. And then he had crashed. Yet, despite his best efforts to run away, people still sought him out. Mattie and Pearsig most of all. He still bore the responsibility for his unasked-for talents. As much as he might try to flee, he knew he could not walk away, could not refuse those gifts, without paying a heavy toll for turning his back on himself.

So, Persig returned the following day and Dayson had to let him take up his labors again, even though he no longer believed the young man would find anything.

The two of them fell into their old habit of silence, though Persig's had a darker quality now. To Dayson's attempts at conversation, Persig refused to give more than monosyllables, and he no longer whistled as he worked. The assurance he'd shown the first few weeks had soured into an unhappy resolve, made grimmer by the prospect that his efforts would prove pointless.

Late in the morning, Dayson interrupted his work of pounding poles to support his green beans and walked over to where Persig was removing sod to expand the scope of his dig. When the young man ignored him, Dayson put a hand on the top of the young man's shovel and stopped him.

"What's up with you?" Dayson asked.

Without looking at Dayson, Persig said, "Up? Nothing." He tried to continue his work, but Dayson tightened his grip on the end of the shovel.

"What's wrong, Frank? Are you wishing you hadn't told me about all that? About your mother?"

Persig stepped away, leaving Dayson with the shovel in his hand, and threw out his hands in a gesture Dayson could read as either despair or anger or both. "I don't know!" He let out a huff of frustration. "Okay. I want to find *something,* something that will make people take notice, make them pay attention to . . ." He ran his fingers through his hair as if he wanted to pull it out by its roots.

"Pay some attention to you?" Dayson tried to pose the question as gently as he could.

"I don't know! All I know is I'm failing."

"Failing?" Dayson scoffed. "You're, what, twenty-five, twenty-six years-old? Okay, you haven't succeeded yet, not like you want to. But you will because you're one of those guys who doesn't have enough sense to give up. The only way you'll fail is to give up on yourself."

Persig refused to look at him. "Sure thing, Governor."

"Enough name-calling, okay? I'm an old man so, yeah, I've managed to do a few things by now. When I was twenty-five I hadn't done anything, was just a farm boy with a year of college behind me."

Persig snorted. "Let me guess. You had grit and determination and you pulled yourself up by your bootstraps, or whatever cliché you like, and you went on to be a war hero and governor of this fair state."

Dayson threw Persig's shovel to the ground. "Look, kid, you don't know what the hell you're talking about, so just shut the fuck up." Martin Dayson threw his head back and worked hard to swallow his anger. "We're a mess, aren't we? You and me both. You feel lousy because you don't think you'll succeed, and I feel lousy because I didn't do as much as I thought I should." He took a deep breath. "Here's a warning—if you're ambitious you can never be satisfied. There'll always be one more hill to climb, one more person to impress." He wanted to stop there, but something more wanted out and he had to let it go. As if letting slip the forbidden name of a dark deity, he murmured, "A person like Ben Rosloff."

"Sorry?"

"You've never heard of him. But it's because of him I lived long enough to get old." He looked at Persig and thought of what it had cost the young man to confess how he had come into this world. And he knew he had to match Persig's valor, so had uttered the name of the man he had never mentioned to anyone but Dorothy.

And he immediately tried to pull it back.

"I'm sorry. I shouldn't have said anything—about me or you or your work. What the hell do I know about anything?" He started to walk away. But after a couple of strides he stopped and turned on Persig. "You say you're lost, been lost from the beginning of your life. Me? I got lost late. Look at us. You dig in the earth. I dig in the earth. And, yeah, maybe we both do it so we don't have to dig into our lives. Mattie's right about that. Which means neither of us will ever find what we're looking for, because . . ." He waved at the torn-up earth. ". . . because we're looking in the wrong place."

Persig walked to the edge of the grass and picked up the shovel Dayson had thrown down. "This is about the war?"

"Yeah, this is about the war."

"I read that you got a medal for something you did on Okinawa, something about leading some soldiers out of a trap."

Dayson gave a barely perceptible shake of his head. "That's what it looked like to people who weren't there."

"Who's Ben Rosloff?"

It took a long time for Dayson to decide he had to answer. And he knew that once he'd said anything he'd have to say everything. He had accepted from this unhappy young man the coin of frankness, and now he had to repay it in kind.

"Met him on shipboard on our way out from Pearl Harbor. Early 1945. We ran into each other on deck a few times. Struck up a conversation one afternoon. Only twenty-three, already a captain. Led a rifle company, about two hundred men. After that first conversation we got in the habit of talking in the officers' mess in the evenings, at first about the usual things. I told him about the farm in Oregon, my family. He talked about growing up near Laredo, Texas. I got the impression he came from a well-to-do family. Damned impressive kid. Got his degree from Stanford in '44 and enlisted the next day. Was wounded on Saipan. Got shipped back to Pearl. Now he was going back out with a new outfit. Me, I'd been sent back for additional training, and a promotion.

"Usually when you get talking with another soldier, you exchange a few words about home, a little about the army, maybe you move on to complaining about the higher-ups or wondering where a guy could get a beer, or a girl. It pretty much stops there. But it's a long voyage out, from Hawaii to Okinawa, and after a while we started talking about other things, about the country, about the world we'd have after the war, what we wanted it to be. I was old enough to be his father. You'd think that'd get in the way, but maybe that had something to do with why he could talk to me as freely as he did. Whatever it was, you knew he was one of those guys who, when the war was over, would go home and remake the country, was going to make sense of what we'd done, make it all mean something. That's what I told him one evening. He kind of laughed, but I could see he felt the same way. He talked about forming a business after the war that would hire vets to build the sort of housing we'd need. Or maybe he would. . ." Dayson felt the breath shaking in his throat. "He said maybe he would get into politics. I told him he should. Should run for something big. He tried to shrug it off, but I could see he'd been thinking about it himself. I even gave him a nickname, not to tease him, but maybe to keep that idea in his head." Dayson waved a hand to erase the words he'd said. "Anyway, it got to where one of the reasons I wanted the war to end was to see what Ben Rosloff would do with his life."

"Nickname. What did you call him?"

"Doesn't matter now."

Persig's silence told him it did.

"I called him Governor."

Dayson tried to say it as if it were a joke, but the laugh caught in his throat. He stopped there, head down, not quite aware he was no longer speaking, the old dialogue continuing in his head.

154

"That's it? The whole story?"

"Huh?" Dayson looked up, startled back into the present. "No, of course that's not it. A few days out from Pearl we were told we'd be assaulting an island called Okinawa and that it would be a tough fight. That's how they let you know that a lot of you are going to die.

"The first landings were on a Sunday. It was Easter—and April Fool's Day. Ben's company went in a couple of days after the first landings. I was G-2, intelligence, for the same infantry regiment he was in, and we landed later the same day. Things seemed pretty quiet at first and we thought maybe it would go easy after all. But the Japanese had dug in deep on the southern part of the island and were waiting for us. The fighting got bad. Lots of kids dying. There wasn't much for G-2 to do other than look over aerial photos and try to make sense of what our own men were seeing. A couple of prisoners came in, guys who had been knocked silly before they could kill themselves, but they wouldn't talk.

"Late one night, after I'd been on the island a few days, a runner from Ben's company came to our tent. He said they'd found something that looked like it might be a map of the tunnel networks the Japanese had dug all over the island. If he was right, it was like finding gold. Could save a lot of lives. The runner said Ben wanted me to come back to his unit with him, take a look at the map. And maybe, when it got light, I could line up this map with the terrain in front of us and figure out if the map was as valuable as they thought. What could I say? I said sure and I went back with him.

"Ben looked ten years older than he had a few days earlier. They'd seen a lot of fighting and not got much sleep. He'd lost a lot of men and you could see what that had done to him. But it was good to see him, to see he was okay. We slapped each other on the back and I told him I wanted to talk to the guy who'd found the papers. Took a while to find him in the dark. A sergeant. Been in charge of a fire team—four riflemen—on a probing mission earlier that evening. They'd been a couple hundred yards in front of the company's position when they'd shot some poor sonofabitch who ran into them. They'd wanted to keep their probe quiet, but he'd seen our guys and was about to give out a holler. So they shot him because that's what you do in war. They searched him like you're supposed to, and they found he had a metal canister strapped over his shoulder. Was a courier of some kind, probably got lost in the dark, thought he was behind his own lines. Anyway, they might as well have let the guy holler, because after firing the shot that got him our guys began to draw fire. They grabbed the canister and scrambled back for our lines.

"After telling me all this, this sergeant tells us something he hadn't told Ben earlier. He was pretty sure the dead guy had two canisters, but they'd left the other one behind when they had to get out of there. Ben and I looked at each other. What we had might be good, but the other canister might have something even more valuable.

"There was a chance the Japanese had found this guy's body by now and dragged him away. But maybe not. Maybe they didn't even know about him. They just heard a shot and fired back. You can't believe how confused war is. We figured we didn't have much choice. We had to go back for that second canister.

"I said I wanted to go with whoever he sent to find this thing. Ben tried to tell me no, but I insisted. He gave me the same fire team that had gone out the first time. You could see they weren't happy about it. And their sergeant is saying maybe we should wait for morning. Ben says no, gotta do it now, before it gets light. Then he picks up a couple of grenades and an extra couple of clips for his Tommy gun. I tell him a company commander shouldn't be going out on something like this. But I understood how he saw it. When he'd asked me to come up to his position he hadn't thought there'd be any need for me to go out beyond the lines, take any real risk. Now he figures he's put me in a bind and he's going to come with me. 'Got to make sure you get back to that farm in Oregon,' he tells me. He kinda laughed, but it was damned serious stuff, and he knew it.

"They give me a rifle and we head out. It feels like it takes forever to cross those couple hundred yards in the dark, crawling around the rocks, staying close to the ground. After a few minutes the sergeant says he thinks this is the place. We're crouching in the dark, everyone tense as hell. The sergeant whispers he's found blood. We crawl over and find a line of blood leading farther into the rocks. 'I thought sure he was dead,' he says, kind of apologetic. He knew that now we'd have to keep going, had to find this guy. No one wants to go after him, especially in the dark, but Ben knows this

156

second canister might have information that could save a lot of lives. So we go scrambling deeper into the rocks.

"We find the guy just a few yards away, trying to crawl back to his buddies, but not really moving anymore. He's through. He's shot in the gut, bleeding bad, and he's terrified, kind of crying. The sergeant has a sidearm, puts it up to the kid's head and leans over him to muffle the shot."

Persig looked shocked. "In cold blood?"

"We were doing him a favor! He was dying and in terrible pain." Dayson knew his anger was only the cover for his doubts. "So we grab the canister and turn around. Before we get ten yards the place explodes. Still not sure what happened. We likely ran into a Japanese probe on its way back, because they're between us and our own lines. Everyone's firing into the dark, wild as hell. The sergeant takes a piece of rock in his eye from a ricochet and yells out. Ben runs over, puts a hand on him to calm him down. We're firing into the dark and they can see our muzzle flashes, just like we can see theirs. A grenade goes off a few feet from me. I'm flat on the ground, firing, so most of the blast goes over me, but I catch some shrapnel in my leg. While I'm lying there, grabbing my leg, a Japanese comes out of the dark, bayonet raised. He's standing over me about to bring it down and end me."

Dayson stopped, his mouth dry. He licked his lips. "I can still see him at night when I'm trying to sleep. Or he wakes me from a dream. I have just enough time to think of Dorothy and Jocie. But before he can bring the bayonet down Ben comes running up out of the dark. Must have been out of ammo and didn't have time to change clips because he swings his Tommy gun by the muzzle and cold cocks the guy with the stock. He reaches down to pull me up, this big grin on his face. I'm thinking he shouldn't have come on this patrol, but am I ever glad he did. I'm starting to get up when he falls onto me, still smiling. I figure I'd pulled too hard on his hand and jerked him off his feet. Or maybe he's joking, horsing around. But there's blood. He'd been shot and his blood's all over me. And I go kind of crazy. I get to my feet, grab Ben by the collar. Gotta get back to our lines. It's the only thing in my head. If I can get him back quick he's going to be okay. It's not really a thought, just an impulse. So I stand up and yell at the other guys to charge at 'em. That's what I said, 'Charge!' Like the cavalry in a western. Got to get through them, get Ben back to our lines. That's all I'm thinking. Not thinking about the danger at all, so it's not really bravery. The sergeant's on his feet by now and firing back, and we run right at 'em, firing as we go."

It was a moment he'd thought of countless times without being able to make sense of it. "We were . . . hysterical. That's not quite the word for it, but that's as close as I can come. The Japanese had to think that if we were attacking them there had to be a lot more of us than they figured. And they probably didn't want to be in that fight any more than we did. Whatever it was, they scattered, and we made it back to our own lines, still firing, still yelling, me dragging Ben by the collar over the rocks.

"It was amazing the rest of the company didn't shoot us for Japanese, but one of our bunch had the sense to keep shouting the password as we ran up, and we got back in the lines without getting shot by our own side. The sergeant ended up losing his eye. I had shrapnel in my legs, not sure how I made it back. As soon as I got through the lines I fell and couldn't walk."

He looked at Persig and knew he should shut up, should have shut up a long time ago. He'd only told this story once in his life, to Dorothy, fourteen years earlier. But it was always there, in his head, pushing him, pulling him. And on this afternoon, with Persig there, it wanted to push its way out for good.

"Couldn't believe I'd made it. And Ben. He'd taken a bullet meant for me, but I'd got him back inside the lines. So in my mind he had to be okay now." A strange sound came out of Dayson's mouth, somewhere between a laugh and a sob. "I still have these dreams where he's back and he's alive and talking to a bunch of us about all the things he's done to make the country better, make it a good place for people to live. And he's fine as long as I don't say—no one says—anything about him being dead. The dreams are good in a way, but they have a feeling of great sadness because I know the truth even if he doesn't, and I know someone's going to slip up and say 'But, Ben, you're dead. Marty got you killed.' Then he'll be gone for good. And all the great things he was going to do would be gone with him.

"The rest of the guys in our patrol had figured we were done for, and they act as if me crying 'charge' saved everyone's life. The truth is I may have been the most panicked guy there, and yelling 'charge' was nuts."

Dayson smiled the saddest smile Persig had ever seen.

"Ben died saving my life. And they give *me* the goddamn medal." He said it with the same shame he always felt when he thought about it. Ashamed for the fact that Ben felt he had to go out to protect him, make sure he got back to Oregon. Ashamed for being alive. Ashamed that, however much he did, he could never do all the things he believed Ben Rosloff would have done.

"I always think of it as being his medal. That's the only reason I can hang onto it. I can't get rid of it because . . . because it's like I'm keeping it for him until he can come back and get it." He tilted his head back and let out an anguished, "Bah!" More quietly, he said, "I should just come out here some night and bury the thing."

Both men looked involuntarily toward Persig's dig.

"Yeah," Dayson said, "let someone dig up that secret a thousand years from now, and let 'em try to figure out what it means." He nodded at the ground he and Persig had dug up. "Sort of a graveyard that's gone into reverse, isn't it? Full of buried things that want to come out, want to dare us to understand them."

Dayson waved his arm in disgust, as if everything he'd said was on a blackboard that he was tying to erase. "Ah! I'm too used to giving speeches. I shouldn't have told you any of this."

"And you've lived your life to make up for—"

Dayson raised a hand to cut him off. "Look," he started, his tone harsh, then, more quietly, "Look, you'll be fine. Forget I said anything. About anything. You're going to be fine."

Leaning forward as if breasting a strong wind, Dayson walked unsteadily toward the house.

"Mr. Dayson?"

He stopped. "Yeah?"

"The second canister. What was in it?"

Dayson tilted his head back and sighed. "Couple handfuls of rice. The kid's supper. Poor bastard never got to eat it."

"And the other one? The first one. What was it?"

"Map of surface roads and a couple of trails. Nothing much we didn't already know."

Dayson's laugh carried all the bitterness of fourteen years living with the guilt of war.

"Keep working, Frank. I'm going inside."

Dayson poured himself a scotch, lay down on the sofa and flung an arm over his eyes, needing to black out, turn off the switch of his mind. He heard Mattie's voice in the back yard. She must have come up along the path and was talking to Frank, he thought. He knew there was something he needed to do for her, but couldn't pull his thoughts together. Drowsy, lulled by the buzz of their conversation, he got the impression that she and Frank talked a long time. He waited for it to stop and for Mattie to knock on his door, but the knock never came.

When he woke he walked into the study and looked out the window. Mattie and Frank were sitting on the grass, only a few inches apart. As he watched, Mattie rose to say goodbye and head for home, but Persig held onto her hand, brought her close and kissed her. She smiled and ran toward the path and her home, glancing over her shoulder as she went. Persig watched her go. Neither of them waved.

A few minutes later Persig walked around to the front of the house—Dayson could see he was whistling to himself again—and drove away.

After he'd waited long enough to be sure they weren't coming back, Dayson went into the bathroom to get some aspirin for his hip. As he closed the door to the medicine cabinet he caught a look at himself in its mirror.

"What did you expect?" he said to the old man looking back at him. "Of course Frank's attracted to her. He told me so himself. And Mattie, well, who else did she have?"

Who, indeed?

Dayson looked at the dirty-gray hair, the bags under the eyes, his face sagging, the skin toneless.

He managed a laugh at the old man in the mirror. "You fool. You fool. You fool. You old fool."

Chapter Twenty-Five

Struggling for
a Soul Not Their Own

He slept poorly that night, plagued by a shift in the winds, blowing now from the east, coming from beyond the Cascades, off the arid interior of the state, a harsh wind, so different from the usual soft westerly breezes. East winds brought the extremes of weather—the most scorching heat of summer and the bitterest cold of winter. By morning it was blowing strong, a hot, dry wind that agitated the spirit and brought to Martin Dayson the recollection of the thing he needed to do for Mattie. It was clear to him now. She might not like it, but he had to do it. For her. She would appreciate it in the end.

After a quick cup of coffee he headed for the path. The wind blew hard, tossing Dayson's long hair, ruffling his beard, blowing like a revelation, pushing him where he had to go.

In the weeks since he had last walked along the footpath, the grass had grown lush, the leaves of the trees a dark green. The Scotch broom was in bloom, the blossoms a bright yellow, glowing with life. In a neighbor's yard apple blossoms had fallen away and the fruit begun to grow.

But the ragged hedge that guarded the old house showed no new growth, and the sun revealed in its tangle of branches an unhealthy hint of gray, as if something were sucking the life from it.

Dayson pushed through the gap in the hedge with a determination born of righteousness. He crossed the yard, bounded up the porch steps and pounded on the door loud enough for Sarah Tannehill to hear from her room on the second floor.

Knowing Mattie was in class by this time of day, he expected no response and got none. He pounded once more and walked in.

Despite the warm day, the air in the old house hung heavy and cold. Nothing had disturbed the thin layer of dust he'd seen weeks earlier.

"Mrs. Tannehill!"

He received no answer, but felt her presence in the old house, as if she and the house were one.

"Sarah Tannehill!"

After a pause long enough for him to doubt the sanity of his actions, her voice came from upstairs, "Who's down there? What do you want?" its seeming strength failing to hide a quaver of fear.

"It's Martin Dayson."

Another long pause.

"If you're here to buy my property, I'm not selling."

"I'm not interested in your property. I'm here to talk about your niece."

"My niece? Why? She's in some sort of trouble, isn't she?"

He walked to the bottom of the stairs and called up to her, "No, she's not in any trouble."

"Then why . . .?"

"Because you and I need to talk."

He could feel her weighing his words, calculating his intent, so she could figure out how to put herself in a dominant position. It was easy enough work with a nineteen year-old girl, no matter how precocious, but the worry in her voice made clear she feared it wouldn't work when faced with an adult.

"I can't imagine why I should speak to you about my niece," she called down to him.

"I'm coming up."

"You're doing no such thing!"

A faint ruffling of bed clothes, a shuffling of feet betrayed her rush to get into place to receive him.

Dayson climbed the stairs and stepped into the perpetual dusk of her room. As before, Sarah sat in the big chair in front of the window, looking like a deposed monarch, her writ reduced to the walls of this small room.

Now that he stood before her, Dayson realized he had given little thought to what he wanted to say, only knew the certainty that he had to say it.

"How do you know my niece?"

"She visits me sometimes."

"How old are you?" she asked, her voice choked with simulated outrage.

"You know who I am and how old."

"Well, you may have been a senator, or whatever it was, but that doesn't give you the right to hold my niece under your sway. She's only a child and I won't—"

"Stop it!" To his surprise and, he thought, her own, she did. And he understood for the first time that what he'd before taken as her anger was in fact fear, the terror of which Mattie had spoken, the fear of being left alone.

He might have felt sorry for her, but he knew she preferred his hostility to his pity. So he gave it to her.

"Your niece is no child. She's a young woman trying to make a life of her own, and it's a damn lonely business for her."

"She is . . . my niece, and now my ward, Mister whatever your name is—"

"You were more convincing pretending you didn't know what office I'd held."

"—and as such I am responsible for her. Matilda is still a child, whatever you might think, and she isn't old enough to be responsible for herself."

Matilda? Really? It was a name for a woman in a horned helmet.

"She's plenty old enough. And she shouldn't have to put up with the grief you cause her. But for some reason she cares about you. And you're taking advantage of it."

"From what I read in the papers, you're a fine one to speak of familial obligations. "

It was a remark meant to anger him, but was so obvious in its manipulation that he nearly laughed.

"You're not raising a child, Mrs. Tannehill. You're helping to form an adult, or should be." Sarah started to open her mouth, but he cut her off.

"Everyone's talking about freedom these days. But they're really only talking about the freedom to conform, to be like everyone else, and it's killing her. Unlike the others around here, she insists on living. Let her do it. Don't lock her up."

"I don't lock her up!"

"You know what I mean."

"She's a confused girl who is caught up in . . . in childish foolishness, thinking everyone but her is occupying some sort of dying world. A notion probably instilled in her mind by those wretched teachers at that wretched school."

"And more power to them. What have we made of this world that she would want to live in it?"

Sarah recoiled at his words, twisting in her chair.

She recovered quickly. "You may be speaking of your own life, but not of mine," she said. "And I suppose you know what she has done with her so-called freedom. Made a slut of herself with some teacher at that school. I found out, never mind how, and I told her I was going to call the school and have him dismissed if he tried to see her again. Ah! That stopped you, didn't it? I can see it in your face. You didn't know anything about that, did you?"

In fact it had stopped him, but not for the reason Sarah Tannehill thought. He had found Mattie crying in the rain that day, and in his certainty about the ways of the world said something that, in that moment, must have been as painful to her as it was mistaken. Lawrence—Donny—had not dumped her. She had broken with him to placate her aunt. And he, Dayson, had presumed to know all about it, when in fact he knew nothing. It was a wonder Mattie had ever spoken to him again. Finally, he understood why she had burned the shack. The part of her that had been trapped was the part that loved Donald Lawrence. That was the part she had to release.

Sarah bore in. "She has amply demonstrated that, having been raised by my addlepated sister and her . . ." She frowned, hesitating. Before Dayson could wonder what lay behind it she continued. ". . . and her husband. She has lacked a strong guiding hand. She has learned nothing about how to conduct herself. She knows nothing about the dangers that lie out there for a woman."

"You talking about her, or yourself?"

Her mouth dropped open. "Well, of all the . . ."

"She needs someone who will love her, not control her."

Even in the dim light Dayson could see her face redden. She pulled herself up straight in her chair, like a cobra about to strike. Dayson braced for the torrent of rage that would come from her.

To his astonishment she brought her hands to her face and, her head shaking, she wept.

Her tears shocked Dayson to silence. For a moment he wanted to dismiss her sobs as one more attempt to manipulate him. But the anguish appeared real and he felt ashamed for thinking to deny it.

Sarah Tannehill gasped and gripped her forehead, seized by the kind of pain for which there is no pill.

While Dayson looked on with pity and horror, she shuddered with the labor of recovering herself, taking up again the imperious manner behind which she hid her fear. It was like watching a film of a vase falling and breaking, but run in reverse, the shattered pieces pulling themselves together and returning to their place. It was an astonishing and terrifying act of will.

Her voice dangerously quiet, she said to him, "You have no idea who she is or what she will do," she said. "You entice her to your place—I shudder to imagine your intent—and you claim to know her. You know nothing of her. Whatever else you might believe, we are devoted to each other. A woman understands things you never will. She is devoted to me, and she will stay as long as I need her."

He watched her tremble as she reached into the well of her anger for a last show of defiance. But it was forced now, unconvincing.

In witnessing her weakness, he saw clearly what he was doing to her, had already done by telling her she had to give up Mattie, the last thing left to her, the last person willing to tolerate her madness. And when Mattie left, as she must, the older woman would be left with nothing.

More gently than he'd thought he could speak to her, Dayson said, "You're right. I don't understand her. But at least I know I don't understand her. To the depth of her soul, she feels that she's something new, unlike anyone else, and it makes her lonelier than you let yourself see. A young girl shouldn't have to be lonely. And if she stays here with you, she'll end up as warped as everything else that grows here."

A renewed access of rage filled Sarah Tannehill until it almost obscured the fear in her eyes. The warring emotions impelled her from her chair. Her blanket fell away, revealing a pathetic nightgown, faded and thin.

"She will stay here! Because deep inside that's what she wants to do, whatever you might think. She will not leave me! Everyone else has. My husband. My sister. Her husband. But, she will stay. She may not understand that yet, but it is true and she will not disappoint me. As for you, you're just one more person trying to confuse her, lead her astray. And you will leave my house this instant. This instant! And never come back!"

She raised her arms like an Old Testament prophet beseeching heaven to strike this infidel dead. It was a performance meant to awe and terrify.

For a lonely young woman, isolated from others by her intelligence and by the certainty that she belonged in a place she hadn't yet found and in a time not yet arrived, her aunt's ability to conjure guilt and fear must shake her young spirit.

For Dayson, it invoked not fear but revulsion, not guilt but disgust.

He threw her words back at her. "Never come back? With pleasure, madam!"

It was a great exit line. But as he stormed out of the house he feared that, for all the righteousness he had felt in coming to the old house and confronting her aunt, he had only made Mattie's life more difficult.

Chapter Twenty-Six

Mattie's Story

For the rest of the afternoon Dayson distracted himself with modest chores, seeing to a couple of small house repairs, washing the dishes, trying to persuade himself he had done the right thing by visiting Sarah Tannehill—and trying to ignore the voice telling him he had made a terrible mistake.

That night he lay awake for hours. Near dawn, he fell into an unquiet slumber.

He woke to sunlight filling the room and the sound of the phone ringing. He looked at his bedside clock and was astonished to see it was ten o'clock.

Bracing himself for another typhoon of abuse from Sarah Tannehill, he fumbled for the receiver. In fact, the call was from Norm Gilkey's secretary, telling him that as much as Governor Gilkey felt honored by Dayson's support he had decided against a high profile presentation of the water reclamation bill. There would be no press, no roll-out ceremony, and his presence would no longer be necessary.

"The Governor was so pleased that you were willing to help him," she said, "And he wanted me to call and thank you."

"Thank me for not showing up, you mean." He knew she was only the messenger and he had no business giving her a bad time. It was Gilkey he wanted to say this too, but wouldn't have the chance.

"I'm sure that's not at all what he meant, Governor. I spoke to Governor Gilkey just this morning and he seemed truly regretful. He thinks very highly of you and—"

"I'm sorry, but I gotta go. Someone's at the door."

He hung up and pulled on a pair of trousers and a dirty sweatshirt.

For the first time, she had knocked at the front door.

She didn't come in but stood on the doorstep, shifting from one foot to the other, her arms crossed tightly over her chest.

"What did you think you were doing?"

He worked to keep his voice level. "Are you going to stand there, or are you coming in?"

"What did you think you were *doing*?"

When he didn't reply, she swept past him to stand in the middle of the living room.

"Why?" she asked.

"Why? Because your aunt makes you miserable. That's why. She tries to control your life. Someone's got to call her on it. Stop her."

"Stop her from what?" Her anger—at him, at herself, at Sarah—amplified every word. "You have no idea what's going on."

"What's going on? Your aunt is making you a prisoner. You've said so yourself. She wants to dictate everything you do. She—"

"She gives me money she can't afford so I can go to school. She gave me a place to live when I had nowhere to go."

"And it only costs you everything you want to be. Your aunt will never let you go."

She flung out her arms and shouted. "My aunt, my aunt, my aunt! Stop it about my aunt! You have no idea what you're talking about!"

"I know exactly what I'm saying."

She raised her balled fists in exasperation. "I kept thinking you'd see."

"See? See what?"

"She's not my aunt!"

Her outburst stopped him cold. "What?"

"She's not my aunt."

"Then what—"

"She's my mother!"

Silence filled the room like the awful stillness after two cars have hit head on.

Her voice emerged from the wreckage, quiet, resigned. "She's my mother."

Dayson's mouth opened and closed as he tried to find words. "But how—?"

"I found out last year." her chin down, Mattie raised her eyes to Dayson's. "My . . . my mom in California was drunk one night. My mom drinks a lot. Just like she does." She nodded toward the house at the other end of the path and gave Dayson a look that said, "Yes, I've always known."

"Mom hated her sister, my Aunt Sarah. I knew that, but I never understood why. And I didn't think of asking why Dad sometimes brought me up here to visit, or why everything was so tense when we came—any more than I tried to understand why Uncle Archie found a reason to leave whenever we appeared. When you're a little kid you don't think about the whys. Things just are."

She tilted her head back and let go a long sigh. "My dad always treated me like I wasn't there, like he didn't want to think about me. Which made it strange that he would drag me along when he came up here. I didn't even know why we came, except that he always needed money. And he dragged me along to make her feel guilty, I suppose. My parents were divorced by then. I was living with my mom. And my mom hated me like she hated Sarah. I never understood that either. At least not until one night last year. She was drunk and roaming around the house whining about how miserable her life was and how terrible Dad was and that Aunt Sarah was a bitch, until I got tired of hearing about it. So I said something about how they couldn't be as bad as she said, nobody was. She laughed and told me how stupid I was and let it all out. How Aunt Sarah and my father had this affair and I wasn't really her daughter, but my dad's and Aunt Sarah's. How Sarah had given me to them to keep so no one would know I was hers. Gave me away to people who didn't want me. That was about the time we'd moved from Sacramento to Bakersfield. They'd always told me it was for Dad's work, but now Mom told me it was so they could go someplace where no one would know she wasn't my mother. No one in Bakersfield would know she'd never been pregnant. They got divorced just after we got there.

"She'd lied to me all my life. She and my dad both. My whole life, and theirs too, was nothing but a pack of lies. Mom told me I should be grateful for all the things they'd done to protect me. I told her she'd only been trying to protect herself. I packed my things and left that night. She didn't even try to stop me."

As he had when Sarah told him that it was she who had forced Mattie to break up with Lawrence, Dayson wondered again at how little he understood. And he thought of how much more tidy and clear politics were than the rest of life—the victories, the defeats cleaner and more quickly resolved than the years-long labor and uncertain results of personal relations. Was that why he had stuck to politics instead of dealing with his family?

Dayson sat in the chair opposite the sofa and said gently, "And so you came here."

"I had just enough money for a bus ticket. When I got to Portland I called Sarah, told her I knew everything. I asked her to come pick me up."

"And she came."

Mattie nodded. "I half expected her to hang up, or tell me to go back to Bakersfield. Or I thought she'd lie to me too and say she didn't know what I was talking about. But she came for me. I'll always remember that. And she told me it was all true. She's never lied to me. But I don't ask many questions."

She took a deep breath, collected herself. Dayson marveled again at her self-possession. *My god, what a strong young woman she was. Strong enough to change the world, if she could only get free.*

Calmer now, she said, "Sarah had always seemed strange to me. Kind of scary. But when I came here from Bakersfield it was all fine, at least at first. Then, every day, she became odder and angrier. Drank more. It was like my coming to live here released all the craziness she'd managed to keep under control. Like she couldn't stand facing what they'd all done—her and Mom and Dad. Couldn't stand facing who I was. I should have left right then. And I didn't. I still can't. Not yet. I'm her greatest shame. But I'm also her last connection to people. If I wasn't there with her . . ." She shook her head at what she could imagine, and what she couldn't.

Dayson looked at the young girl before him, searching so hard for a new world while the weight of the old one threatened to crush her before she could find it.

"I'm sorry, Mattie." It was a rote expression of regret and it made no impact. "I suppose I should say it's none of my business and have the good sense to stay out of it. But I can't. Okay, I shouldn't have gone to talk with your . . . with Sarah without speaking to you first. You've got reason to be mad at me. But I knew if I'd told you what I was going to do, you'd have told me no. And she needs to see what she's doing to you."

Mattie shook her head. "You don't understand her. I don't know what you said, but she's terribly upset. Worse than ever. She's frightened. I'm frightened for what she might do."

"Believe me, Mattie, you have to leave that house. You have to get away."

"And go where?"

He wanted to tell her, "Here. Come live with me," but he knew that the strength of his hope was exactly the reason he couldn't ask her.

Now Dayson understood what Dr. Kimmel had told him about Sarah once disappearing for several months, and why Mattie had got upset when he mentioned it to her. He tried to imagine where Sarah had gone, how she had managed to hide her pregnancy from this small community. The realization hit him hard. My god, he thought, she'd gone down to Sacramento. He could see it clearly. She had lived with the sister she'd betrayed and the husband who was the father of the unwanted child. What an unholy stew must have filled every corner of that unhappy house. What an atmosphere to have been born into. And, later, how could Archie have taken Sarah back? It was hard to imagine that he had loved her, but love could be a hard thing to fathom. And what else could explain it? Kimmel had spoken of other times she had left. Did she have other lovers?

On so many occasions, over so many years, he had always found the right words to say. This time, with no audience but this young girl, all he could do was whisper, "My God, my God, the secrets we keep. They're killing us. Look at us, Frank and me, trying to dig up ancient secrets from the back yard because we can't face the ones we already have." It was both too much and not enough, and he added, "Isn't life the most godawful mess you ever saw?"

Mattie drew a shuddering breath. "The land, her house, she's told me they're all mine when she's gone. It's supposed to be a gift, but it feels like a trap. She thinks her promise to give it all to me will make me stay with her until she dies. The truth is she has no one else to give them to. She has no one. Only me."

The emptiness of Sarah's life filled Dayson with horror and an unwanted surge of pity. Yet it made him reflect on who, what, did he have to fill his own life? He'd had so much and lost it all, had failed to do what was required of him to hold onto any of it.

It took the young girl to ask the obvious. "Why can't people find what they're looking for?"

He was surprised how quickly the answer came to him. "Because they don't know what it is they want."

For a long time Mattie sat with her head in her hands, her elbows propped on her knees, breathing slowly. Dayson again marveled at her resilience, at the rock of her truest self. He supposed he had met challenges of greater scope—the corrosive bleakness of the Depression, the terror of battle, the quieter battles of politics—yet throughout them all he had known the brotherhood of a people sharing deprivation, the support of a nation at war, the popular acclaim of the electorate. He had known, too, the love of a family, a family he had asked to sacrifice so much to his ambition. Mattie, though, faced all of it alone, the betrayal of everyone who should have taken care of her, the cowardice of those who were meant to guide her life. And, alone, she sought a new world where she could make a home. He, of all people, should understand, Dayson thought. They both struggled to find a better world. But his ambition, strong as it was, had only allowed him to imagine making the current world a little better. She wanted a new one altogether.

After a time, he saw that she had focused on something lying in the clutter of his coffee table. She reached out and tapped the piece of paper lying on the coffee table, half-covered by a book.

"This is that law," she said.

"The bill, yeah."

"Did you go down to Salem, like you said you would, and tell them what was really happening?"

"I got disinvited. I think they figured out I wasn't really on the team."

"They did it without you?"

"As far as I know they haven't held the hearing yet."

"So you decided to just let it go?"

The look on her face hit him hard.

"Like I say, they don't want me down there talking about it."

"Can't you just go down anyway?"

He spread his hands in an equivocal gesture. "I suppose . . ."

"Isn't it everyone's capital?"

"Well, yeah, I guess." He waggled his head uncertainly, not happy about where the conversation was leading nor about suffering a lecture on civics from a teenage girl.

"But what's happening here isn't important enough to you," she said.

"Of course it's important," he snapped.

He didn't want to tell her the truth, that he'd been willing to return to Salem as an honored guest, speaking as a public figure of still-considerable weight. The prospect of going back when he wasn't wanted, hat in hand, pleading for leave to speak, bruised his already battered ego too badly to contemplate.

With the second sight that belongs to the young and lonely visionary, she sensed what was in his heart.

"You're ashamed."

"Ashamed? What have I got that I should be ashamed of?"

"Of losing the election, of going down there and seeing everyone after you've been rejected."

"I'm not . . . ashamed."

His denial came out as a quibble over semantics.

She sat up straight. "I'll come with you."

"No!" Then more gently, "No. That's good of you, but . . . it's not like people here are counting on me to go down and speak for them."

"They would be if they understood what was happening."

"I'm not sure I understand what's happening. Do you really care that much if they buy your place?"

"Everyone around here cares about what happens to Topping. It's their home."

"Then one of them should take the lead down in Salem. I'm not the only one around here who could do this."

"Yes you are. I saw all those letters on your desk. People are still asking you to come speak to them. They still want to hear what you have to say. They still want you to help them."

Could she have put it more naively? More truthfully?"

"And we still have time," she said.

"Time for what?"

"You said there'd be hearings. Maybe we could get some people down there and try to keep them from passing that law."

Even Dayson was surprised by the laugh that burbled out of him. "My god, you're a wonderful girl. I only wish you were right."

He didn't want to admit that her words had stirred something in him he thought dead. Batch was right, politics was still in his blood. The thought of engaging in battle again, rising from his political grave to haunt the state once more, had been unbearable. For months, he had hidden in Topping, nursing his wounds and falling back on cynicism to justify his inaction. And what was cynicism but a sophisticated-seeming excuse to do nothing?

They were interrupted by the sound of the door to the utility room opening and shutting and, a moment later, the sight through the kitchen window of Frank carrying his tools across the lawn.

Dayson thought of the fruitless digging with which he and Persig had passed the spring. Maybe it was exactly as he had told Mattie, they had found nothing because they didn't understand what they were looking for. Or perhaps they didn't understand they had already found what they needed to find and didn't value it.

He remembered the uncanny feeling he had so often felt when working out in the back yard.

"Mattie, do you spy on me?"

He expected a quick denial, but she said nothing, only watched Persig, who had dropped his tools on the ground and set his hands on his hips, trying to work up the courage to go to work once more when he knew he would almost certainly find nothing.

After a while she raised her shoulders and let them drop. "I used to watch you sometimes. I stood in the poplars, or at the edge of the woods and watched you work."

"Why?"

"I wanted to see what a normal person did."

"How long did it take to figure out you picked the wrong guy?"

She nodded through the window toward Persig. "Maybe he'll let me see what he does."

He wanted to tell her that Persig wasn't normal either. But who was? When it comes to people, there is no normal.

He understood. She needed to get outside, to leave behind the words they had said, the conflict that had spurred them. And he knew he had to let her go.

After she'd gone out Dayson made his bed, got properly dressed and fixed a piece of toast and a cup of coffee before following her outside.

He wasn't keeping an eye on them, he told himself, just wanted to join them.

Persig had interrupted his work and was sitting on the edge of his dig, his feet resting in the dirt. Mattie sat near him, her legs curled under her long skirt, her fingers fiddling with a blade of grass. They had been holding hands when he came out, but quickly withdrew them, speaking to an intimacy not yet matured. They looked up as Dayson walked across the yard, his fingers around the necks of three brown bottles.

"I suppose eleven o'clock is a little early for a beer, but it's a warm day and I figured you could use something to drink." He handed Persig one of the bottles, then made a show of holding back Mattie's. "You old enough to drink this stuff?"

She knew this wasn't really the question and she gave him a faint smile to let him know things were all right between them. She told him, "A few weeks ago you were wondering if I was old enough to drink coffee."

The winds had shifted once more. A soft, warm breeze from the west stirred the tall firs. Their trunks creaked pleasantly, like old men stretching their legs.

Dayson took a sip of his beer, nodded toward the apple trees. "Maybe I should get someone over here to prune those things, take out the deadwood, see if I can't get a good crop next year."

"And you'd have a better view of the hills." Mattie gave him a signifying look. "And of the path. You could see people coming and going better."

Dayson smiled, his heart glad at her joke, meant to be understood only by the two of them.

Persig added, "If I extended my dig that far, I could take out those blackberry vines for you." His remarks spoke too much of obsession to allow anyone to smile.

"Heard anything from your dissertation committee?" Dayson asked.

Persig shook his head.

Mattie looked first at Dayson, then at Persig. "You're getting a PhD?"

The young man shrugged. "Maybe. Ask my committee."

Dayson could see it hadn't occurred to her that Persig was a scholar, rather than just some guy he'd hired to do some digging.

"You're not from around here," she said. It was less a question than a realization.

The young man looked at her out of the corner of his eye. "Family's from Bend," he said, pausing before adding, "But I suppose you are. From around here, I mean."

Their eyes darted toward each other, then darted away, like startled goldfish, each struggling against a current of words left unsaid, their tentative exchange barely audible.

"I guess so," she said. "For now." Concentrating on twisting her blade of grass into a knot, Mattie said, "Is your father as tall as you are?"

The young man looked toward Dayson.

The older man gave the younger one a faint nod, telling him, yes, this was something he had to do.

Frank laced his fingers together to cover the shaking in his hands. "I'm not sure. I never knew my father. I was adopted."

Mattie nodded in a tentative way, expecting more. When Persig remained silent she realized that this was all she would get, that he had left out of his story everything crucial.

It struck Dayson how much this young man and young woman had in common, something so obvious he had overlooked it. Though in different ways, they had both been deserted by their parents, until they doubted the legitimacy of their birth, their right to be in this world.

"I'm from Bakersfield," she confessed.

The two of them leaned back, exhausted by their exchange.

Mattie recovered first and looked for safer ground. "You dig up things. From the past, I mean."

Persig smiled at her shorthand version of his profession. "Yes, I guess that's pretty much it."

"And what will you do when you find something?"

He waved his hand at the ground he had dug up. "Maybe we'll understand something about who came here, what they were doing. Why they left." He closed his eyes and a sad smile played across his face. "More likely, we'll only think we understand. We'll pretend we've got it all figured out."

Turning to Dayson, Mattie asked, "And why is it you can dig in the ground here, too, but you can't sit down at your desk and dig into your own past."

Dayson had been enjoying the awkwardness of their exchange and didn't like the spotlight turned on himself. He wanted to tell her to leave his unfinished memoirs out of this.

"You haven't touched your beer," he said.

She regarded the bottle for a moment, then jumped to her feet. With two light steps she leaped into the torn-up earth of Persig's dig. Her eyes glistening, she spread her arms wide and began to turn in a circle. As she pirouetted, she tipped the bottle, spilling its contents onto the thirsty ground as if it were the finishing touch to an obscure ritual.

Her eyes burned with an intensity that killed the impulse of either man to laugh, catching them up in a sense of ancient magic.

When the last drops had fallen into the dirt she dropped the empty bottle and looked up to judge the position of the sun. "I'll be late for class," she said, throwing off the spell she had cast. "Next week is finals."

Persig rose to his feet. "I'll walk you down to your place."

She tried to keep smiling, but Dayson saw in her eyes the shadow of anxiety over what would happen if Sarah saw her with a boy.

"It's all right. I know the way," she said with a sigh.

She walked backwards a few steps, still looking at Frank, making sure he stayed put, before turning around and running toward home.

Persig looked at Dayson for an explanation.

The old pol shook his head. "Funny girl."

Later that afternoon, as Herb Greenburg rang up his purchases, Dayson nodded toward the highway. "That repaving job looks pretty good."

Greenburg paused and looked out the window while sacking Dayson's groceries. "Yeah, I guess so."

Was he aware of the frown that flickered across his face as he spoke?

Dayson again thought of the farmer he had spoken to a couple of months earlier and his unhappiness about the repaving, saying how folks would only speed through Topping faster than ever, treating it as if it didn't exist, until one day it wouldn't.

Hardly even hamlets, really, these tiny communities were strung along Highway 26 like beads on a necklace, still spaced roughly as far apart as the range of a Model T's gas tank, much the way similar waysides had once marked the distance a stagecoach could go before needing to change horses. And, just as the stagecoach stops had died, killed by motored jalopies, so the modern car with its greater range threatened the survival of Topping and Rose Arbor, Timber and Elsie.

The cost of progress. How many times had he said words to that effect while signing one bill or another to encourage new businesses, build bigger suburbs, lay out faster highways? As he became accustomed to it he'd said it with diminishing pangs of regret. But what kind of progress was it that ate up farms and forest simply so people could drive faster and live farther from where they worked?

He asked Herb, "Are you hearing anything about people trying to buy up land around here?"

"Listen long enough and you'll hear anything," the grocer replied with the hint of a smile. "But, yeah, they're even buying land up in the hills. Can't figure that one out."

A vaguely formed notion that Dayson had carried in his head for weeks came suddenly clear. If someone put in a dam, the area would have enough reliable water for a spreading blotch of new homes on what had been farmland. And with a better source of electricity, they could pump water into the hills, cut down the filbert orchards and build houses.

Folks might debate whether such development helped or hurt, whether the transformation of tiny burgs like Topping was worth the cost. But they couldn't discuss it if they didn't know about it, if the decisions were being made without consulting them. And, by keeping it quiet, those few who knew what was about to happen would grow rich by taking advantage of those who didn't.

The two men looked out at the highway and watched a car speeding past.

And Martin Dayson decided he had something important to do.

He called Ernie Fonseca, director of State Lands, who told him, "I was thinking of calling you this afternoon." Senate committees, he said, were close to shutting down as the legislature sprinted toward adjournment, and Senate Bill 468, as the water reclamation project was now officially known, would receive a hearing at ten the following morning. Rather than mounting a dog-and-pony show for its passage, with VIPs grinning for the cameras, the governor's office had persuaded the Senate president to let the bill slip quietly through committee as a non-controversial item.

"They think they can get it through that fast?" Dayson had asked.

"They say they'll have it on the Senate floor the next day and the House may get it that afternoon. House committees don't shut down until Thursday. So, yes, they've got time."

"Did you ever get a look at the bill?"

"Got it this afternoon. I'm supposed to lead off the hearings in the morning, which is odd, considering we had nothing to do with drafting it. I'll probably still be reading it to myself while I'm sitting in front of the committee. By the way, I heard that when they scaled down the presentation of the bill you got yourself uninvited for the hearing."

"It might be the other way around. They scaled it down so they could find a reason to keep me away. But a neighbor girl reminded me that I'm a citizen like anyone else, and no one can tell me I can't attend a hearing."

"Or sign up to testify."

"Or sign up to testify."

Ernie wished him luck, adding, "I'm still looking for whatever it is you think they're trying to hide in this thing, Governor."

"If I'm right, it's all in plain sight, Ernie. I'll see you tomorrow."

He returned to the Greenburgs' store later that afternoon and told Herb and Rose about the bill and the danger it posed to Topping and other communities like it. He told them of the committee hearing scheduled for the following day, asked them to attend and, if they could, persuade a few neighbors to come with them.

From the expression on Herb's face and the way Rose defensively lifted her hand to the base of her throat as he explained what he had in mind, he knew he might as well be asking them if they wanted to be shot out of a cannon. To his surprise, they said they'd do it.

"If you think it would help," Herb added.

"It might," was all he could honestly tell them.

Anxious to know where things stood, Mattie stopped by Dayson's place before evening set in. When he told her of his conversation with the Greenburgs and their promise to come down to Salem she leapt from the chair and hugged him.

"Easy, girl," he laughed. "The grange boys will be there, and the developers and people from Gilkey's office. They're all on alert now." He saw that he hadn't dented her hopes at all. "It's an eight o'clock hearing. We'll have to get up early."

Chapter Twenty-Seven

Babylon Revisited

Earthbound and boxy, the marble-clad state capitol lacked the gravitas of its classically-styled predecessor, destroyed by fire more than twenty years earlier. The current building, with its bulky stone dome surmounted by a gilded statue of a pioneer, had been described as a shoe box topped by a bowling trophy.

Whatever its sterile modernity, the building had once been the center of Dayson's life. After years spent in its halls, first as a legislator, then as governor, he had often joked that he knew the building better than he knew his own home. In the end, the joke had been on him. He hadn't set foot in either place, his former home or the Capitol, since the rainy January afternoon when he had left office.

Before leaving the house that morning, Dayson had combed back his long hair and patted down his beard but, regarding himself in the mirror, he thought he still looked more like one of the early pioneers than he did like the state's previous governor.

As if to confirm his impression, he attracted only a few curious glances as he pushed through the Capitol's revolving doors and walked in. Nor did anyone pay much attention to the tall young woman who walked beside him, except perhaps to remark to themselves how nice it was that this old man had brought his granddaughter to see the Capitol.

As they crossed the rotunda Dayson stopped and pointed to the enormous state seal set in the floor. "See that? A lot of folks here think it's the center of the world, the navel of the universe. Me? I used to think it might represent a different orifice." His laugh echoed under the high dome. "Even the best of them can get so caught up with what's going on in this building they forget there's a real world out there."

Mattie looked at the seal, then at Dayson. "But we won't."

He could only smile.

If no one had recognized Dayson as he walked through the Capitol with Mattie, by contrast nearly everyone in Hearing Room B stopped in surprise when he showed up for the eight o'clock hearing.

Dayson had often said that he could open the door of any hearing room, see which committee was in session, take a look at those waiting to testify, and know which bill was under consideration. So even if he hadn't seen the agenda posted on the hearing room door, he would have known he had the right place.

In the front of the room, near the long, curving dais around which the committee members sat, Ernie Fonseca was shaking hands with Asa Meeker, the committee chair. A couple members of the grange sat in the front row in their Sunday suits, reverent as parishioners awaiting the sermon. Sitting behind them in the second row, Tom Heidigger of the Farm Bureau shuffled through his three pages of testimony.

Nearly a dozen people from Topping had come. The Greenburgs had closed their store for the morning. Even Dr. Kimmell had driven down with his wife.

It took Dayson a moment to spot the ones he knew would be there, the men whose presence told him he'd made no mistake about the bill's intent. Three men in expensive suits, lobbyists for real estate developers, sat in the back row of the hearing room. Though well-known to Dayson, they were unfamiliar figures to the farmers who made up most of the audience, and they attracted little attention, which suited them fine. They would speak only if necessary, trusting the farmers to carry the day for them, even if—especially if—the farmers didn't know that's what they were doing. One of them—Dayson couldn't remember his name—greeted the former governor with a nod and a cool smile.

Dayson leaned toward Mattie and said quietly, "Find a seat near the back. I've got some old friends to say hello to."

Mattie looked around in wonder. "You know all these people?"

"Pretty much." He smiled, seeing that she finally grasped how big his world had once been.

For a moment, the men standing in the front of the hearing room backed away from Dayson as he came up to them, just as gazelles and zebras keep a wary distance from a lion in their midst. Then, remembering he'd been defanged the previous November, they came forward to shake his hand and welcome him back, though he could see their puzzlement at his presence.

Asa Meeker, noting the stir, looked up from talking with Ernie Fonseca. His owl-like eyes popped wide.

"Well, Governor, what a great surprise to have you here with us this morning."

An eleven-term legislator, Meeker had long ago acquired the tic of making everything he said sound like part of a speech. A burly, balding man of sixty-four, Meeker possessed an aura of probity and strength, a tribal elder in the particular village that lived in the Capitol. His eyebrows rose as he repeated, "A great surprise."

The two longtime colleagues shook hands and Meeker asked, "To what do we owe the honor of your presence?"

"Good to see you, Asa. If you have time for me, I thought I'd testify on SB 468."

Meeker squinted curiously at Dayson.

The ex-governor wondered if Meeker knew of Gilkey's original plan to give the bill a high-profile introduction, or the reason why he had canceled the big roll-out and told Dayson to stay home. Likely so, but his committee had been so preoccupied with a rewrite of the Forest Practices Act and Gilkey's amendments to the Willamette River clean-up he probably hadn't given it much thought. With farm groups all in favor of the bill and with Gilkey's assurance it would cause no ripples, Asa would happily approve it that morning on the committee's last session before adjournment.

Former political allies and rivals alike, the other senators came out from behind the long dais to shake his hand, decorum and respect more important than the remembrance of old scores. Tom Heidigger, the Farm Bureau's man, clapped him on the back. The boys from the grange, good Republicans all, shook his hand, happy to have, they assumed, such a distinguished supporter for what they saw as their bill.

Asa Meeker put a hand on Dayson's arm. "I suppose we'd better get going. We'd be honored to have you lead off the hearing, Governor."

"I dunno, Asa. It doesn't seem like I should speak until the committee's heard a summary of the bill. Let me go after Ernie."

Ernie Fonseca gave Dayson a quick, bleak smile, meaning he still didn't understand the bill or the former governor's problem with it.

"That'll be fine, then." Meeker looked over his shoulder to the committee secretary. "We'll have Mr. Fonseca lead off, followed by Governor Dayson. Then Mr. Thayer."

Dayson looked out over the half-filled hearing room and wondered how he could have missed Art standing near the window at the other side of the room, a manila folder in his hand.

At what point, Dayson wondered, had Art found out what the bill was really about? He had no doubt his former aide understood it thoroughly by now. He'd been a good staffer, always up on his brief.

"How are you, Governor?" Art said as he crossed the room and shook Dayson's hand. "It's good to see you."

Like hell it is, Dayson wanted to say, but couldn't help but give his former protege a wink and a smile. "Good to see you too, Art. You're here to testify for the Governor's office? A real mark of confidence from the old man."

"Thanks. I'm sure the Governor would want me to say hello for him."

They both knew that if Gilkey were aware Dayson had shown up he'd be spitting out words of one syllable.

Asa Meeker gave the two men a narrow-eyed frown. He had walked these halls too many years not to sense the tension between them, and was wondering about its source and what it meant for his hearing that morning.

"All right," Meeker said. "We'd better get going if we want to pass the bill out to the floor today." Still standing in front of the dais, Meeker leaned across it and raised his gavel, ready to bring the committee to order. "Ernie, why don't you take your seat at the table and start us off.

With a sidelong glance at Dayson, Ernie told Meeker, "I'll be awfully quick, Mr. Chairman. I only received the bill yesterday and haven't had time to do a formal analysis."

His gavel poised in the air, Meeker stopped and looked in turn at Dayson, Fonseca and Art Thayer. His nostrils flared at the unexpected stink rising from Senate Bill 468. His voice audible only to the three men around him, he asked, "Ernie, didn't your office draft the bill?"

"No, Senator, we didn't."

Dayson knew that Meeker took pride in running his committee well, conscientious about giving each bill its proper consideration. To allow SB 468 only a pro forma hearing before passing it to the full Senate, he needed the bill to be as non-controversial as advertised. The displeasure he directed at the three men betrayed his growing suspicion that the bill wasn't everything the governor's office had promised.

"But you did read it," he said to Ernie, seeking reassurance.

"I went over it last night."

"Fine, then," Meeker said with an expression that made clear it wasn't fine at all. He banged his gavel on its wooden block. "The committee will come to order," he said, and walked around the dais to take his chair.

Dayson looked back and gave Mattie a fleeting smile as he took a seat in the front row.

Fonseca sat before the committee and, at Meeker's direction, gave a brief summary of SB 468, apologizing on the record for having no more than a passing acquaintance with the bill, which authorized the construction of six water impoundment dams with some minor hydroelectric capacity. One dam, the Tyee, would be sited on the John Day River, with the other five in the Willamette Valley at sites not clearly specified, despite the naming of a couple of water courses. Funding for the construction of the dams was already contained in portions of the state budget passed by both houses the previous month, he said.

With that, he folded his hands and waited for questions, the entire summary having taken no more than two minutes.

A couple members of the committee rubbed their foreheads at the sketchiness of Fonseca's description. When their questions about the exact location of the dams in the Willamette Valley were answered with a polite but firm, "I don't know," their unease deepened. At this point in the session, to ask for more time to consider the bill would be tantamount to killing it.

And they had no appetite to kill a measure they still wished to regard as routine, the money already approved, even if they hadn't noticed that particular line item at the time.

Despite the brevity of Fonseca's testimony, they didn't ask follow-up questions and let it go unchallenged, though they didn't look happy about it.

Asa Meeker thanked Ernie for his testimony and asked Dayson to come forward, introducing him with effusive references to his years of service to the state and the honor he lent the committee by his presence that morning. The woman who served as the committee's secretary came out from behind her desk and asked Dayson for a copy of his testimony. Dayson enjoyed the surprise on her face when he waved her away, saying, "I haven't got anything written down."

Perplexed, the committee secretary looked toward Meeker, who nodded her back to her desk, giving her the frown he meant for Dayson. "There's no law says a witness has to have written testimony." For a moment he gazed unhappily at Dayson. "And now, Governor, why don't you tell us why you're here today?"

His hands folded before him, Dayson said, "I've been asking myself the same question, Mr. Chairman. I originally meant to come down to Salem at the Governor's request and speak in support of this bill. However, I find I can't do that. I should tell you that I live near where one of the dams may go, but this bill won't affect me much, not personally. I'm here today, instead, to speak for the people working on family farms and for the communities that have shared the dignity and the risks of making their living from the soil."

Behind him, the grange and farm bureau guys sat up a bit straighter, tilted their chins a little higher, not realizing they were only getting their heads closer to the chopping block.

"Perhaps most of all I'm doing this for a young neighbor who maybe sees better than I do what this bill would do to those communities." Though he hadn't mentioned her directly, Dayson smiled as he saw Asa and a couple of the other committee members instinctively look toward Mattie at the back of the room. "I want to thank the chairman for his references to past glories. But I'm just a private citizen now, one who respects the institutions on which our civic life depends. I want, as all of you do, a government that is trustworthy, well-informed in its deliberations, sure in its actions. My neighbors want the same. But in the rush to get SB 468 through this committee, a rush deliberately created by its sponsors, you're being denied the opportunity to look carefully through its provisions and make a considered judgment on its merits."

The senators, like a chorus of Greek actors, their true faces hidden behind the graven masks of their public selves, sat behind the long arc of the dais wearing uniform frowns. The grange members slumped in their seats.

Dayson understood. The senators didn't have time for a proper hearing, and they knew it. They figured they'd scheduled a measure that could sail through committee without controversy, a two-foot putt of a bill. Weary from the demands of the six-month session, staggering toward adjournment, they resented this political ghost traipsing in to tell them they were being gulled.

With no papers in front of him, no notes, Dayson spent the next few minutes trying to persuade the committee of things for which he had no clear proof—that the new administration hadn't simply expanded the scope of the original bill but transformed it into something altogether different from its purported intent. Yes, the Tyee Dam would fulfill its promise. The other dams, though, were sited in the Willamette Valley, where there was no shortage of water to justify their construction. "In fact," he said, "I'm morally certain this bill isn't designed to help farmers at all. I believe it will only lay the groundwork for water systems that will displace them to make way for construction of housing tracts and commercial development. The same farmers who support this bill today will find themselves driven off their land as the property taxes skyrocket beyond what farm incomes can meet. No one has told them they're being used as a cat's paw for those who know what it's really about. By the time they figure it out, it will be too late. Even now, development companies are quietly buying up land near the dam sites. We need to slow this down, think it through. Despite what you've been told, there's no rush on this. I know this won't be a welcome suggestion, but you need to delay consideration of this bill until next session, when the governor's office will have to make clear to you what this bill really does. It's been put off before, back when I sat in Governor Gilkey's chair. It can be put off again."

Dayson watched the members of the committee squirm in their chairs. As a legislator he had sat on the other side of the dais, listening politely through countless hopeless cases, and he could see he was losing them, had in fact already lost them. They didn't buy his argument for the simple fact that they didn't have the time for him to be right.

He felt the impulse to get up from the witness chair and walk away, but reminded himself he had known all along he had virtually no chance. He hadn't come to win. He had come to keep faith with Mattie and the people of Topping, and he would see it through.

When he'd finished, Meeker leaned forward, resting his large frame on his elbows, and said, "You realize, Governor, we have biennial sessions . . . I hardly need to tell you that when we adjourn in a few days we won't be back for two years."

"Yes, Mr. Chairman. I don't say this lightly."

Asa Meeker passed his hand over his face and looked down at the bill before him. He and Dayson had been friends and allies for years. "Are you sure about what you're suggesting, Governor? Can you give us the names of the companies that will profit from this? Do you have some evidence that these people buying the land have had prior knowledge of this bill?"

To each of these questions, the former governor, no longer with any staff or the weight of the various departments to support him, gave a humiliating series of "I don't know," "I'm not entirely sure," and "I haven't got that information yet."

Dayson had tried to deliver his testimony with quiet confidence, tried to make clear that the lack of clarity regarding the bill's details, as demonstrated by Ernie Fonseca and himself, was sufficient reason to vote against it. Instead, he had come off as someone who couldn't back up his assertions—a crank or, worse yet, a radical at a time when conformity ranked as the country's greatest survival reflex. Short of time, short of patience, comfortable in their intent to do the right thing, the members of the committee needed him to be wrong. And so he was, no matter what he might say. In any case, some of the committee members would see nothing wrong with turning farmland into housing tracts.

Embarrassed at the need to shoo his old friend from the witness table,

Asa Meeker thanked Dayson for his testimony and again praised his years of service to the state, his commitment to the causes in which he believed, his words serving as an unintentional valedictory to the end of Dayson's public life.

With two more bills to consider that morning, Meeker wanted to move on. He looked over the audience and said, "If there are no more witnesses signed up to speak in opposition to this bill I propose we move on to its proponents."

When Mattie stood, Dayson, for a confused moment, thought she had risen as some sort of tribute to him. Or maybe she thought they were supposed to leave now.

It took him a moment to see he was wrong.

Nervously clenching and unclenching her hands, she stepped into the aisle and called to Asa Meeker, "I'd like to testify, sir."

The chairman's eyebrows shot up in surprise. With a quick glance at the committee's secretary, he asked Mattie, "Honey, have you signed up on the witness list?"

Her voice wavering, she asked, "No. Can I do that now?"

Meeker swiveled in his seat and glanced at the clock above him.

"I suppose we have time. And I don't wish to deny a young lady a chance to speak. Please, come on up," Meeker said, motioning her forward.

Her footsteps were the only sound in the room as she came up to take a chair at the witness table.

Nervously twisting in her seat, she looked over her shoulder at the lobbyists in their expensive suits, the grange members, the government officials. It would have been a daunting sight for even an experienced witness, Dayson thought.

She took a deep breath, turned toward the chairman and the committee members. And she could say nothing.

The silence grew to an eternity that might have been all of ten seconds. Dayson felt a sweat break out on his hands. "Come on, Mattie," he whispered. "Come on, girl."

Meeker leaned forward in his seat and said gently, "We're all ears, honey. Maybe you could start by telling us your name and where you're from."

Once more she glanced over her shoulder, and this time found Dayson. He nodded and smiled, trying not to betray his own nervousness. She returned the barest of smiles and looked toward the Greenburgs, the Hofstadters, the Gaffneys, the Kimmels.

"Just relax," Meeker said, smiling. "Now, what have you got to say to us this morning?"

"I'm . . . I'm here to . . ."

She fluttered awkwardly, like a young bird trying to fly for the first time.

Dayson, helpless, dug his nails into the palms of his hands. An uneasy murmur ran through the hearing room. Mattie licked her lips, said nothing. Dayson fought the impulse to run up and join her at the table, say something, do anything to get her past this moment. But he knew she would never forgive him if he did.

And at that nadir, the young bird, toppling toward the earth, steadied herself, arrested her fall and took flight.

In a clear, strong voice she said, "My name is Mattie Reed. I'm from Topping, Oregon."

Her identity established in ways the senators could not appreciate, she continued. "I'm here to talk about the future. I don't think it's right to build this dam, the one near Topping. We . . ." The term seemed to surprise her as it came from her mouth. "We. We are a farming community. My neighbors grow the food all of us eat. No one gets rich at it, but no one complains. That's what they do. That's who they are. We live in a beautiful place. The fields are so green. The hills around us are covered in forest. I wake up every morning to the birds singing. If this dam goes in everything will change. The fields will be covered with houses. They'll chop down the filbert orchards. And when they've done that they'll start tearing out the forest to put in more houses. The cities aren't full yet. Let more people live there. They can build more houses there and leave the countryside alone. Don't let them buy up our land and make us leave."

Meeker held up a hand to stop her. "I'm sorry to interrupt you. I know it's not easy for you to be talking to a bunch of old men like us, but I keep hearing everyone talking about 'them,' and how people are afraid they'll buy up all the land. Can you tell me who they are, young lady?"

No more "honey," Dayson noted.

"I . . . I don't know their names. But they've been coming to the door, trying to buy the land that belongs to my . . . my . . ." Her head dropped, and Dayson feared she had come to the words she could not say, yet could not avoid. But she raised her head and said, "To my mother."

A small stir coursed through the people from Topping. Dayson watched them frown in confusion. They were thinking she must have misspoken, or perhaps exaggerated a bit to make her point. They traded a few winks and let it go. She was just a young girl.

Meeker shook his head as if trying to get her words out of his ears. "Who are these people you talk about? Whose land have they already bought?"

"I don't know, sir."

Meeker sighed. "Well, join the club. The committee has before it what we have been assured is a non-controversial bill, one to help farmers, not hurt them. And all I'm hearing from opponents is that someone, somewhere, somehow wants to build a bunch of houses on what is now farmland. But they don't give me any evidence. Sweetheart, I very much appreciate such a young girl as yourself coming forward to speak—"

"You can't do this!"

A flush spread over Asa Meeker's cheeks at this disrespect. "That's enough, young lady. Please return to your seat."

"But I . . ."

The members of the committee, weary and overworked, sat back in their chairs or leaned forward on their elbows, wanting simply to move on.

Seeing how it was, Mattie said, "Yes, sir. Thank you for letting me speak."

She went back to her chair next to Dayson. For a moment he thought she might cry. But she clasped her hands in front of her, sat up straight and retained her composure.

He put his hand over hers and squeezed. "I'm proud of you, Mattie."

Dayson felt the collective sigh of relief as no one else rose to speak against the bill and Art Thayer took his seat at the witness table. His one-time aide smiled magnanimously, his victory already assured, ready to tell the committee what it wanted to hear, that this was a good bill, one that merited expedited consideration and a quick "yes" vote. The farm groups would follow, testifying to their support of the bill and their hopes that it would go over to the House as quickly as possible.

While Art spoke, Dayson rose with the weariness of a defeat foretold and retreated down the aisle. As he did, he glanced at the developers' lobbyists. They looked even more complacent than when he had entered. This one was in the bag. Their testimony would not be needed.

Mattie fell in behind him as he pushed through the doors of the hearing room and stalked down the corridor.

"Aren't we going to stay?" she asked.

"What for?"

"But you don't know how the committee's going to vote."

"Yes, I do. And so would you if you knew anything about it."

"So what do we do now?"

Dayson stopped abruptly. "Do? We get in the car and go home, that's what we do."

"That's it? You're just going to leave, without trying anything else?"

"There is no anything else. We lost."

"You said it had to pass a House committee too."

"It's controlled by Democrats, and they'll do what Gilkey wants them to do. This was our only chance and we lost."

A small crease of confusion wrinkled her young brow as she looked over her shoulder toward the hearing room, trying to figure it out. Dayson realized she truly did not understand what had happened. How could he expect her to? For all the many times she had schooled him on singers and movies and books—Simone de Boo-Boo, Joe Baeza and the rest—she couldn't grasp his world any better than he did hers.

"You don't think they understood what you were saying?" she asked.

With a shake of his head, Dayson, too, looked back toward the hearing room, not puzzled, but resigned, seeing it all as clearly as if the walls were made of glass—Art Thayer urging the committee members to vote yes, the grange members giving their testimony, the lobbyists leaning back in their seats, smiling.

He regarded Mattie and felt the urge to protect her from the part of the world she didn't yet grasp.

"Understood? They couldn't afford to understand, Mattie. They don't have the time."

"They were all listening to you. All of them. I could see it.

"They're a polite bunch. I'll give 'em that."

He saw the shock in Mattie's face. Defeat came to the young unanticipated but merciful in its swiftness.

Over many years, he had usually won his political battles, but had always felt the disappointments more keenly than the victories. Now he had lost his last battle without much of anyone but Mattie and a few others even noticing. Maybe he could tell Persig not to worry anymore, the charisma that had offended the young man, his ability to bring people around to his point of view by sheer force of personality, had expired, overtaken—like his eyesight, his hearing, his energy—by advancing years.

"Believe me, Mattie, I know what defeat looks like. It looks like what just happened in that hearing room. The bill will go out on the Senate floor and then over to the House before any opposition can form. Gilkey will sign it and, as part of the deal, the farmer's will throw their support behind his revenue bill and it'll pass too. Gilkey will make sure that they won't know they've been fooled until after they've helped him win the next election."

After watching Dayson leave the committee room, the people from Topping, after some hesitation, followed him out. Catching up to him in the corridor, they gently clapped him on the back, squeezed his arm, thanked him for his effort. Herb, with Rose beside him said, "We came close. Maybe we can win when the House votes on it."

Dayson wanted to tell him, "That's not how it works." But he smiled and said, "We'll see."

He wouldn't tell Herb and Rose, Mattie, the others, that he hadn't expected to win. Instead, he would say to them in all honesty that their effort wasn't wasted. They'd come together and fought the good fight, had shown, if to no one but themselves, that they were a real community and they were not to be ignored.

While they spoke quietly in the hallway, Art Thayer, who had finished his testimony, sought him out and shook his hand. Out of respect, he spared Dayson any expression of condolence. "It's good to have you back here where you belong. I've always believed in you. I still do. You're going to come down next session, give us hell again?"

Art didn't let go of his hand until Dayson, touched by his obvious sincerity, chuckled and told him, "I suppose I will, Art. And I'll see that you don't win 'em all."

"I know you will. Governor."

It would be a long process, siting and building the dams, securing the funds from the federal government, getting the necessary permits. The good people of Topping might yet manage to stop them somewhere along the line, and he would fight with them every step of the way. Though he didn't like the odds, he was learning not to underestimate his neighbors.

Chapter Twenty-Eight

Temples and Burial Grounds

Martin Dayson—former governor, former state representative, former war hero, former husband, former everything—drove home along the back roads through countryside that lent its measure of solace to the former farm boy from Yamhill. Beside him, Mattie sat silently, her furrowed brow and far-away gaze making clear she was still puzzling over what she had seen and what it meant, both for her and for the man she had persuaded to make the trip.

They passed through the tiny hamlets along the way—Wheatland, Unionvale, Cove Orchard—motoring along the rolling farmland, his heart's home, the land where he had grown up, married, worked. Now each mile wove a shroud of melancholy around that same heart, a shroud that gave the landscape a darker hue despite the presence of the hopeful young woman sitting next to him. How much of this land would one day see its last crops plowed under to make way for tract homes, gas stations, burger joints? Though born with this soil under his fingernails Dayson knew he had, during his years in Salem, fostered this very brand of progress, encouraged the encroachment of pavement and postage-stamp lawns over the very fields that fed the people who paved them over. With each new industrial development, every new suburb he would think, "There, that's exactly what was needed." And the following year there were more inroads on the farms, the forests, the coast, each one, considered in isolation, justifiable even laudable. One good decision followed another until they resulted in disaster.

In what the pipe-smoking arbiters of opinion called the Age of Anxiety, with an entire nation, an entire world, caught between the threat of tyranny and the menace of annihilation, economic development stood in for righteousness. Industriousness became a way of keeping terror and doubt at arm's length, even while it destroyed what it meant to preserve.

And who was he kidding? The farmers themselves had once formed the forward edge of this kind of progress. His grandfathers had cut down the valley forests, pulled the stumps, planted the corn and wheat, driven the dusky savage into the shrinking wilderness, onto land no one else wanted, at least not yet.

"Poor bastards," Dayson thought, unaware he had muttered the words aloud until he noticed Mattie looking at him. "Poor bastards," he repeated, a little louder ignoring the worry in her eyes.

A hawk glided over a field, conjuring up the image of the great wooden mask that held within it the soul of the forest, of Deer, Bear, Beaver, of the People—the mask itself a token of what could be seen and, equally, what could not. Now the great bird lay in exile, caught and hung by a nail in a basement office, the symbol that once invoked the unity of man and nature reduced to an artifact.

He glanced at Mattie looking sorrowfully out the side window. Something in her face remained untamed, not yet weighed down by the opinions of people she shouldn't care about. Again, he thought of the fertility icon, His girl, as he sometimes called it. Nothing like it. Not around here at least. It had walked unbidden into his life, or at least not consciously bidden—though the mind seldom knows what the heart seeks—following a long and obscure path that somehow led to his garden.

Or was he again getting two things mixed up?

When had he ceased to have answers, he wondered, and replaced them all with questions?

"I don't know what to do, Ben." This time he knew he had said it out loud.

He dropped Mattie off at the college and glanced at his watch. "I guess you'd better hurry or you'll be late for class."

"No classes this week. Finals. Remember?" She saw in his eyes that this wasn't a good day to tease him. "I'll come by later today."

"You don't need to."

"I know."

He pulled into his driveway and started toward the house. Halfway up the walk, he stopped, halted by the suddenly unbearable thought of once more shutting himself inside. So he walked through the back yard, past Persig's sad little dig and his own flourishing garden until he stood at the edge of the path. A soft breeze nuzzled his back like a tap on the shoulder, urging him forward. He looked down the path to where it disappeared into the patch of woods and began to walk, buoyed by the feeling that, rather than running away from something for once, he was walking toward something. The fact that he had no idea what it was made it all the more compelling.

As before, the birds grew silent when he entered their home. A small epiphany lit up a sleeping part of his mind, telling him that the spirit of the great mask, even from its exile in Robert Bachelder's office, still inhabited this holy place.

He'd read somewhere that the earliest Roman temples were circular, their roofs supported by a ring of thick wooden columns in an attempt to recreate the sacred groves in which their ancestors had first worshiped, first sought the answers to the mystery of their own existence. Walking now among the great trees, their branches meeting overhead in a canopy of green, he understood why they had built their temples as they did.

After a few minutes he came to the clearing. From the edge of the woods he looked at the remains of the shack, black and fallen now, like the house beside it. Already, the grass had grown over the faint path worn by Mattie as she had crossed the meadow to meet her lover, leaving no trace. The shack and Lawrence and what they meant had become the past. Mattie, child of the uncertain future, had burned it down in order to be free. What could be more clear?

To the degree his walk had followed any intent at all, Dayson had vaguely meant to stop here and go back. Yet the path continued and, after a moment's hesitation, he decided to keep going.

Once beyond the clearing, the path rose steeply into the hills. To his left, the woods grew increasingly dense, the ground under the firs a carpet of ferns dotted with vine maple. To his right, he could see through the trees that he had risen above the fields in back of his house. Though the wooded slope curved around to meet the hills of the Coast Range, the path continued straight.

While he wondered where the path could be leading him, it grew narrower and rose more steeply. Puffing now, the limp from the shrapnel in his hip growing sharper with every step, he became increasingly determined to keep going, determined to see where the path would take him.

As he began to think he was only following a deer track that would lead deeper into the forest then fade to nothing, he came to a clearing at the top of the ridge, man-made, roughly fifty yards square, bounded by tall trees on three sides, with the fourth open to the west.

Like so many pioneer cemeteries, the spot had been chosen well, set on a hill apart from the little town, a green and peaceful haven that lent itself to repose. The open side of the clearing afforded a vista of the little valley in which Topping rested. Dayson wondered how its beauty could have escaped him until now—the well-kept fields, the modest cluster of homes, the Greenburg's store a couple of miles away, the far hills covered with orchards on their lower flanks and the dense forest above, all of it glowing like an emerald in the sunlight.

Some people avoided cemeteries, wishing no reminder of the end that awaited them. Dayson, though, had always liked these modest country graveyards, the feeling of connection he gained from them, their ambience of rest and continuity.

He left the woods behind him to walk among the graves, each surrounded by a green border consisting more of weeds than grass, but neatly trimmed. Fresh flowers decorated a few of the graves. Those buried here were not forgotten, were still part of the community. He recognized a few local names—Gaffney, Strachan, Hofstadter. A Josiah and Clara Greenburg were probably Herb's parents, Dayson thought, until a second look at their birth dates made him realize they had to be his grandparents, come from Illinois, their marker said. This was characteristic of pioneer cemeteries, a statement on the gravestone of which faraway place the residents had quit to come out west, a last humbly proud statement of the challenge they had accepted, the great journey taken.

How many of them, he wondered, had meant to stay in this area for only a year or two before moving on to yet greener pastures, only to slowly realize they had ceased their wanderings and would pass the rest of their days here. He recalled Batch telling him, "We're all just visitors."

The sound of car tires on gravel caught Dayson's ear, an old Ford coming up the hill. It pulled into the cemetery and a gray-haired man got out. He wore a dark, wide-brimmed hat and suspenders over an old but clean shirt that must once have been blue but had faded almost to white. In one hand he carried a modest bunch of flowers, probably picked that morning from his garden. In the other hand he carried a coffee can. Walking a bit unsteadily, though straight-backed and with dignity, he made his way to one of the graves. There, he took a handful of faded flowers from a vase set against the gravestone, replaced them with fresh ones he had brought and poured water from the can into the vase. The man lingered a few moments, head bowed, hands clasped in front of him. Then he raised his head and, refreshed, walked back to his car and drove off.

Dayson continued his stroll through the cemetery. When he stopped, he told himself he had not been looking for this particular grave. But once he had found it, he knew it was the one he'd been looking for.

Archibald Tannehill had been born in Ransom County, North Dakota in 1889, making him quite a bit older than his wife. Had the difference in their ages caused problems? An empty plot lay next to his. The gravestone already carried Sarah's name and birth date, with the date of death left open. *Bound by Love* it said. Who was he to judge that it might have been otherwise?

He stretched his back, aching a bit after leaning over the gravestone.

All right, he had failed down in Salem. And it mattered. He'd demonstrated to Mattie how little weight an ex-governor threw around there. For her sake he would try to give the impression he didn't take it too much to heart. He wouldn't let her think that by persuading him to attend the hearing she needed to bear the burden of his failure.

His mood lifted by a new resolution he would share with Mattie, his spirit cleansed by his visit to Topping's mothers and fathers, he headed back down the path toward home.

Though hard on his aging knees, the journey back seemed far shorter than the trip out. When he came out of the woods and into his back yard he found that Mattie hadn't waited long before coming to see him, and that Frank had come too, and the two of them were sitting in the grass. They were holding hands, but once more dropped them as he walked up, interrupting whatever mood they'd been sharing.

"We were wondering where you were," Mattie said.

Shading her eyes with her hand, she looked up at him in a way he hadn't seen before and he knew they'd been talking about him, that Frank had told her of his war and of Ben Rosloff and how he'd come to be who he was.

His gut twisted in aggravation. Why in the hell had Frank felt he had to tell Mattie about Ben and all that?

The answer came readily. It was because he had secretly hoped Frank would.

Brushing the dirt from her long skirts, Mattie got to her feet and said, "I'd better get going. I just came by to say hi." She didn't need to say she had come to see if he was all right.

Frank jumped to his feet. "I'll walk you back."

Mattie glanced at Dayson before saying, "All right," the uncertainty in her voice undercutting the sureness of her words.

Dayson understood. She wanted him to call Persig back, find a reason to keep him from going with her. And part of him wanted to do it. But he understood the selfishness in his impulse and decided he wouldn't step in.

Something about the look she gave Dayson made Persig say, almost by way of apology, "I'll be back in a little bit."

As the two of them walked toward the old house Mattie looked over her shoulder at Dayson, her eyes clouded with uncertainty. He knew she feared Sarah's reaction if she saw her walking with a young man.

When they had disappeared down the path, Dayson stood alone at the edge of his garden. It was a warm day and the sun felt good and he tilted his face to the sky. Yes, he was alive and the day was fine and his old heart was too accustomed to sorrow to break over a young girl.

Chapter Twenty-Nine

Chasing the Future,
Chasing the Past

The Greenburgs were in a chatty mood the next day and kept Dayson for quite a while, talking about the early days of the store, established by Herb's father. Dayson didn't mention that he had walked up to the cemetery the previous day and seen his grandparents' graves, fearing it would seem somehow an invasion of the storekeeper's privacy.

When he returned home he was surprised to find Persig standing beside his plot, head down, arms folded. He didn't usually come two days in a row. Next to him he had gathered his tools into a pile.

"What are you doing, Frank?"

Persig looked down at his tools as if they were friends who had failed him, then nodded at the ground he had torn up over the past weeks, trying to force from it the secrets it did not wish to surrender. "I can't make any sense of it. Can't find anything, and can't figure out what that statuette was doing here."

Dayson sensed the young man's mood came from something more than his frustration with his dig, something to do with Mattie. What could have changed so abruptly after the previous day's growing intimacy? It wasn't hard to imagine.

"So what do you do now?" Dayson asked.

Persig stuck his hands in his pockets. For a long time he said nothing, then made a little shrug, no more than a twitch of his shoulders.

"I meant to tell you the other day. I ran up to Seattle last week to defend my thesis. My committee has accepted it—and me." He gave Dayson a sidelong glance to catch his reaction.

"You got your degree?"

Persig nodded.

"Well, congratulations!" He slapped Persig on the back, but the young scholar acted like he was accepting condolences at a funeral.

Lots of people can't handle bad news, Dayson thought, but this kid can't even handle good.

"I suppose I'll have to call you Doctor Persig now."

"Not unless you want me to call you Governor." He said, trying to smile.

"What's going on?"

He took a long time to answer. "A couple of months ago I got an offer for a position at Indiana University. Contingent on getting my degree. Tenure track position." He said it as if confessing to a vice. "I suppose I can take them up on it now."

"That sounds great."

Dayson wanted to ask him why he didn't have enough sense to be happy. But he had come to understand that the young man's capacity for happiness had been buried under layers of emotional scar tissue.

Dayson nodded at the dig. "Where does that leave us?"

Persig took a couple of deep breaths. "I guess I have to tie things up here and accept Indiana's offer."

"And leave behind nothing but a big question mark? Is that what's bothering you?"

Persig responded with an ambivalent lift of the eyebrows.

Dayson had occasionally wondered how he would react if Persig were to give up trying to find the truth about the stone figure. Now that moment had come and, to his surprise, he felt relieved.

"You've told Mattie you're going?"

Persig looked off across the fields toward the hills.

"Yeah."

"And maybe you told her how nice Bloomington is in the fall, how she might like it there."

Persig's silence was answer enough.

"And what did she say?" He tried to make it sound casual.

"Didn't say anything." A troubled look clouded Persig's young face. "There was kind of a scene."

Dayson wanted to ask him what he had expected. The girl barely knew him. But he was a lonely young man, and lonely young men can push things too hard.

Persig picked up an armload of his things and carted them toward the driveway. Dayson took up the rest and followed. The two men tossed the tools in the trunk and Persig slammed it shut. He offered his hand to Dayson.

"Sorry I didn't discover anything for you."

Dayson clasped Persig's hand in both his own. "I think we discovered all we needed to. Maybe stuff we didn't want to know. Stuff that makes our lives harder, not easier."

Of course, Persig misunderstood him. "No. You're wrong," he insisted. "We have to know. We have to find out where things come from."

Dayson didn't mind. After all, understanding the past was the kid's job. But he hoped Frank would not always look for meaning in a hole in the ground, would look up and see what today offered, not just yesterday.

He lifted his head to the sky, knowing what he had to say. "Frank, go back to her. Give it another try."

"I . . . We're going in two different directions."

"Then turn around and go with her in her direction."

Persig's mouth worked silently until he said, "I can't do that."

"Why?" When he got no answer, he asked, "What happened yesterday?"

Frank's face worked with emotions he would not express. "She'll tell you."

"That's it? One setback and you walk away? You may think this dig is ridiculous, but you learned a lot and met a wonderful girl."

"It wasn't ridiculous!" Persig shouted, then caught himself. "I just failed, that's all."

"Okay, maybe it's not worth digging up any more here. But don't give up on Mattie. And don't give up on yourself." Exasperated with the feckless young man's silence, Dayson growled, "All right. If you haven't got any more guts than this you don't deserve her.

"Mighty bold talk from a guy who lost an election and went off to live like a hermit."

Dayson felt the anger rising in his chest, but the memory of the previous day in Salem and his willingness to throw in the towel in front of Mattie made him understand that he too had fallen short.

"Yeah, maybe you're right. Do what you need to do, Frank."

Having managed to get Dayson to drop the subject of Mattie, Persig's mood lightened slightly. "Like you say, maybe we found some things we didn't know we were looking for."

Dayson repeated, "Things we didn't know we were looking for," the words resonating deeply. He offered the boy his hand. "I'm grateful for everything you did, Frank."

"Thanks . . . Marty." Persig allowed himself the ghost of a smile.

Dayson waved to him as he backed onto Hayward Road, but couldn't see if the young man waved back.

Dayson sat at his desk, pen in hand, telling himself he was ready this time to plumb the uncomfortable truths of his life. But as he looked down at the empty page before him he knew he could not write about his life because his life made no sense to him.

Propping his head in his hands, he closed his eyes, a deep weariness pulling at him, less of body than of soul. A few months earlier he had still possessed the energy of a younger man, ready to work morning to night, exhilarated by the challenges he shouldered. Now, though it was only late afternoon, he felt exhausted.

He shuffled the few feet to his room, fell into his bed and sank into sleep like a foundering ship.

"Dorothy."

Dayson woke to the sound of his own voice. Muddled, he blinked vacantly, unable to remember where he was or whether he was waking into day or night. He sat up slowly, fully clothed, the late afternoon light streaming in the window. Would there be more moments like this, life increasingly seen through a wavering lens of uncertainty and confusion?

Though baffled, a sharp impression pierced the fog—he was not alone. He squinted toward the opened bedroom door.

"Good god!"

"I knocked and you didn't answer," Mattie said.

Dayson grunted with the effort to sit up and swing his feet onto the floor.

"So you just waltzed in."

"You shouldn't have let Frank come to the house with me."

It occurred to him that Mattie never said "my house" or "our house" or ever called it home.

"How was it my job to stop him? If you didn't want him to come, you should have said so."

"I couldn't."

"Why the hell not?"

"I just couldn't, that's all."

Uncomfortable with the idea of this young woman standing in the doorway while he sat in his bed, Dayson rose and squeezed past Mattie and limped down the hallway to his study.

When he looked behind him he found that Mattie had followed him, standing now in the doorway of the study.

"Why do I feel like I'm being herded?" he grumped.

"You shouldn't have let him come," she said again, then, more tentatively, "He shouldn't have come."

"I saw him this morning. He told me something happened while he was at your place."

She crossed her arms over her chest as if to protect herself. "He said I should move to Indiana with him. He's going to be a professor there."

"And your . . ." What should he call her—Mattie's aunt, her mother, Sarah? "And she heard him?"

Mattie scuffed across the room and looked out through the window, her back to him. "I shouldn't have let him in. She heard him and actually came out of her room. That shows how scared she is. She flew into a rage, accused him of all kinds of things."

"And you let her run him off for you."

"No," she said, dropping her head. "He let her run him off."

"And what did she say to you after he'd left?"

"It doesn't matter." Mattie waved her hand as if whatever Sarah had said, she had said it so many time it had lost any power to hurt her.

Dayson understood. Whether Mattie wanted to acknowledge it, even to herself, she was beginning to break away, unraveling the ties holding her to Sarah Tannehill.

Looking out the window, her back to him, she said, "The part I don't understand . . . After Frank left she became so calm. It was like she didn't want to show how upset she was. It seemed like she'd made up her mind about something and felt better. That scared me more than anything."

"You know, Frank's an impressive guy in his way."

Mattie turned her head to look at Dayson's reflection in the window. "He thinks the answers to all his questions are lying behind him. He's stuck in the past."

"While you're stuck in the future."

"The future will arrive. The past is gone." She expelled an exasperated breath. "Because I'm pretty, boys think they love me. What they really want is to make me 'theirs.' They think they want to protect me. But really they want to conquer me, like I'm some kind of castle they have to storm, and they'll be heroes if they capture me."

"And you'll miss your chance to be part of the new thing that's coming."

She searched his words for mockery. When she found none, she said quietly, "Yes."

As he had so many times before, Dayson picked up the statuette and searched its face for a revelation. As ever, it gave him nothing. It did not prophesy, only served as an avatar of old truths. Like Mattie, he would have to figure things out for himself.

He turned it over in his hands, absorbed by a half-formed notion that the new life Mattie saw coming and the ancient life reposing in the stone were connected in ways he did not understand, that the little goddess pointed into the future as much as it did into the past.

He put down the lump of stone and said to Mattie, "You know you're going to have to leave her."

"Yes."

"She knows it too."

He stood behind her, watching her reflection in the window, how it revealed her sadness as well as the composure that inhabited the same space as her untamed soul.

"Last week, I didn't think I could stand it anymore," she said. "I actually bought a bus ticket."

"Not back to Bakersfield."

She snorted. "You know where."

"Is that where the future is going to start? San Francisco?"

"Don't make fun of me."

"I'm not making fun of you. Believe me, Mattie."

She lowered her head. "I'll be letting her down terribly."

"And she's hoping that will stop you. She's set you up for it, counting on your good heart to keep you from leaving."

She spun around, her face red with emotion, recalling to him the day he had found her crying in the rain.

"It's so hard. I've only now found out that . . ." For a moment she seemed on the verge of tears. "That she's my mother!"

"Giving birth to you and then giving you away doesn't make her your mother. Not really. And if you don't free yourself now, when will you?"

"When she doesn't need me so much."

"She'll always find a way to need you if that's what will keep you in that house."

She turned back to the window to face her reflection, face herself. After a moment she bounced a wavering smile back at him. "Besides, I can't leave. I have you to take care of now."

There are so many forms of love, he thought, and yet we only use one word for them all, and we end up confusing one thing for another. He told himself she must never understand how much he wanted at that moment to cross the room and take her in his arms.

"Mattie, you're going to have to grow a more ruthless heart. We're the old world, Sarah and me, and you need to leave both of us behind."

He wouldn't tell her the truth, that every generation sees something new coming, something exciting and unprecedented. We don't realize—and thank God for it—that we'll betray ourselves by growing old and scoffing at our younger, better selves. We'll laugh at how naive we had been when we were young, when in fact, as we got older, we simply ran out of energy and confidence.

Maybe, for Mattie, it would all happen as she wanted it to. She would liberate herself and take on the hard work demanded of her ideals.

Her reflection in the window made her appear to be outside and inside at the same time, standing before him even as she floated above the torn earth outside, as if it were she that he and Persig had been looking for all this time. Yet they had both missed it because they kept digging into the ground rather than looking up to see what stood before them. And, as she said, they had wanted to capture the past, trap its meaning in a net and pin it to the specimen board of their expectations.

Instead, he and Frank would have to settle for the thin satisfaction of knowing that she *was*, and could not be possessed any more than one could possess the spirit of the great mask or the life-giving power of the stone figure in his hand. You can't own these things. You can only live in accordance with them.

As he looked at her reflection, he saw that Mattie was looking back at him. Abashed at being caught at it, she abruptly turned to face him, no longer an image floating in the air, but a very real young woman.

When she knew he saw her clearly she said, "I have to go now."

She had said the same words so many times, yet he had always taken consolation in the certainty she would come back. One of these days, and soon, she would mean it, and it would be the last time. Would he recognize the moment when it came? Would he be any better prepared than Sarah?

Though she had said goodbye, she didn't move.

"What is it?" he asked.

"I'm scared."

"That she'll be angry with you when you get back to the house?"

She shook her head. "I'm scared I'm going to be crazy. Like her."

"Afraid that you'll never fit anywhere?"

She nodded.

"Everyone's crazy, Mattie. It's the cost of living in a world so full of contradictions, full of fear. Our craziness protects us from seeing things too clearly."

"I want to see things clearly."

"Maybe you will. You're the bravest girl I've ever known. If anyone can, it's you."

Still, she didn't move, and he knew that, like everyone else, her courage had limits.

She tilted her head back and clasped her hands in front of her. "I'll be fine."

She walked past him and out the door.

Chapter Thirty

Into the Abyss

At night he read in his chair in the living room rather than in his study, where unanswered mail lay on his desk—letters from party leaders pleading with him to attend a meeting, a dinner, or just have a cup of coffee for crying out loud—and where he faced the blank pages of his unwritten memoirs, where he bent under the weight of the medal he did not deserve, where the stone figure spoke more loudly to him every day but in a language he couldn't understand, where he thought too often of the young woman trying to span two worlds, one known, the other obscured by the opaque glass of the future.

He wondered if the band that buried the bit of stone in his back yard might have been right in believing that winds, streams, rocks—his hunk of stone—possessed life as surely as trees and birds and people.

"Enough," Dayson muttered and went back to his book.

A tumbler of scotch perched on his stomach, he had turned a page of Guthrie's "The Way West" when a pounding at the back of the house startled him into spilling half the drink down his shirt.

Only one person ever knocked at his back door and his heart rose at the sound. But when he heard the panic in her voice his chest went cold.

"Mr. Dayson! Mr. Dayson! Martin!"

He rolled off the couch. Before he could cross the room she had burst in.

"Quick! Come! You have to help!"

"Mattie, what's wrong?"

"The house! The house . . ." She waved her hands in front of her face. Too upset to speak coherently.

"What's wrong with—"

"The house is on fire!"

"Wait a minute. What?"

"She's set the house on fire!" Panting, Mattie grabbed his hand, pulling him toward the door. "Please, hurry!"

Baffled, he pulled back.

"Wait. Are you serious?" But he could read the answer in her face. "I'll call the fire department."

"Hurry!"

She ran after him as he rushed into the kitchen to find the number.

The call to the fire station went to the home of Arlo Gorsline, the chief of Topping's volunteer fire department. Working hard to remain calm in the face of Mattie's panic and against the pressure he felt in his chest, Dayson quickly told Gorsline about the fire. "Yes, the old Tannehill place," he told the chief. "What? I don't know. Just a moment." His hand over the receiver, he asked Mattie, "Where's Sarah?"

"She's in the house! She set the house on fire and she's still inside."

Dayson spoke again to Arlo Gorsline, "She may still be in the house. . . . No, I'm just a neighbor. My name? Marty Dayson." He frowned. "Yeah, well, thanks for your vote. I . . . Look, I'm running over to the house. I'll see you there."

He had hardly dropped the receiver back into its cradle before Mattie seized his hand and pulled him toward the door. He started to tell her they should take his car, but realized that by the time he found the keys and opened the garage and backed out onto the road it wouldn't be much faster than the path. So he followed her across the yard.

Once away from the lights of his house, Dayson could see nothing, and balked at her insistent pulling. But she would not relent, and he understood that her young eyes could see things his could not. He would have to trust her.

Already, he saw the glow of the fire against the night sky and smelled the smoke.

* * *

A few moments later they pushed through the gap in the hedge. There they stopped, arrested in awe and horror. Most of the upper floor was already consumed by the fire. The heat had shattered the windows and flames were licking at the eaves. The lower floor, too, had started to burn, the fire crawling downward, hungry to devour the whole decaying structure.

Dayson recovered himself first. "Come on. Maybe she got out and she's around front."

Raising an arm against the heat of the fire, Dayson started toward the front, but had got no farther than the side of the house, the only part not yet engulfed in flames, when, over the roar of the fire, he heard Mattie shout, "There!"

At first he saw only the dancing flames through the window of the upstairs hallway. Then a clutch of leaping shadows coalesced into the figure of someone wandering along the hall, as if sleep-walking. Sarah had become yet one more apparition in a neighborhood Dayson had once seen as earthbound and practical, but which he now understood to be as spirit-filled and haunted as any ancient castle.

Behind him, he heard Mattie, pleading, "Sarah! Sarah!"

Unheeding, probably unable to hear the girl's voice over the fire, Sarah Tannehill walked toward the worst of the flames.

Dayson's body went slack with dread. Mattie stood in front of him, crying, "Sarah! Wait! Mother, don't go!"

But the woman and the house had merged into each other, become a single thing. One could not die without the other dying too.

Dayson felt his breath grow short. His head spun and his chest felt as if squeezed by the pincers of an iron crab. Would he end this way? Tonight? The thought didn't frighten him, only filled him with regret to end with so much left undone. And this young woman still needed him. As his knees began to buckle he threw his arms around Mattie like a man grabbing a life ring. Steadying himself, he managed to say, "No, Mattie. You can't help her now."

The young woman turned into him and sunk her head against his chest, sobbing, "Mother."

Over the roar of the fire they heard the siren of an approaching fire truck.

* * *

Too late to save the house, the firemen could do little but play their hoses over the roof and the chestnut trees to keep the fire from spreading.

Arlo Gorsline found Dayson and Mattie standing near the side of the house. The pain in Martin Dayson's chest had abated and he found he could breathe almost normally again as he told Gorsline how they had seen Sarah Tannehill walking into the center of the burning house.

Gorsline looked at the blazing house, flames shooting through the roof now. "Poor old girl." He glanced at Dayson. "It's shock. Fire does that. People don't know what they're doing. They think they're walking away from the fire when they're really walking into it."

Dayson couldn't bring himself to tell the chief that he thought Sarah knew exactly what she was doing.

For a moment Gorsline seemed about to say something about Sarah being half-crazy, but he looked at the girl staring at the fire and held back.

After all, whatever people thought of the girl, she was the woman's niece.

A few minutes after a fire truck from Forest Grove arrived, the upper floor collapsed into the lower part of the house, sending a cloud of sparks into the night sky, and briefly triggered a renewed intensity to the fire.

With the girl's house destroyed, Gorsline asked Dayson if there was somewhere for her to stay. Dayson had released his hold on her and she stood a little apart from them, a lone figure looking at the dying flames of the house.

"Marta Larson has an extra room," Gorsline said to Dayson. "I know she'd be willing to take the girl in for a few days while she figures out what she's going to do with herself."

Willing. The word struck Dayson badly. It meant unwilling except for a sense of obligation.

The chief caught something of Dayson's expression and coughed discreetly. "No one's concerned about her reputation now."

Dayson knew Gorsline was right. Topping was a good community of decent people. They looked after each other, even the Magdalene's and the exiled strangers in their midst, because, like Batch, they understood, we're all just visitors.

"It's all right," he said to Gorsline. "She'll stay with me for a while."

Gorsline regarded Mattie as she watched her house burn.

"We'll have to wait until things cool down to look for her aunt," the chief said. He nodded at Mattie, and continued to speak as if she could not hear. "I don't think she'll want to be around for that."

"No."

"I understand she's from California. I suppose she'll want to go back home. A girl that age needs her mother and father."

There was so much he could have told Gorsline about her mother and father, stories of betrayal and cowardice, hard-heartedness and jealousy, but also of love, however badly realized. He said none of it.

Gorsline held out his hand. "It's really good of you. Taking her in like this. Thanks, Governor." He smiled to show he knew how to address a former office-holder.

"Sure. Happy to." Dayson thanked Gorsline for all that he and his men had done, then walked over to where Mattie stood, laid a hand on her shoulder and led her back toward the path that led to his place.

Chapter Thirty-One

After the Fall

As he had before, Dayson made a bed on the sofa, then went into the kitchen to make Mattie a cup of tea.

While he stood at the stove waiting for the water to boil, he wondered how the young girl in his living room would take the loss of the woman who had given birth to her, though had never been her mother in any real sense. Mattie must have hoped for something more when she came to Topping, hoped for an opportunity to cut through the tangle of Sarah's defenses, overcome the woman's fears and form a bond. She had stayed in that house all these months, struggling not only with her own demons, but Sarah's too. Gutsy girl. A shame no one gave medals for that kind of courage.

When he returned to the living room, he found Mattie sitting on the edge of the sofa, staring into the void. She took the cup of tea without seeming to notice it.

Dayson took the armchair opposite her. When he thought she was ready, he said, "Tell me what happened."

At first she seemed not to have registered his words, then slowly shook her head. "I'm not sure." After a moment she corrected herself. "Yes, I am," then lapsed back into silence.

Dayson knew not to push. Whatever it was she knew, he would have to wait until she was ready to tell it.

When she spoke, it came out in disjointed fragments. "I told Frank to stop at the hedge, but he followed me into the house and maybe I let him. He told me he was going to Indiana and that I should come with him. I told him not to ask me that, to please not ask me to come with him." She twisted her mouth into a grimace. "I told you, Sarah came down and accused him of all kinds of things. But she shouted at me too for bringing him into the house. She called me terrible names. Like always. For the first time I realized these are the names she's called herself. That's when I understood. She hated herself. Hated herself for giving birth to me. Hated herself for not being a mother—and then for trying too late, when she was already crazy. All this time she's been afraid, not just for herself, but for me too. She's been afraid I would be like her. And right then I saw it clearly, seeing her for who she really was. That's when Frank stepped in between us, told her she couldn't talk to me like that." Mattie looked at Dayson, her eyes beseeching him. "Why do boys think they have to do things like that?"

Mattie let out a long wordless sigh that stood in for all the answers she didn't have.

"I thought my . . . that Sarah would go wild at Frank talking to her like that," she said. "Instead, she just got quiet. She asked him to leave. Politely. But while she said it she was looking at me as if she had a secret, something she held over me that I didn't know about. It scared me. That look in her eye. . . . He looked at me too, still waiting for an answer. Whether I would go with him or not. And I couldn't say yes. I couldn't do it. When Sarah saw that, she smiled at him. And he walked out the door."

Mattie related all this with great care, weighing each word, seeing now the things she hadn't seen before and what they signified, and how they led where they did.

"After Frank left, I went up to my room. I could see she had been going through my things. She did that sometimes. I'd tell her to stay out of my room, but she'd say my judgment couldn't be trusted. She'd found my bus ticket, the one for San Francisco. Found it in my desk drawer. Or did I leave it out?" She took a long time to think about it, knowing that if she had left it where Sarah was bound to find it everything that came after was inevitable, something she had set in motion.

"I looked up and found her standing in my room. Just standing there, looking at me. It was like her body had gone silent, but her eyes . . . She'd crumpled up the ticket and left it on my desk so I would know she'd found it. I told her that, yes, I'd bought the ticket, but I'd decided not to use it, that

I wouldn't be leaving, that I'd stay with her. She shook her head and told me not to lie. The funny thing is, I still don't know if I was lying or not."

Mattie twitched her shoulders, throwing off the question. "She got angry, balled up the ticket and threw it at me. Then she left. After that she was quiet the rest of the evening. I made some dinner for us. I brought hers up to her. We never eat together. I could tell she'd been drinking. It's funny what it does to her. Sometimes the drinking drives her sort of crazy angry. And sometimes she gets all sentimental. When I put her plate on the table, she touched my hand. She never does that, never touches me. That scared me more than anything. Before I left, she told me she was cold and her stove oil was running low, and could I bring some up. I thought I'd filled her reservoir tank only a couple of days earlier, but I didn't want to say no. So I went downstairs to the tank outside the kitchen and filled her can and brought it up to her room and lifted it to pour the fuel oil into the reservoir. But she stopped me, told me she would do it herself and to put the can on the floor. Something about it made me feel uneasy, but I couldn't put it together in my head. I couldn't imagine that . . ." She looked troubled by a sudden thought. "Or did I want to pretend I couldn't see what was coming?

"I went back to my room to read, but I couldn't concentrate. I looked out the window, and the stars were so beautiful. I turned out my light and watched the stars appear, like someone had spilled sugar across the sky. I wanted to go up in the sky and live among the stars." She looked at Dayson with such sadness in her eyes that he had to look away. "But I'm down here, aren't I?"

Her tea had gone cold and she put the cup on the table beside her. "She must have been very quiet, because I didn't hear her at all. The first thing I noticed was the smell of the fuel oil. I thought maybe she'd spilled some as she tried to fill her tank, so I got up to see if she needed help. I guess that impulse to help her is what saved my life, because when I opened my door I found her standing in the hallway, pouring it on the floor. The only thing I could think was that she'd gone crazy. She put the can down and opened a box of matches. I wanted to scream, but I was too scared. Then she said something to me that . . . that . . ."

As gently as he could, Dayson asked, "What, Mattie? What did she say?"

"I . . . I don't know."

He waited a moment before saying, "Yes you do."

She turned on Dayson, her eyes wide with fear as the scene clawed at her. "She said, 'I'm doing this for you, you know.' And for the first time ever, I thought I saw love in her face. She looked so loving. How can love be so terrifying?"

"I don't know, Mattie. There are so many things I still don't understand."

His confession brought a wavering smile to her face.

Dayson asked, "What did you do?"

"I ran. I was so scared."

"Right past her?"

"Yes."

"She made sure you got away before she set the fire."

"I . . . I didn't think of that." Mattie tilted her head back, her eyes wide at this new thought. "It's like all of her life she's been piling stacks of wood around herself, waiting to tie herself to a stake and set a match. And when she thought I might leave her . . . that's what made her decide. I feel like I killed her."

"No, Mattie, you didn't."

It hit him like an epiphany. He hadn't killed Ben Rosloff either. Both Sarah and Ben had made their choices, one from a sense of duty and rightness, one from the illness in her soul that mistook as love the impulse to possess. Neither of them would want anyone else to take the blame.

As best he could, Dayson formed the words he needed to say. "I think she died, at least inside herself, a long time ago, and she was looking for a way out. I think she was counting on you coming out of your room before she set the fire. I know this sounds strange, but in the only way she knew how she wanted to set you free."

Finally, she began to cry. She'd been holding herself together for hours and now she could let go. She held her arms out to Dayson just as, years ago, Jocie had held out her arms to him when she'd stubbed her toe or been stung by a bee. He rose from his chair and sat beside her on the sofa and put his arms around her. She laid her head against his chest and sobbed.

She cried for a long time, nineteen years' worth. Eventually, her sobs began to subside and he felt her slowly relax in his arms. As she fell asleep her young face relaxed and she began to breathe slowly, peacefully.

Dayson reached up and turned out the light.

For fear of waking her, he kept his arms around her, understanding that he loved her and not worrying about what kind of love it might be. It was all kinds merged into one.

Looking across the darkened room as Mattie had earlier that night, he saw the stars appear through the kitchen window, flickering in the blackness.

No, he thought, I've got it wrong. Whether we look to the stars for guidance while crossing oceans and deserts, or look to the sky for the auspices that will tell our futures, the stars remain constant. It is we who flicker. In the eyeblink we call our lives we shiver with fear, quaver with uncertainty, vibrate with joy. We search for happiness, try to find meaning in our work and lives. And all the time, what we seek is love to ease our way through this short journey.

Mattie stirred in his arms. Her young brow furrowed momentarily, troubled by a dream, then smoothed again as she turned and nestled her head more deeply against Dayson's chest. He held her in his arms deep into the night, thinking all the time that she was right—in spite of everything, there was beauty to be found in this night, however hard won.

Chapter Thirty-Two

The Exorcising of Ghosts

In the morning Dayson feared that, as before, Mattie would be gone when he rose, and this time for good.

Instead, he found her sitting on the couch in the long dress she had been wearing the night before, contemplating the crumpled bit of paper in her hands that was her ticket to San Francisco.

She looked up as Dayson came in. "After she threw it at me I picked it up and put it in my pocket. I lost everything but this. Not that everything was very much." In her eyes lingered the horror and shock of the night before. Yet she was already gathering her strength to accept its tragedy and keep going. She managed a bleak smile and said, "I saved the one thing I needed to save."

"We'll buy you some clothes and whatever else you need."

"I can't have you spending a bunch of money on me."

"You'll be able to pay me back. I was thinking about it during the night. There'll be an insurance settlement on the house. It may take a while, but it'll be clear that you're her heir."

Her eyes opened wide. "I'll have to tell my parents?"

"At some point. You're not twenty-one yet, so they may have some say in things."

Dayson let her think it over for a moment before adding, "And, counting the grounds of the house, you have about five acres of what may, like it or not, turn out to be prime real estate. In the meantime, I'd better make us something to eat."

It was a lot for Mattie to take in and he started toward the kitchen to let her begin the work of putting it together.

But she surprised him by taking her thoughts—and his—somewhere else.

"You didn't fail."

He turned in the kitchen doorway. "What in the world are you talking about?"

"In Salem. You didn't fail."

"I'd like to know what else you'd call it."

"You just lost this time."

He started to tell her how little she knew about politics, then remembered his conversation with Persig about failure and success, how he had set himself up as the voice of experience speaking to callow youth. Now she had reversed the roles, with callow youth doing a pretty good job of speaking truth to the old man.

"I suppose you'll tell me that whole disaster there was for my own good. Got me out of the house."

"You got yourself out of your house. You *did* something."

He stood in the doorway, trying to think of a suitable come back. And there wasn't one."

"Martin." She smiled at his look of surprise as she called him by his given name. "Martin, that other man, Ben, is gone. You're still here."

Dayson started to raise his hand to cut her off. No one but he had the right to talk about Ben Rosloff. But his gesture died half-born because, by caring for her, he had given her the right to speak to him about what mattered most. For fifteen years he had held Ben's memory as his inspiration, saw Ben's life as the ideal which he lived to fulfill. He had used it to drive himself to high office, to statewide fame, to myriad accomplishments, however dubious. And it had never been good enough because Ben's approval lay beyond his reach.

A couple of times Dayson had dared to reflect that perhaps Ben Rosloff would have done none of the things they had both imagined. He might have come home from the war, got married, had kids, taken a regular job, ended up taking his comfort and meaning from the quiet rewards of daily life. Dayson didn't want to admit that he had formed the path of his life not only for Ben's sake but for himself, that he had always wished to accomplish important things. He didn't wish to consider the possibility that he had made Ben's memory a hostage to his own ambition, allowing neither of them any peace.

It hit him like a wave he hadn't seen forming. Mattie was right. She wasn't the only one free now. He could liberate himself, if he could find the guts to do it.

The knock at the door startled them both.

Dayson saw the car in the driveway, the seal of the county sheriff on the door. "Well, old girl, it looks like breakfast is going to be delayed."

Over the next half hour, Mattie recounted to the sheriff the events of the previous night, including the fact that she was Sarah Tannehill's daughter and the sordid story of her parents' relationship. She spoke of Persig's presence that evening and how deeply it had disturbed Sarah.

The sheriff, a short, graying man in an inexpensive suit, wrote her statement in a pad, waiting patiently when Mattie wept a couple of times. At the end, he folded up his notepad and thanked her. "It's pretty clear your mother wasn't responsible for her actions last night." He didn't use the word "insane" but his meaning was obvious. He saw the troubled look in her eyes and gently added, "And you're not responsible either."

As he rose to leave, he pulled Dayson aside. "The medical examiner called from Hillsboro to say he'd have to identify Sarah's remains from dental records. There won't be any point is asking Mattie to come down to his office to identify her." He nodded at the girl, still sitting on the sofa. "I guess she'll be okay staying here with you for a while?"

"She can stay as long as she needs."

The sheriff shook his hand. "Thanks, Governor."

After a morning rain, the day of Sarah's funeral broke sunny and warm. Dayson had made arrangements with a Forest Grove funeral home for a simple graveside service at the Topping cemetery.

Perhaps twenty people—the Greenburgs, Dr. Kimmel and his wife, others Dayson had never met—gathered at the hilltop to see Sarah to her rest, laid beside her husband. Whatever demons had made her so difficult, she was, after all, one of them, a neighbor in a town that was probably dying too. They owed it to her, and to themselves, to be there. Even Donny Lawrence came, his wife holding their baby girl in her arms. Dayson made a point of shaking his hand, thanking him for coming.

As chief mourner, Mattie accepted condolences, most of them given in a minor key over a quiet accompaniment of ambivalence about this girl who had upset the order of their little community.

The new world Mattie wanted would start like this, Dayson thought, with a funeral putting the old world to rest.

To Dayson's surprise, most of the mourners shook his hand too, mentioning how good it was of him to take Mattie in and thanking him for calling the fire department that night. This time none of them felt compelled to tell him they had voted for him. He understood, they were acknowledging that he was their neighbor, a member of the community.

Chapter Thirty-Three

Don Quixote and the Notary Public

When Jocie called this time she asked to visit Dayson at his place—no rendezvous at a restaurant, no imploring him to get out of his house. After they agreed to meet on the coming Friday and Dayson had started to say goodbye Jocie broke in, "Oh, Daddy?"

"Yeah, Joss?"

"Would it be all right if I brought Mom along? She said she needed to talk to you."

He started to say, "So, that's what this is about," but let it go.

"Daddy? You still there?"

"Yeah, Joss. Sure, bring her along."

The two women took the sofa across from him in the living room, the three of them—Dayson, his not-yet-ex-wife and his daughter—sitting a little too straight, all of them struggling for words.

Mattie, on hearing of their planned visit, discovered that she needed to go over to campus and pick up a copy of her transcript. Dayson wanted to tell her she didn't have to go, but they both understood that he didn't want to explain to Jocie and Dorothy how a nineteen-year-old girl had come to live with him, even temporarily.

Jocie leaned forward on the sofa and said, "You were in the papers last week, Daddy. For being down in Salem."

"Yeah, I saw it too. But there's nothing all that new about having your old man's name in the paper, is there?"

"It's been a while."

"Yeah, I guess so.

"I'm sorry you lost. I thought you were dead right."

He spread his hands in a what-have-you gesture. "The papers made me look like Don Quixote taking a run at an iron windmill."

"It was good to see you down there," Dorothy told him.

He started to dismiss the fight over the water reclamation bill as just one more defeat. But he knew he owed her the truth. "It surprised me, how good it was to be there. I thought it was the last place I ever wanted to see again." He waggled his head. "Maybe next time I'll win."

The implication of a next time made Jocie smile.

Funny, he thought, how they both liked the idea of his getting back into the ring again when it had been the very thing that had torn them apart. Things change. He had changed. After suffering the loss in November, his motivation had changed too. He'd gone down to Salem because he wanted to, not because a dead man's memory compelled him to go.

Dorothy opened her purse and pulled out some papers, bringing home to him that life wasn't simply a series of second chances. Some losses were permanent.

"I got these from my lawyer the other day," she said. "They made their unhappiness clear, but wrote it up as you and I agreed."

"Mine weren't very pleased either," he said and nodded toward the study, where his set of papers lay on the desk.

"Shall we go ahead and sign them?" she asked.

He considered the documents in front of him like a condemned man considering a noose. He understood now. It had been Dorothy's idea to come over, and she'd asked Jocie to make the call. But it was all right. Everything was fine.

A question came to him. "Don't we need a notary?"

He'd hardly let the words out of his mouth when the obvious occurred to him—his daughter's job with the law firm. "But, yes, you're a notary, aren't you, Joss?" He laughed with pleasure. "You two really thought this through, didn't you?"

Jocie chewed at her lip. "I still don't know if I can do this," she said more to her mother than to him.

He wondered if she meant she couldn't bring herself to officiate at the end of her parent's marriage, or that she worried about its legal propriety.

"It's between your mother and me, Joss. You're not legally involved. I think it's okay"

Jocie looked from one to the other of her parents, searching for a reprieve. "Your lawyers won't like it."

"All the better," Dayson said, cajoling her with a smile. "Where's your seal?"

"I've got it out in the car."

"Well, go get it," Dayson said.

Once she'd left, Dayson and Dorothy looked at each other across the coffee table. Behind the wrinkles, the graying hair, the worry lines, he saw the twenty-six year-old girl he'd married so long ago.

"I'm sorry, Dot. Sorry about all of this."

"Yes, me too." She made a little shrug and, with that gesture, their life together ended.

"We'll be good to each other? And to Jocelyn?"

"Of course we will."

When Jocie came back in, Dayson fetched his papers from the study. They both signed each set, wordlessly pushing the copies across the table to each other, then to Jocie. Their daughter signed them and affixed her seal.

Dayson leaned over and put an arm around his daughter's shoulders and she wept quietly for a moment.

Dorothy, too, put her arms around her. "It's okay, honey. Really it is. I'm still your mother. He's still your father. That doesn't change."

One last time they embraced their daughter together, and they knew Joice had, however unconsciously, cried so it could happen.

After a couple of minutes of small talk, Dorothy rose to go. She and her now-ex-husband, shared a hug and a peck on the cheek, for Jocie's sake and for their own.

In the end, they didn't trust themselves to say anything beyond "Goodbye."

Chapter Thirty-Four

The Child of the Sixties

Though she too had been affected by their defeat in Salem, Mattie recovered more quickly than he had. Another gift given to the young. During the day, she helped Dayson with his garden. In the evening she looked through his books. He felt gratified when she took a couple of them from the shelves to read. They ate dinner together but, while they enjoyed each other's company, their conversations often sputtered into long, awkward silences, a reminder of the pain Mattie still needed to work through and, whatever their affection for each other, a reminder of how little they had in common.

She would disappear at times, and Dayson knew she had taken the path back to what was left of the house she had shared with Sarah. Once he saw her returning from the other way, where the charred ruins of the shack still stood.

It had taken two fires to clear her path, one she had set and one she had needed to flee from. Together, they had set her free.

After these sojourns she would say little, remaining quiet, her young features troubled. In her own way, she was doing what he too had been working on, reconciling the scattered threads of her life so she could move on. When she had resolved the puzzles and paradoxes of her long struggle and sudden freedom, she would leave.

After a couple of weeks, the day came. She told him it was time to go.

He knew not to try to talk her out of it. She was free, but at a terrible cost—like so many of those liberated by the war in which he'd fought.

There are, he thought, all kinds of wars, and many paths to peace.

* * *

They signed the papers to make Dayson her agent. He would arrange to pay the taxes on her property, and to sell it when she decided the time had come.

"Or maybe I won't sell" she told him. "Maybe I'll come back to live here someday."

They both knew she wouldn't, and that this was all to the good.

A few days later he drove Mattie into Portland to catch the bus to San Francisco. As a Californian, she would get into the university cheaply, finish her degree. Until her insurance money came, she would find work to pay for room and board. And with luck she would find, too, other people who wished to make a new world.

To the young the world was always new, Dayson thought, just waiting for their generation to realize the endless possibilities life offered. And—who knows?—perhaps this time they'd be right.

At the last moment, as she shuffled in line to board the Greyhound bus, she broke away and ran to Dayson and threw her arms around him.

"I love you, Martin."

"I love you, too, Mattie."

They both knew they meant slightly different things, but that was all right.

He held her out at arm's length and smiled. "When you get there, be sure to get Ferlinsphaghetti to take you out for Italian."

"And I'll say hello to Simone de Boo-Boo for you if she comes to San Francisco."

Was her voice a little choked?

It would embarrass them both, he knew, to tell her how courageous he thought she was. Besides, she would know how he felt when she got to San Francisco and found his medal in her suitcase. It would finally go to someone who deserved it.

She stopped on the top step of the bus and turned back to him. "I have to go now."

They both smiled at the familiar words.

"I know you do. Godspeed, Mattie."

She found a seat and waved to him from the window.

He waved back until the bus pulled away and he lost her from sight.

Chapter the Last

Returning to the Earth
that which Belongs to Earth

"I liked your speech to the City Club, Marty. I hope Gilkey was listening."

"Thanks, Batch."

The two men settled into their armchairs in Dayson's study, cradling their drinks, gin and tonic rather than scotch on such a hot day, the kind of day that can come in September. Indian summer they call it.

"And I couldn't help noticing you'd shaved your beard off."

Dayson sipped at his drink. "Got tired of it. No big deal."

"Best thing for you, getting back into the game, putting all that other stuff behind you."

Dayson only grunted. He wanted to say that getting out of his shell hadn't made him feel ten years younger, as Batch had once promised. And he wanted to tell him that a nineteen-year-old girl had briefly given him a second flush of youth, as a doctor might give a patient a jolt of electricity to get his heart pumping again. And he'd decided that youth was best left to the young. But he kept that to himself too.

"Frank Persig came by my office the other day. On his way to Indiana. We only talked for a couple of minutes. He didn't say anything about how things finished up out here. Did he ever find anything more? Ever make any sense of what that little statue was doing here?"

"No. Nothing we can do but guess how it got here. We'll never know."

"Must be a big disappointment."

"A couple months back I might have thought so too. But in the end I decided maybe the most important things are unknowable—what a bit of stone is doing in my garden, what it might have meant to whoever made it. Or what another man's life might have been if he'd lived long enough." Martin Dayson saw the quizzical look in his friend's face, and knew not to explain further. "I'm thinking it's better to leave a few mysteries where they are."

"You still working on those memoirs?"

Dayson shook his head. "Been too busy lately. I'll leave the story of my life for when I'm through with it."

The two old friends finished their drinks and Dayson said, "Come out back. See my garden."

As they rose, Bachelder looked at the book on the table beside Dayson's chair. "'The Second Sex.' Sounds like pornography," he said with a laugh. "Who's Simone de Beauvoir?"

"A friend recommended it to me. It's pretty good. C'mon, let's go outside."

They went out the back door, and Batch marveled at the garden, by now burgeoning with carrots and cucumbers and lettuce and tomatoes and pole beans. As before, he remarked on the view. "It's peaceful. It's . . . I don't know . . . Perfect somehow."

Dayson looked past the apple trees and the line of firs, across the fields, tall with corn, toward the distant hills blanketed by the forest.

"Yeah, I know what you mean. Maybe it is. Perfect."

Batch nodded toward the path. "Does that girl still cross your place?"

He wondered why Dayson took so long to answer.

"No. Not anymore. She's gone."

"You finally ran her off?"

Dayson looked down the empty path. "I think maybe she ran herself off."

"I see you planted over most of Persig's dig."

"Yeah. Spent a couple days putting back the topsoil he'd dug out."

"You left that far corner unplanted. Why's that?"

He only grunted and asked, "You want a couple of cucumbers?"

With the modest pride of the successful gardener, he walked around to the far side of the garden and plucked two cucumbers.

"Hey, Marty, you're not limping."

"Huh? Oh, yeah, I finally had that shrapnel taken out a couple of weeks ago. Figured it was about time." He knew his friend wouldn't understand if he said he'd done it to let a guy named Ben Rosloff rest easy in his grave. The war was over now.

They talked a few more minutes, a couple of gray-haired guys happy to stand in the warmth of the sun. Then Batch said he had to get going, hefting the cucumbers in thanks as he said goodbye.

That night Dayson took his shovel and went out to the yard. Batch had been right about his garden, everything was growing well. He looked toward the path that led toward Topping and the ruins of Sarah Tannehill's house.

They had come from there. Dayson knew this bit of the unknowable as clearly as if he could see them walking from the north along this rise, the image coming not from memory, or at least not from his, but from the memory held in the land itself.

Not a large band, perhaps forty adults and a dozen children, the latter representing the fragile promise that their clan would not disappear. They called themselves simply the People. The band had wandered for generations beyond measure, long beyond the memory of any one of them, though not beyond their collective memory of having come from a land on the other side of the world.

They had journeyed through terrible cold, through forests where the sun hardly penetrated, over mountains and across rivers. Throughout their great trek, they never lost the sense of who they were, nor the certainty they would survive, for they carried with them the icon, the spirit from the old land, a talisman that defined their existence and promised them that, whatever they must endure, she would keep them close to her heart and let them prosper, make them the physical manifestation of herself.

Eventually, they came to this long, low ridge that afforded a clear view of the land around them. A stream, clear and quick-flowing, ran along its edge. The woods were thick with game, the streams teeming with fish, the edges of the woods filled with berries.

They built shelters, temporary at first, but soon replaced with wooden lodges. They kept the stone icon in one of the lodges, augmenting its power with wooden carvings invoking the spirits of Bear and Salmon and Beaver and of the great Sky Bird, servant of the tribe's abiding spirit.

When the other carvings threatened to diminish her preeminence, they decided to bury her in her own place in the earth, over which she held sovereignty. They didn't need to see her to know she was there. With ancient songs and ritual dances, with the pouring onto the earth of libations to please and sustain her, they placed her in the ground and covered her with her earth.

When the People moved on many years later they left it behind and went on their way, assured that she was always with them.

So they left the land for a dream of a better place. And they left the icon, for whoever came after them, for whoever would need it when their fortunes were dark.

When Dayson had dug down far enough into the bit of unplanted ground Batch had noticed—not too deep, only a foot or two—he went inside and took from his desk the icon—his girl, as he had so often called it—as well as the piece of shrapnel he'd asked the doctors to give him after the surgery. He placed them together in the hole. He was about to fill it in when he understood he had to one more thing to add, however difficult. After twenty-seven years, the ring didn't want to come off, but he pulled and twisted until it finally freed itself. Without it he felt oddly naked and free himself from one more talisman of the past and filled it in.

When he'd finished he looked into the sky at the half-moon and at the sprinkling of stars visible on the horizon. And, in the stillness of the night, he heard from the woods the beating of the wings of a great bird.

About the Author

Stephen Holgate has led a varied life. In addition to serving as a diplomat in American embassies overseas, he has: worked as a congressional staffer; acted with the national tour of an improvisational theater group; served as a crew member of a barge on the canals of France; and lived in a tent while working as a gardener in Malibu.

His novel Tangier received the Silver Medal in Fiction from the Independent Publishers group and made Bookreaders ten-best list in the Indie Mystery/Suspense category. Madagascar, met with similar critical success, receiving a coveted starred review from Publishers Weekly as well as another listing from Bookreaders among the ten best Mystery/Suspense novels of the year.

Contact Stephen Holgate at:
StephenHolgateWrite.com

~ ~ ~

Thank you
for reading *The Goddess and Martin Dayson*. If you enjoyed it, please think about writing a short review at one of these websites.
Amazon.com | Goodreads.com